the
straight
road
to
Kylie

More delicious titles from Simon Pulse

A Girl Like Moi
by Lisa Barham

Disenchanted Princess
by Julie Linker

Honey Blonde Chica
by Michele Serros

Price of Admission
by Leslie Margolis

DRAMA!
a new series by Paul Ruditis

the straight road to Kylie

NICO MEDINA

Simon Pulse

New York | London | Toronto | Sydney

This book is a work of fiction. Any references to historical events, real people, or real locales are used fictitiously. Other names, characters, places, and incidents are the product of the author's imagination, and any resemblance to actual events or locales or persons, living or dead, is entirely coincidental.

SIMON PULSE
An imprint of Simon & Schuster Children's Publishing Division
1230 Avenue of the Americas, New York, NY 10020
Copyright © 2007 by Nicolas Medina
All rights reserved, including the right of reproduction in whole
or in part in any form.
SIMON PULSE and colophon are registered trademarks of Simon & Schuster, Inc.
Designed by Steve Kennedy and Greg Stadnyk
The text of this book was set in Swift.
Manufactured in the United States of America
First Simon Pulse edition May 2007
2 4 6 8 10 9 7 5 3 1
Library of Congress Control Number 2006935867
ISBN-13: 978-1-4169-3600-8
ISBN-10: 1-4169-3600-9

For Erin and Rachel,
my constant sources of entertainment and inspiration

THE STRAIGHT ROAD TO KYLIE
A Kylie Minogue Mix by Jonathan Parish

1.	Step Back in Time	00:01
2.	Celebration	00:16
3.	Drunk	00:25
4.	Can't Get You Out of My Head	00:44
5.	Word Is Out	00:56
6.	Come into My World	00:69
7.	More More More	00:83
8.	I'm So High	00:97
9.	Put Yourself in My Place	01:05
10.	I Guess I Like It Like That	01:28
11.	Shocked	01:41
12.	Spinning Around	01:69
13.	Kids	01:83
14.	Too Far	01:92
15.	On a Night Like This	02:17
16.	Say Hey	02:31
17.	Limbo	02:41
18.	Your Disco Needs You	02:49
19.	Still Standing	02:69
20.	Confide in Me	02:81
21.	I Should Be So Lucky	02:91

the straight road to Kylie

1. Step Back in Time

I really wish I wasn't gay right now.

Seriously.

If I wasn't gay right now, I wouldn't be having sex with Alex.

No, not Alex*der*.

Alex*dra*.

That's right, ladies and gentlemen. Jonathan Parish has done the unthinkable. Out-and-proud Christina Aguilera–worshipping, Diesel shoe–wearing, lover-of-large-sassy-black-women-and-skinny-white-heiresses Jonathan Parish is having sex with a *girl!*

These were the thoughts running through my head that insane night. I did *not* know what I was getting myself into.

Maybe I should recap.

My best friend, Joanna Marin, decided to throw herself a turning-eighteen birthday bash. Originally, her mom, Orlando-suburbanite-wishing-she-were-Winter-Park-Park-Avenue-chic divorcée Marsha Marin, was going to take her out for brunch and to a cute little boutique on Park Avenue. But, in true Marsha Marin fashion, she had to cancel on her only daughter to take over a fellow flight attendant's Orlando-Atlanta-Paris-and-back flights. This left Joanna alone on the weekend of her eighteenth birthday—alone and angry . . . but with an empty house and a fistful of I'm-so-sorry money. What else was there to do but throw the party to end all parties to celebrate Joanna's official passage into adulthood?

When she'd told me just before sixth period that she'd gotten a voice mail from her mom about the change of plans, we'd agreed to meet at Aretha (my 249,982-miles-young '91 Volvo) after school let out to drive to Amigo's for chips, salsa, quesadillas, and some serious planning. After ruling out a day at Disney World (too young for us—she was turning *eighteen* for Christ's sake!), Islands of Adventure (that was getting old—we'd bought ourselves annual passes the year before), or the beach (it was possibly going to rain), we decided to throw a debaucherous alcoholic bingefest. Yes, we were quite the original duo.

"We'll need a handle of vodka," I said, starting out our list.

"So go ahead and put cranberry and orange juice on there," Joanna added.

"And limes."

Joanna and I loved making lists. For anything. Party supplies. Party CDs. Guest lists. To us, the most exciting part of a party was hunkering down and writing out the lists. Über-cool, right? "If we're getting limes already, why not tequila and salt for body shots?" Joanna suggested. She had a tear in her eye, I think. Nothing made her happier than people licking her stomach. Give her a few drinks, and she soaked up the attention like a sponge.

"Okay. But I'm gonna want beer, too. How many people are we inviting?"

"I don't know. Do we have to know that right *now*?"

"Absolutely!" And I was dead serious.

Joanna blew out a horsey kind of sigh. "You are way too anal."

"People who live in glass houses and make lists for fun shouldn't throw stones."

Joanna took a gulp of her Diet Pepsi and let out a belch in response. The chips-and-salsa boy—whom both Joanna and I had been drooling over since we were able to get to Amigo's on our own—replenished our supply and chuckled. Joanna was mortified.

"Oh my God, Jonathan," she whispered. "What do you think he *thinks* of me now? I mean, how disgusting *am* I?"

Yay. Damage control. Why did my best friend in the world have to be so typically outgoing, but *so spastic* around cute members of the male race?

I mean, Joanna is pretty, a natural beauty who looks amazing with or without makeup—but she still feels she has to wear it to get guys to notice her. (It's always sort of bugged me.) She's got shoulder-length dirty-blonde hair that bounces when she walks, just like shampoo commercials say that hair should. Her skin is TV-star flawless, and she has pale blue eyes. She works relatively hard on her body, and that—coupled with a rapid metabolism—shows in her tight, fat-free frame. At five-foot-eight, she stares right into my matching blue eyes. But despite what she's got going for her, she never seems to get the good guys. Call it dumb luck or a curse or whatever, but it can really get to her. Which then sometimes leads to wallowing in self-consciousness, and still not getting the good guys—it's a vicious cycle, really, but if I told her about it, I'm afraid she might kill me. She doesn't take to criticism too well, no matter how constructive.

While we're on descriptions, I'll go ahead and say—*toot, toot!* goes my own horn—that I am also pretty, with or without makeup (although a little eyeliner for special occasions never hurts). I've got an okay body (flat tummy, cute little biceps, hard legs and ass, thank you very much), dark brown hair, and bright blue eyes. Everyone says that's the best part about me—the dark hair–light eyes combo. And even though I'd always sort of wanted to be a blond, I had to agree.

But back to my damage-control duties . . .

"Sweetie—"

"*Don't* call me 'sweetie,' okay?" she interrupted. "I love your gayness and all, but if you start using 'sweetie' then the next step is capri pants and excessive eyebrow-tweezing. I can't have a *Queer Eye for the Straight Guy* correspondent for a best friend."

"Easy, killer," I said. "And besides, capris went out years ago. Sweetie."

"Eat me."

"So . . . can I take your order?" Perfect timing. Did they train waitresses for this? Oh, well. At least it wasn't the cute chip boy.

"Oh . . . uh . . . m'kay," Joanna stammered, turning a bright shade of Amigo's-signature-salsa red. "I'll take the . . . uh . . . veggie quesadillas."

"And you?"

"Chicken chimichangas, please," I ordered.

The waitress collected our menus and told us it'd be just a few minutes. Joanna's face returned to its normal shade.

"Anyway, let's get to that guest list," she said. Apparently, spitting out a vulgarity in front of our waitress made her forget about not-so-daintily belching in front of our favorite chips-and-salsa boy. Wow. No more damage-control responsibilities. It must have been my lucky day.

If only the luck could have lasted through the weekend.

"Not too many, right?" I asked. "We don't want it ending up like some cliché high-school party from the movies, do we?" It just wasn't our style.

"No way."

"Good. Let's do it, ho."

Our parties usually had anywhere from ten to thirty of our closer friends, plenty of booze, sometimes other substances (nothing nasty), nonstop party mixes, and usually a lot of dancing. I, being the good best-gay-friend that I was, was usually the ringleader for the dance portion of the party. I'd pull people off the couch and out of their shells, and put them right up to my waist to grind the night away.

By the time our food arrived—luckily while Joanna was behaving—we had a list of thirty-three names. Probably around twenty-five would show. Figure that with the vodka, tequila, and rum (newly added to the alcohol list), everyone would consume around two and a half beers on average, which made a little more than sixty-two beers. Round it up to seventy-two to buy six 12-packs. We could always have a leftovers party. We had this down to a science. Who said math was useless?

- One handle vodka—Smirnoff
- One biggish bottle of rum—Bacardi Limón
- One biggish bottle of tequila—Jose Cuervo
- Two 12-packs Bud Light
- Two 12-packs Amber Bock
- One 12-pack Smirnoff Twisted Orange (They taste like Flintstone's Push-Pops. I had to add it.)
- One 12-pack Killian's Irish Red
- One bottle sour mix
- One bottle triple sec

That was the list for my brother to take care of. Jesse's a senior at UCF majoring in Civil Engineering, with a minor in Providing Alcohol to His Kid Brother. He takes his studies seriously.

The list for Joanna and me to take care of was:

- Six limes
- Orange juice
- Cranberry juice
- Sprite
- Coke
- Diet Coke
- Five bags chips (Unspecified—hey, we couldn't plan *everything*. Some things have to be left to decide on a whim, right?)
- Dip
- Salsa
- Three gallons water
- Excedrin

It was three thirty, Thursday afternoon. I was in charge of the party mixes; Joanna was in charge of the phone calls. We'd both follow up with everyone at school on Friday. We should do this for a living.

Thirty minutes later, I was heading toward the on-ramp for the East-West Expressway after dropping off Joanna. In order to afford the spacious, grandiose home that matched her impossible taste, Joanna's mom had to buy so far from the actual *city* of Orlando that it was practically on the coast. Forty minutes to the east was the beach and Kennedy Space Center. Forty minutes to the west was Disney. And smack-dab in the middle of her far-out house and Disney were the cities of Orlando and Winter Park, and our school—Winter Park High.

Our school is pretty much your typical high school. Jocks. Nerds. Drama Nerds. IB Kids (International Baccalaureate—our magnet program for "exceptionally exceptional" students from the area). Normal kids. A couple of (out) gay kids. A few more (closeted) gay kids. A few poor kids. Middle-class kids. Rich kids. A few very rich kids. And then the *super*-rich kids who didn't even know what to do with Daddy's American Express Black Card.

Winter Park has a *lot* of rich residents. All sorts of well-off people: big-shot lawyers, Orlando Magic players, Carrot Top (seriously). Rumor had it that even Madonna bought a house near Park Avenue for, like, two seconds, before she resold it. Winter Park's welcome/city-limits sign, which reads WELCOME TO WINTER PARK, PLEASE DRIVE WITH EXTRAORDINARY CARE, more often than not has the last *E* of "care" crossed out. Cute, huh?

My group of friends is pretty much right in the normal, middle-class middle of the student body. We drive used and hand-me-down cars from the decade of our birth, but at least we have cars to drive. And we live in nice houses in good neighborhoods, but for the most part not extravagantly. I live right where northeast Orlando meets Winter Park, on the Winter Park side. Carrie and Shauna live out east, toward UCF. Others are scattered around my neighborhood and Winter Park Pines, right by the high school.

And then there's Joanna, who's way out in BFE (Butt-Fucking Egypt, in case you were wondering).

I cursed her mother's affected Park Avenue tendencies and inexplicable need for a four-bedroom house for two people as I waited in the sweltering heat to get on the East-West Expressway, the heavenly stretch of highway that would whisk me back to civilization in twenty minutes.

My old beat-up Aretha might break down all the time and *definitely* not have air-conditioning, but at least she has a stereo. Driving (and life, for that matter) means nothing to me without my music. And life is hardly worth living without my favorite Australian pop princess (*queen*, actually, in my opinion) Kylie Minogue. I pulled out two CDs and considered them: Kylie's *Fever* and Garbage's *Version 2.0* (my favorite album by my favorite band—hands-down, the best album ever made, and I don't care if Lauryn Hill won the Grammy that year!). Seeing that it was over ninety degrees and humid, I decided that the weather called for Kylie's "Burning Up." So I put *Version 2.0* away for the moment and popped in *Fever*, skipping to the twelfth track.

I let the infectious disco-y beats popping out the speakers mix with the impossibly heavy heat sinking into my car, and embraced the sweat pouring down my body as I danced my ass off and Kylie sang about summer madness. Although it was technically fall, it was early October in Central Florida, where summer weather could stretch until Halloween—the heat and humidity were just things I had to embrace. The cars in the right-turn lane inched toward the on-ramp. The music slowed, cooled, broadened, stretched out. My car was up to the red light. I was next.

As the song exploded into its grand finale, the light turned green and I gunned it (as best I could) onto the highway. The rushing air rejuvenated me, and I glanced down at the odometer and smiled as dirty old Aretha hit a quarter of a million miles. The song wound to a close, and I decided it was time to celebrate the act of motion by singing and dancing to some "Dirrty" by Christina Aguilera. Out came *Fever*, in went *Stripped*. A day this sweaty called for X-Tina.

I pulled out my faux-drag-queen act, singing, dancing, and hand-motioning as much as anyone can do while driving a one-ton stick-shift Swedish tank of a car down an expressway. Not that I'd actually *seen* a real-life drag queen in person before, but I'd watched them on TV and YouTube and stuff. Song ideas for the party CDs crackled and sputtered in my brain as I drove toward the Orlando skyline. "Impressive Instant" by Madonna. "Cherry Lips" by Garbage. The Britney Spears–Chris Cox MegaMix! "You Gotta Lick It Before We Kick It" by 20 Fingers and Gillette! I'd expose these people to some *culture*, dammit!

As soon as I got home, I ran into my room to get started on the party mixes. I couldn't let my excitement die down. I threw my bag onto my bed and kissed Kylie hello. Kylie's picture, that is.

See, I have this wall. . . . So when those Christmas gift calendars go on sale on January second, I raid the malls of Metro Orlando to gobble up all the ones of Kylie Minogue. They're tough to find, but I find them. Not to mention, of course, the CD cases, album advertisements, stills from when she played the Green Fairy in *Moulin Rouge*, and magazine articles. Needless to say, the resulting Kylie Wall is fabulous. And it makes me happy no matter what mood I'm in. I come in after a shitty day at school, Kylie greets me all cute and sexylike from her motorcycle in the desert, and all is right in the world. So naturally today, glimpsing Kylie in her fabulous one-piece on the rocky beach only heightened my already happy mood. She was so cute I could pinch her!

Joanna hated the wall. She said it creeped her out, which I can sort of understand. I think the straw that broke the faghag's back on that one, though, was the stand-up cut-out of Kylie from her *Fever* era (thank you, eBay!) that hung out in front of the Kylie Wall. Joanna always makes me store her in my closet when she sleeps over, saying, "I can't deal with one more set of Kylie eyes looking at me!" Please. She should *be* so lucky.

I thought it was perfectly natural for a boy like me to have such an adorable Kylie shrine. And, what with my perpetual lack-of-boyfriend, it was nice to have *something* to give a little kiss to every day. . . .

I remember when I came out to my parents and older brother and how unsurprised and sweet and supportive they were—till my dad asked me, "But, Jonathan? What about Kylie?" To which my brother just chuckled in response.

I settled myself into my desk chair and started going through CDs to burn.

This party was going to be the best.

I absolutely could not wait.

Friday at school was a blur. I was way too excited about the next night to concentrate on anything. Being a senior (finally!), planning/having/throwing parties was what I lived for lately, so the unit test in statistics; the bullshit skit my Spanish group and I had thrown together and performed (involving a cheating husband and an angry *esposa* throwing a *grande* glass of *agua* on him); and the lectures on God-knows-what, the cardiovascular system, and the legislative branch, in English, anatomy, and government classes kind of melted together for me. I probably couldn't tell you the difference between a capillary and an artery, or exactly how many seats there are in Congress, but I *could* tell you the track list for "JOANNA TURNS 18 PARTY MIX 1," since that's what I was *really* listening to all day. In my head, anyway.

Whatever. I had a four-point-oh average and I was allowed to have a BS day.

I'd checked in with Joanna in Spanish before our skit, during lunch, and after school in the parking lot, and we had twenty-three yeses, eight nos, and two maybes.

"Carrie is coming, though, right?" I asked. "I haven't gotten a chance to ask her myself." Besides Joanna, she was the most important person to me. "Oh, and Shauna?" Shauna was Joanna's best girlfriend, and was quickly becoming one of my favorite people.

"Carrie said she'd be there with tassels on her nipples and nothing else, and Shauna said she wouldn't miss it for the world. Now let me see those mixes."

I handed her the six CDs I'd slaved over until two a.m. the night before. Maybe that's why everything had been such a soupy, foggy mess that day.

Carrie Adams and I had met by the vending machines on the first day of junior year. I'd just come out of the closet that summer and was ridiculously paranoid that it somehow showed. Like some big, gay snake shedding its outer closeted skin to reveal a bright and shiny-new rainbow-colored layer. I felt like everyone was watching me, judging me (or loving me, depending on the person). As if not everyone in school didn't *already* think I was gay—but it just felt different.

Eventually, though, word got around. Pretty quick, actually. Because first I had to tell the most important friends, then it turned into my closest, like, fifteen friends . . . and then before I knew it, it was all over school. Not that that was a bad thing, really, since I didn't feel like I had to parade around school with a sash over me that read OUT AND PROUD to get the point across. No. Everyone just suddenly *knew*.

Admitting to my friends and family that I was gay didn't feel wrong; in fact, it felt wonderful. I was happy to be an out-and-proud sixteen-year-old. But my pride went only so far. I still lived in the South (as liberal as Orlando can seem, it definitely has its Pensacola moments—really, they should just hand the Panhandle over to Alabama, in my not-so-humble opinion). I still knew hardly any out gay kids my age. And the closeted ones were . . . let's just say they didn't have enough self-esteem. I still had no idea how to meet other gay kids (except, of course, for the Internet—but there was no *way* I was gonna get into that). And it was all still so very new to me.

I fed my quarters into the vending machine, and as I bent down to retrieve my Diet Coke, I felt a hand slap my ass. Hard.

"Oh, *baby*, is this seat taken?!" some girl yelled.

Startled, I whipped around to see a tall, wild-haired, gorgeous girl in flip-flops (she got written up for those later), Seven jeans, and a tight thrift-store T-shirt that read CARNIVAL CRUISE LINES: I'M IN SHIP SHAPE! She had some major ass-kickin' Asian features—with her severe jaw line and high cheekbones—and kind of looked like a badass female samurai, but with this big, fantastic Afro of jet-black hair. I loved her instantly. But I suppose my shy smirk didn't really show it.

"Oh, I'm sorry! I mean, you're gay, right? All my gay friends at my old school loved it when I did that, and I thought it was a better way of introducing myself than the usual hi-how-are-you? kind of thing. *So* boring. And I'm bi anyway, so it's only, like, *half* offensive if I slap your ass."

I was still too dumbfounded to say anything. This girl was awesome.

"Shit . . . you *are* . . . gay, right? Well, if you are, my name's

Carrie. And if you're not, my name's still Carrie, but maybe we could go out sometime. Ha-ha-ha-ha!"

Somehow, hearing a perfect stranger say out loud that I was gay wasn't as bad as I'd thought it could be. Carrie had an incredible vibe to her, and I instantly wanted to be her friend. Not to mention that she had just said "all my gay friends." So I loosened up, let out a laugh, and stuck my hand out for her to shake.

"Hi, Carrie. I'm Gay, but you can call me Jonathan. Care to share some of my Diet Coke?"

She took my hand in hers, lifted it to her face, and kissed it.

"And before you ask," she said, "it's half Korean and half black. And *no* I will not do a Margaret Cho impersonation for you, and *no* I will *not* do Wanda Sykes for you, either."

"Marilyn Manson again?" an annoyed Joanna said, yanking me suddenly out of my reverie. "Jonathan, are you trying to *ruin* this party?"

"It's his cover of 'Personal Jesus,' Joanna," I said. "Come on! Who wouldn't appreciate that?"

"*Me!* And it's *my* birthday." She had her arms crossed and was pouting at me.

"But, look—all your favorites are on there, too," I said, pointing out various tracks on the CD—OutKast, Ludacris, Ciara, Cher. "You know I aim to please." I reached out and pinched her butt.

"Ouch!" she screeched, slapping my hand away.

A couple of guys from the football team saw this and were laughing. "Go, Parish!" they yelled. I didn't know quite how to take it.

But Joanna did. "Shut the hell up!" she yelled at them. Then, to me, "But what's all this other stuff on here for? Placebo? Peaches? Goldfrapp? The Faint—?"

"Don't you dare say anything about Kylie or Garbage," I threatened.

"Wouldn't dream of it," she said, rolling her eyes. "But the list goes on: Thunderpuss? Muse? Hooverphonic?" She paused. "*Hooverphonic?* Is that what happens when a vacuum cleaner and a phone have sex?"

"I *refuse* to cohost a party where the music is all stupid, predictable Now-That's-What-I-Call-Music-Volume-Eighty-Three crap. You know I have to expose these people to something different!" I smiled. "It's my lot in life."

"Sure."

I saw the corner of her mouth move up slightly into a half smile.

"It all works great as background music, too," I lied. That was always the way to get her.

"Fine. As long as your brother doesn't back out on buying the alcohol."

"He won't."

This little music battle, like the list-making, was another party ritual of ours. She pretended to hate my music, I pretended to care, and she eventually caved. The CDs were always a hit, and we both knew it. This time would be no exception. I had even made smooth, slow, background-music types of CDs for chilling out in rooms other than the main living room. This party was going to be the party to end all parties—somehow I just knew it.

2. Celebration

"One, two, three, *go!*"

Joanna, Carrie, and I licked the salt off one another's necks, threw back a shot of Jose Cuervo, and immediately popped lime wedges into our mouths and sucked them dry. The liquor hit me like a *truck*! I let out a little yelp and flopped my wrists up and down like I was trying to fly. I couldn't help it; it's what tequila makes me do.

"WHY DO I ALWAYS DO TEQUILA SHOTS WHEN I KNOW WHAT THEY DO TO ME?!" I screamed through my scrunched-up pug face.

Joanna—probably already feeling a little tipsy from her one shot—giggled and said, "Quiet, Jonathan, you'll wake the neighbors."

We all busted out laughing. It was still light out—only six o'clock. The party wasn't till eight, but we felt like getting a head start. We weren't *usually* such drunken lushes—but it was a special occasion. And I *especially* deserved it, after kicking off my weekend with a Friday-night closing shift and a Saturday-morning opening shift at Target, where I worked. Not exactly my idea of carefree bliss, but I'd picked up the Friday-night shift for some extra cash.

"So, honey, any good stories from Target for us?" Carrie asked, mixing up some major tequila sunrises.

"Well," I began as I searched through my messenger bag for the DVDs I'd brought over, "some jackass lumbered in tonight and tried to return an obviously used phone in a brand-new phone box. And when I told him that there was a problem with the phone he was trying to return, he was all, 'Well that's how you *sold* it to me.'"

And I wasn't even kidding. Maybe I'd embellish on my stories a little sometimes, but people would try to get away with anything, and nothing surprised me anymore. I pretty much had a new story like that every other week.

I found what I was looking for in my bag—*Strangers with Candy*, Season Two—and took a long swig of my drink.

We heard the front door creak open.

"You guys started without me?" Shauna interrupted meekly as she walked in.

We all dropped what we were doing and ran to Shauna, screaming joyfully and showering her with hugs and kisses. Our drunken way of saying we loved her and would catch her up in no time.

Petite, blonde, and adorable Shauna Smart had been best friends with Joanna since elementary school. I'd known her and Joanna since the beginning of ninth grade, when we all started at Winter Park. Joanna and I almost instantly became the best of friends; Shauna and I had taken longer to get to know each other. I'd always *liked* her, don't get me wrong. But it just took a little extra push to get us to really connect. For one thing, she was already, like, Joanna's *best* friend, and for another thing, she was kind of debilitatingly shy. Sweetest thing, though, but *so* shy. So, like I said, our friendship needed a push.

That push had been our impromptu trip to Myrtle Beach, when we were in the ninth grade. I was only fifteen, but Shauna had started school a year later than everyone, so she already had her license. During one of my and Joanna's musical disagreements, Joanna had said, "You act like Garbage is the fucking *Beatles* or something!" to which I of course replied, "No, I don't— they're *better!*"

Before I knew it, Shauna had told me of her love for the newest Garbage album (which got next to no promotion or airplay, so I was impressed), I had complained about how they weren't coming to Florida on their tour, she had asked where else they were playing, we had made respective phone calls to our parents, and we had started making plans for a little road trip to see them in Myrtle Beach, South Carolina. Fifteen hours in the car, a cheap hotel with sheets that smelled like butter, countless gas-inducing fast-food meals, and a few hours standing in an at-capacity club to see your favorite band (for the most mind-blowing concert of your life, naturally) can make or break a friendship. Luckily for us, we loved every second of it. And it had given me the chance to really break her out of her shell, at least when she was with me.

She was still super-bashful most of the time, but after that trip, I could almost always bring out the wild-and-crazy side of her. Like the time I dared her to grab Mickey Mouse's crotch during a photo at the Magic Kingdom. And ask Pluto when he got off his shift so she could take him out for a drink and a hot dog. She'd always run up to me after, giggling like a middle-schooler, and give me a playful slap, pretending that she hated me for convincing her to do it.

"Don't hate us!" I cried now, hugging her obnoxiously.

"Yeah!" Carrie and Joanna agreed. "We love you!"

Shauna surrendered to our love shower for a few seconds and then asked sweetly to be caught up. Then she bounced up to Joanna's room—and I definitely mean "bounced," because Shauna is stacked—to drop off her bag as Carrie poured her a shot and a drink. Joanna and I moved to the living room and collapsed backwards onto the couch.

"So, Joanna," I said.

"Yes, my dear?" she replied.

"Tell me who's gonna be here tonight. . . ." I gave her a little wink. She knew what I meant.

"Well . . . lots of people. Vanessa and Marie and—"

"I think he's asking about men, baby," Carrie interrupted. "We know about all the girls who're showing up."

"Oh . . . right," Joanna said, furrowing her brow suspiciously.

"Could the reason you're acting coy be that the crush of your high-school life might be coming here with a Miss Alexandra Becker?" I ventured.

"You mean Trent Kessler?!" Shauna called in mock surprise as she came down the stairs, her blonde hair swishing with each step.

"Howdidyouknowshewasbringinghim?" Joanna sputtered off at rapid speed.

"Because I ran into the young lady today at Target, and when I asked if she was bringing any friends to the party, she mentioned the good Trent Kessler's name." I stirred my drink with my index finger and took a long pull from the glass. I was already feeling a little warm around the edges.

"Well, yeah, she'd mentioned bringing him when I followed up with her on Friday in calculus," Joanna admitted. "I just didn't want to bring it up because I knew you bitches would be *nagging* me about it!"

"Oooooh, c'mooooon," cooed Carrie.

"We'd never do that," I chimed in.

"Never," Shauna confirmed.

We paused for a second to let Joanna release the breath she'd been holding before we went in for the kill.

"So what're you gonna wear?"

"Do you wanna borrow my perfume?"

"What's his favorite beer?"

"Did we *get* enough beer?"

"What color underwear are you wearing?"

"Are you gonna slip him some roofies?"

"And then show him who's boss?"

"Are you on your period?"

"Did you wax your—?"

"JONATHAN!" they screamed at me.

Oops.

"I was gonna say eyebrows," I lied. "Honest."

Everyone erupted in laughter, even Joanna . . . a little.

Trent Kessler is this adorable surfer god–type guy who Joanna had been hopelessly crushing on since he'd transferred to Winter Park from Satellite High, over on the coast, in freshman year. Unless he was a tanning-bed whore, he definitely went back to the beach as often as he could, because he was still the same bronzed god that Joanna had laid eyes on that fateful day in biology. And he just seemed like a really great guy, while Joanna's few past boyfriends were anything but. But, of course, Joanna being Joanna, she never snagged him. Borderline flirtatious chatter during group projects in class was as far as she'd ever gotten.

After a minute of uncontrollable tequila giggles, Carrie, Shauna, and I noticed that Joanna wasn't busting as much of a gut as we were, so we regained our composure.

"Does my misery bring you joy?" she asked us.

"Not unless you want it to, drama queen," I replied, smiling.

Joanna sighed and took a deep breath. "I'm wearing my tight-in-the-ass black pants, that cute pink top from Betsey Johnson, and I'm still debating the shoes; I don't want to borrow your perfume because it makes me sneeze; I don't know what Trent's favorite beer is, but with as much of it as we *bought*, I'm sure we have it; Jonathan, do *not* worry about supplies right now, you *freak*; I'm wearing black underwear, but not because I think I'll be showing it to anyone tonight; I will not be slipping Trent Kessler any illegal date-rape drugs; I'm menses-free; and yes, Jonathan—I went downtown today and got my eyebrows waxed."

I guess that answered our questions. All of them, in fact.

"Anyway, I'm gonna go refresh my drink," Joanna said, and stood up and went to the kitchen.

I thought she might be a little upset, so I motioned for Carrie and Shauna to start up the *Strangers with Candy* DVD and headed after Joanna. She had hauled a bag of ice out of the freezer and was starting to beat it against the countertop, trying to break up the ice—and her frustration, I guess—into smaller, more manageable chunks.

Thunk. Thunk.

"Joanna, wh—?"

"What's wrong?" she finished for me. *Thunk.*

"Well, yeah, we were just—"

"Messing around?" *Thunk thunk!*

"Um . . . I guess so. It never seemed to—"

"Matter before?" *THUNK THUNK THUNK!*

Carrie turned up the volume.

Shauna sipped at her tequila sunrise.

Joanna picked up a knife.

Now *I* was nervous.

I opted for humor.

"Isn't it sweet that we finish each other's . . . ?" I paused, waiting for the obvious.

"Sentences?" Joanna replied, smiling a bit. She took a breath, and then a few rapid stabs at the big chunks of ice.

"Whoa, easy there, Sharon Stone," I joked. "This isn't *Basic Instinct,* okay?"

"Sorry. It's just that tonight's different, Jonathan." She sighed. "I've been gushing like a fucking idiot about Trent since we were, like, fifteen. *Fifteen!*"

"Jesus, don't I know it!" I feigned exasperation.

"I dunno—just after all the past loser boyfriends, maybe it's time I actually *really* go for it with Trent. I was just hoping that tonight, now that I'm an official . . . adult"—we looked at each other and mock-cringed—"I could finally suck it up and talk to him for *real*. I'm talking actual conversation here."

She looked at me, and I looked at her. I took a deep breath and then a sip of my drink.

"Wow," I said. "I'm a little surprised."

"What do you mean?"

"It's just that . . . well, you *know* you're beautiful. At least you should. And you should know that you do deserve the best boyfriend in the world. You just . . . don't seem to know that. That's why I'm surprised." I took a deep breath for what I was about to say. I never really told Joanna how I felt about stuff like this. "You know, I don't think you need that extra little bit of makeup, the push-up bra, and all the stuff like that—"

"Really?" she asked.

"Well, yeah . . ."

"Well, what right do you really have to say that? I mean, it's not exactly like you're looking at girls and deciding if they're cute enough to date or kiss or sleep with, right? So why should I listen to you?"

"Look, don't be so hostile—"

"I'm not being hostile; I'm just being realistic. It's not exactly like you're following any of your own advice, you know. I don't see you raking in the guys."

"Ouch."

There was a pause. "I'm sorry, Jonathan. . . . I'm just freaking out today."

"Just . . . listen to me. I may not look at girls and decide if they're hot enough to go out with, but I can tell when they try too hard. And I think you sometimes do. So, I want you to think about this. You were just saying how you had to *try* something with Trent. . . . I just want you to try *not* to try. Wear that outfit you were talking about, because it's fabulous—"

"Okay, 'fabulous' sort of reminds me too much of 'sweetie.'"

"All right, whatever, fuck off—I'm gonna use it."

"Fine." She let out a little chuckle.

"The outfit is fabulous, but so are you, *sweetie*. Just don't try too hard with all the makeup and the gussying-up and everything. Just act normal—act like you do with me—and see what happens. You're an *adult* now"—another mock-cringe—"so try to be adult about it." I paused for a second. "Did that sound lame? I feel lame." Tequila does *that* to me, too.

Joanna looked at me sweetly and leaned over to give me a quick—but sincere—hug. "Not at all, sweetie. Thanks. Sorry I was kind of a bitch."

"No problem. Happy birthday," I said as I reached my arm down and pinched her butt. She jumped back and screeched. "And expect seventeen more of those—one for every year."

3. Drunk

The party ended up being a hit. A fucking hit! Everyone was drinking and talking and socializing and shmoozing and mingling and every other synonym for talking. And, of course, a few people had come up to commend me on my CD-making efforts—which made my night.

And Joanna ended up taking my advice to heart, going for some very subtle sun-kissed-skin-looking makeup treatment, with just a little mascara, eyeliner, eye shadow, and lip gloss. She looked great. Her just-skimpy-enough blouse hugged her torso in all the right places, as did her jaw-dropping pants.

Appropriately enough, "Me So Horny" kicked in just as Trent Kessler came through the front door with Alex Becker. God, Trent looked gorgeous; Joanna was right to have been crushing on him since God-knows-when. He had on a pair of very faded jeans that hung halfway down his perfectly toned surfer-god bubble butt (which is probably why the damn pants weren't slipping down to his ankles) and a tight vintage T-shirt that read DAYTONA BEACH.

"I see Alex is in her usual garb," I said to Carrie as we spotted them and waved them over to us.

"Aww, take it easy on her," Carrie said.

"Oh, I totally am—I love her to death, but she acts like she's still getting used to her post-pubescent body. And she'd be totally cute if she just retired those old jeans and big baggy shirts."

"If you say 'makeover,' I am so outta here," Carrie told me jokingly. "Now shut up, they're coming over."

Trent ambled in, his right hand running through his curly blond hair. Mmm!

Alex clomped awkwardly—but cutely and charmingly, nonetheless—over alongside him.

"Dude," he said (I know—how appropriate, right?), "you're, like, the only other dude here!"

"The curse of being a gay boy in high school, I suppose," I replied. "Hi, Alex."

"*Hola*, Jonathan."

"Joanna wants her fucking rug back."

"I don't know what you're talking about," she said, all deadpan.

We smiled at each other and broke out into laughter.

Maybe I should mention that Alex Becker is the other girl in my Spanish group with Joanna. She was my mistress in the last skit, who'd stolen Joanna's—or, rather . . . *Soledad*'s—husband (me) and *alfombra* (rug). Boy, did it get messy that day! Totally fun.

"You guys are crazy," Trent said. "So, seriously, no other dudes?" he asked. "We're not gonna break out the *Ya-Ya Sisterhood* or something, are we?"

"But then we get in our panties and have a tickle fight!" I giggled. "But what do you care if you're the only available booby-lover in the room?" I asked. "This should be a dream come true for a red-blooded all-American boy like yourself."

"No, man, I think I need a drink first," he said. Awww, how cute. Surfer-boy was the nervous type. "What do you guys have?" Perfect.

"Well, why don't you go see the birthday girl? She'll hook you up." I couldn't resist, and pointed him in Joanna's direction.

"Awesome." And he was off.

"So, lady, what can I get you?" I asked Alex.

"I dunno—something sweet?"

"Vodka and cran?"

"Uh . . . sure," she answered. "What service!"

"Pleasing you is my pleasure," I said (God, do I have to flirt with *everyone*?), and walked to the kitchen, where Joanna was nervously—but not too nervously (I was proud of her)—giving Trent a tour of the alcohol table. I poured Alex and myself two generous vodka crans, squeezed a bit of lime into them, added a glug of orange juice, and headed back to the living room. I swung my head around as I walked away, waggling my tongue at Joanna and checking out Trent's adorable ass at the same time. I believe in multi-tasking.

Another hour into the party, and everyone had shown up. Somehow, word had gotten out, and there were a few extra people there, but some of them brought more to drink. Liquor was flowing, people were dancing (yay!), and whoever wasn't dancing was clamoring for body shots. Joanna moved all of the alcohol off the dining-room table and onto the kitchen counter to make room. "Who's up?" she called.

"Me!" called Carrie, leading a shyish-looking cute brunette

boy to the table with her. I think his name was Nick and that he was there with our friend Erin.

"So, what would you prefer to lick off of me?" she asked him as she lay down on the table. "Or does it even matter?" She gave him a sexy smirk, and when his response came—which I believe was "Uhhhh . . ."—I took the liberty of licking Carrie's abdomen and shaking some salt onto it. Next, I placed a lime wedge below her belly button, just above the waistline of her low-rise jeans. Then I poured a shot of tequila into a shot glass.

"Now, Nick . . ." I began. "It's 'Nick,' right?"

"Uh-huh . . ." He looked a little embarrassed.

"Good. Now, you're gonna have to lap this up fast, okay? Because this is a very expensive knockoff Italian table, and we don't want to make Mrs. Marin mad at us. . . . And you don't want to offend Carrie, either, do you?"

"Nope." He pushed his glasses up to the top of his nose.

"And if you don't lick it all up fast enough, I'm gonna do one off you," I threatened.

"No, Jonathan!" Carrie screamed in her most dramatic stage voice. *"He's MIIIIIIIIIINE!"*

"Okay, Nick—one, two, three, *go!*"

The little crowd around the table hooted and hollered and screamed as I poured the shot into Carrie's belly button and Nick licked off the salt and started slurping at her stomach like a Labrador retriever. After a few seconds, Carrie sat up and gave him a big kiss and the crowd cheered. As she walked past me, she leaned into my ear and said, "Bagged another one." I love Carrie.

"Who goes now?" Joanna called.

"I think *you* do, birthday girl," I taunted, pinching her two more times. "Only five more to go," I whispered.

"Oh, fine," she said, acting all put out.

I noticed that Trent had been hanging around her since he'd arrived at the party, so I naturally put forth the suggestion: "And how about you do the honors, Trent?"

"Sweet," he said. Good sign. I think.

Joanna sent me a quick, stabbing look (did she not *know* I was gonna do that?!), but her expression quickly softened. She'd been slugging back vodka and Sprite for a while, and she definitely wasn't against having Trent Kessler lap up liquor from her body.

I had Trent set up a pile of sugar, a lemon wedge, and a shot of chilled vodka, and sat back and watched as he proceeded to lick, suck, slurp, then lick again, and then bite into the lemon wedge with a slightly dazed look on his face. Joanna giggled, threw herself into sitting position, and yelled happily, *"Fuck this! It's my birthday and I wanna DAAAANCE!"*

Joanna ran out of the dining room, corralling everyone through the archway and into the living room. Lords of Acid's "Spank My Booty" was playing, and all of a sudden the room just exploded full of dancing, shaking, and grinding bodies. Carrie grabbed my arm on the way and pulled me into the kitchen, where she'd poured some shots for me, herself, and Shauna.

"Here's to debauchery," Carrie said.

"And friends," Shauna added. Too sweet.

"And to how hot Trent and Joanna look together!" I said.

"I know!" Carrie said. "He's got me sweatin' like a whore in church with that ass of his."

"Agreed," I replied. "Okay, enough toasts. Wow, that's hard to say. . . . Anyway, one, two, three, *go!*"

The tequila drop-kicked me like a ninja on crack. I was in the middle of my wrist-shaking fit when Carrie shoved a Bud Light into my hand and yelled, "Chaser!"

Without thinking—I wasn't doing much of that at this point—I slammed the beer bottle upward and chugged deeply from it, trying to dull out the tequila burn. By the end of this, I was completely dizzy, all my senses dulled out. I wasn't sick yet, though—hopefully, it'd stay that way.

"I'm gonna fuckin' kill ya, Carrie," I slurred in a fake hick accent.

"You're fucked up, Jonathan," Carrie informed me.

"News flash! News flash!" I cried.

"All right, kids," Carrie called out over the music, ignoring my idiocy. "Let's dance!"

"Oh, I'm not sure I want to—" Shauna started to say.

"Of course you do, baby," I said, and pulled her into the throng of people.

The dance party had gotten nuts, and I was loving every drunken minute of it. In hindsight, maybe I didn't *really* need to try to drink my weight in alcohol, but I was feeling euphoric as I bounced from girl to girl on the living-room-slash-foyer impromptu dance floor we had cleared, grabbing waists, riding asses, and shaking my nose in cleavage all along the way.

At one point, I couldn't help but notice that I was surrounded by a crowd of girls, all sort of tag-team nasty-dancing with me. It was a sort of gay Lord-of-the-Dance-esque orgy, but with clothes on, and with all the girls' boyfriends standing off to the side, looking perplexed, jealous, and intrigued, whispering to one another. At one point, this girl Kristen Samuels whispered sloppily into my ear, "Tom *never* dances with me like this—I wish he *would!*" I laughed, glanced up at her boyfriend, Tom Matthews—who was this muscular, brown-haired football stud I'd had the hots for since tenth grade—and politely passed her on to him, saying, "You should take her to some backseat somewhere."

If this was the extent of the action that I was ever going to get—girls riding me, having their dance-floor way with me, while their hunky boyfriends gave me smoldering looks—then I'd take it. I have to admit, I kind of liked it. Not as much as I'd enjoy a reciprocal sexual attraction, but oh, well. Not like *that* was gonna happen.

"Heeeey, Jonathan," Kenny Daniels said nasally, breaking into my crowd of horny female dance partners. "Wanna dance?"

Ugh.

Kenny Daniels was, like, the only other out kid at Winter Park. He was *sort of* cute, but in that trashy bleached blond–pierced nipple sort of trying-way-too-hard kind of way. I found him pretty obnoxious, and wasn't too keen on hanging out with him, as I'd heard from some of his girlfriends—who were *always* trying to set us up—that he "dated" heavily online. And that just isn't my thing, really. And he was way too forward and—I realized as he grabbed me by the ass—touchy-feely.

"Oh, Kenny!" I yelled over the Pussycat Dolls. "I'm vibrating!"

"Hot."

"No, not hot—really, I'm vibrating," I said, pointing to my pocket. "It's my phone; I have to go."

I ran to the kitchen and flipped open my phone. Totally saved by the bell. Or buzz. Or whatever. It was my brother.

"Jesse!" I yelled into the phone. "How the hell are ya?"

"I'm great, bro—how're you?"

"Drunk as aaaall shit."

"You sound it." He laughed. "Look, I was just calling to see if everything was going all right with the party. Anyone gotten sick or anything? No one's driving out of there as drunk as you are, are they?"

"Noooo, Jesse," I said deliberately. "Everything's good! And thanks for the al-co-hol."

"You're-wel-come," he replied, mocking me. "Just call me if anything happens, okay? And drink some water!"

"Water! That's *brilliant!*" I turned to the people milling about the kitchen. "Hey! Someone get me some water!" Someone handed me their drink. It wasn't water. Oh, well.

"See you later, bro."

"Laters."

I hung up the phone and surveyed the scene—the party seemed to have reached epic proportions:

I saw Kenny Daniels taking over my place in the sea of hot-and-bothered girls who had boyfriends who wouldn't dance with them. Whatever. So *not* touching that, ever.

I spotted Joanna and Trent sort-of-talking-sort-of-dancing at the far end of the room. Good!

A few feet to the left, I saw Shauna sandwiching Jake McKay

with Marie Acosta. Go, Shauna! I wondered how drunk she must be to act so boldly.

And then I spied Carrie leading Latest-Conquest Nick upstairs, presumably to one of the "chill" rooms. Glad *somebody* was getting some action tonight. Carrie was always getting action, actually—with plenty of guys, and even a few girls. But guys were easier. Apparently. Not like I knew, or would *ever* know. "Ugh—I am *not* gonna turn into a bitter drunk gay boy," I said out loud to myself, looking around and noticing a couple people looking at me strangely. I laughed. I should have known *then* how drunk I was.

And then I saw Alex, dancing by herself near the window. She turned her head and saw me, and waved. I smiled back, took a swallow from my beer, and danced over to her, mouthing the words to "Like a Virgin." She laughed as I held out my hand, gesturing her to dance with me. She accepted, and I semi-bowed/semi-fell to one knee and gave her delicate hand a not-so-delicate kiss.

"Very gentlemanly, Jonathan," she said through a gutteral, gurgly, groggy-drunk laugh as she wiped her hand on her jeans.

I grabbed her by the waist and locked hips with her, swaying back and forth to the synthy eighties beat. And then she was smiling at me, really big.

"And kudos on the CDs," she continued. "It's quite a mix you have. . . . Marilyn Manson followed by Madonna?"

I said something idiotic like "Variety is the spice of life" or something. Then, "Oh, whoa, was that cliché or *what*? God, I'm drunk—did I say that out loud?" I leaned forward and gave her a peck on the cheek.

She threw her head back and laughed some more (she must've been pretty loaded; I'd never seen her act so wild), and I tilted her body back, supporting it with my right arm, while we continued to grind our hips back and forth, back and forth, forward and backward.

"Jesus, Jonathan, you're an incredible dancer," she said, clasping her hands behind my neck. "A girl needs to be on birth control to dance with you—"

"Aaaaaahhhhh!!!!!" I interrupted her. I couldn't help it—Britney had come on. My favorite club mix. "I fucking *love* this remix—the beat is just brutal!"

Our dancing and grinding pumped up into hyper mode. We shook our bodies to the relentless beat. We vibrated our pelvises to the intense rises and buildups. And our bodies erupted, arms and torsos flying and flailing, to the techno explosions that followed. Our bodies contorted, our muscles screamed against the lactic-acid buildup (I guess health class taught me *some* stuff), and we could feel the sweat dampening our clothes.

"Don't you love it!" I beamed.

"Totally," Alex said through ragged breaths, leaning forward to kiss *me* on the cheek now. She was getting totally into it.

And then I started to notice things: some of the other party-goers looking at us, talking into one another's ears. Trent looking away from Joanna momentarily and staring at Alex, then me, then quickly away (kinda weird). Alex's incessant grinding against me, even when the song slowed down and blended into the next. How my hands were totally grabbing her ass, and hers mine. And the weird, never-quite-before-seen bedroom eyes I think she was making at me.

"But," she said, "I think I need a break—I might've pulled a leg muscle thanks to you. Do you wanna come take a breather with me?"

"Sure."

Apparently, noticing strange things and connecting them in your brain to possible consequences is something that gets screwed up with copious amounts of alcohol.

We stumbled off the dance floor and through the kitchen, slowly lumbered up the stairs, and wound up falling down very ungracefully ("Timberrrrrrrrr!" was all that was running through my head) onto the bed in one of the empty guest rooms. (Guest room? Again, not thinking.) I could have easily just passed out right there. I mean, why not? I'd already had a ton of fun, my girlfriends were occupied with other guys, and I sure as hell wasn't gonna hook up with Kenny Daniels or anything. . . .

"Hey, Jonathan," Alex interrupted my dizzy thoughts, "are you and Kenny together?"

I let out a burst of laughter. "No!"

"So are you seeing anybody?" She sat up in the bed and pulled her knees up to her chest, hugging them.

I laughed again. "Other than my left hand and a few teen heartthrobs in my dreams? Hardly." I sat up, too, and leaned my head against the wall for support. It wasn't doing so well on its own.

"Well, why not?" she asked. "You're totally hot, and such a sweetheart."

"Oh, go on," I chuckled. "Haven't you noticed? I'm, like, the *only* gay guy at Winter Park that is less than hideous!"

"Well, Kenny isn't hideous."

"In ways he is, though." I exhaled. "I don't want to date some pill-popping kid who puts on house music to make out to, you know? Plus, I don't think he'd want to *date*, really. He's just kinda sleazy . . . and I'm not really interested."

"Huh."

"But, you know, it's kinda starting to suck," I said. "I'm seriously, like, the only gay guy at Winter Park I'd date. And I'm not gonna go online to meet anyone, 'cause that kind of freaks me out, so what does that leave me?" Why was I just going on and on about this? All of a sudden, the words just kept coming out of my mouth, and I couldn't stop. "And, *God*, I can't take one more party where I see everyone else coupling off and leaving me with nothing. . . . It's getting old. *Anyway*, Carrie *has* been promising to introduce me to some of her other gay friends from Dr. Phillips— their magnet program's for drama and the arts, so that school is *crawling* with 'mos."

"That's nice."

"Yeah, but I'm sick of waiting!" I said. "God, I just think sometimes it'd be easier to be straight. Maybe *then* I could couple off with someone and head to a guest room. . . ."

I realized my slipup and the resulting awkwardness, and looked at Alex and laughed nervously.

"Well, I'm not dating anyone, either," Alex said now, wringing her hands, like she was drying them off with a hand towel but without the hand towel. "I haven't *ever*, really."

"That's kinda hard to believe," I told her. "I mean, you're way cute—maybe you just don't know how to work it."

"Hey, same for *you*, Jonathan! You're totally hot."

"You said that already."

"Did I?" She looked away from me and studied her feet, hugging her knees closer to her chest. "Anyway, it's so annoying—and this party's gotten me thinking. . . . I'll be eighteen soon, too. I mean, that makes me a woman, right?"

"Well, technically doesn't womanhood start the day you get your first period? I think I learned that on a *Cosby Show* rerun."

She laughed loudly at this. "God! You're so funny!" she choked out. "The thing is," she continued, "I still don't feel like a woman yet, I don't think. I feel like I need to go through some rite of passage or something."

The only light in the room was coming from a little lamp on the bedside table and a sliver of light peeking in from the hallway. I could hear Kylie singing "In Your Eyes" through the din of the happy partygoers and longed to be down there. Away from this room. And this situation . . . whatever it was. I'd never been seduced before, but this was starting to feel like it . . . and I didn't know what to do. If I couldn't handle getting myself a glass of water, how could I take care of *this* situation?

"So maybe I should just have sex once to get it over with, right?" she blurted out.

Whoa! Um, okay. Twisted. Weird. Illogical. Sad. Interesting. "Sure, why not? As long as you're safe." Who was I to lecture while intoxicated? Didn't they give tickets for that?

"Well, it should be with someone I care about, I think . . . so it's special." She leaned closer to me and put her hand on my knee. "Someone like . . . you? What do you think?"

"Who-ho-ho-hooooah," I managed, drunkenly trying to swat her hand away like a fly. "Are you serious?"

"Well, yeah . . ." She pulled her arms back to her side of the bed and resumed her former knee-hugging position, all of a sudden looking crushed. "You were kinda flirting with me a lot while we were dancing and I thought you wanted to . . . I dunno. But maybe you could? If you don't mind, that is. . . . I didn't think you would, actually. . . . Is that crazy?"

"*Mind?* Alex, I'm *gay!* Of course I mind. I like *guys.* I think boobs are nothing more than superfluous orbs of fatty tissue. I impersonate Cher after too many cosmos. I *drink* cosmos! I consider Madonna to be higher than God. And Kylie Minogue to transcend even *Madonna's* status! Are you seeing a pattern? Plus, I'm . . . I'm not in the frame of mind. It'd be . . . taking advantage of me if you made me have sex with you. I don't even know my own *name* right now. Am I making sense?" I was scrambling for a way out of this.

"Sure, you're making sense. . . ." Alex said, looking kind of embarrassed. "But consider it," she continued, seeming to get more confidence. "We know each other really well, and you've been a great friend to me since I met you. Remember when you stuck up for me in Señora Lopez's class that time? In the middle of class, right when she was reaming me for not knowing the past tense of some verb, and you just raised your hand and were all like, 'Señora Lopez, why do you hate Alexandra?' She didn't know *what* to do—it was so wonderful!"

"Actually, it was '¿Por qué detestas a Alexandra?'" I corrected her.

"Exactly! You're brilliant. And when we would eat lunch together sometimes in junior year and you'd listen to all that stuff about my parents and everything?"

"Yeah," I said, softening up a little. "I remember. I mean, it was no big deal or anything—I was just helping out."

"I *know*. But that's why you're so special to me."

"I dunno, Alex—"

"And you're just such a sweet, amazing guy," she continued, interrupting me, clearly aware that she was on a roll, "and I know I can trust you to be gentle with me, and to just be . . . well . . . *Jonathan* about it. You mean a lot to me, and it'd mean a lot to me if you were my first."

Well, actually, this was really nice to hear. I wished it was a *guy* saying it, but beggars can't be choosers, I suppose. Alex *was* a good friend, and I liked the idea of being her first, and being someone she could trust. And getting genuine physical attention for once was also pretty cool . . . even if it meant sleeping with a—

Wait. *Hello, this is Logic checking in.* "But won't things get weird?" I asked.

"I dunno," she said. "Probably not."

"'Cause you don't, like, have a crush on me or anything, do you?"

"Me?" she laughed. "Well . . . no! That'd be crazy . . . because you're *gay*, right?"

"Way gay," I clarified. "So we couldn't get weird, okay? Wow." I paused, contemplating. "Have you considered a career in selling insurance? You've almost got me sold."

"That's the sweetest thing anyone's ever said to me," she said, laughing again.

Could I? Would I? I was, of course, still pretty shaky on the idea. I mean, come on! Having sex . . . with a *girl*? Was I this desperate for physical affection? It would be special . . . for *her*. Because when I pictured myself losing my virginity, it was with a guy, not a girl. So losing my *girl* virginity wouldn't exactly do anything for me. So, by that rationale, maybe . . . I could do it?

"I don't know, Alex. I think . . . maybe . . ." I stammered. "But, maybe it's just because I'm so wasted. I mean, don't you think I'm too . . . wasted?" For lack of a better word. Apparently.

"Well, let's see. . . . Pop quiz: What did Madonna say to her cabdriver when she first arrived in New York?"

"'Take me to the center of everything!'" I replied proudly.

"Then I think you're good to go."

"Wait! That one was too easy—!"

And I don't know what came over her, but the next thing I knew, Alex was straddling me and holding me in a wet, tongue-y lip-lock. Hate to admit it, but it was pretty great—kissing is just fun in general, regardless of gender. After a little while of that, she started rubbing against me as if we were back on the dance floor and putting her hands up my shirt. This was bizarre. It felt all wrong. But I just couldn't stop. It wasn't like I was *enjoying* it, though. I mean, yes, after five minutes or so, I popped a boner, but I was a seventeen-year-old guy—I could give myself an erection by fumbling around for my cell phone for too long!

O, Madonna (Ciccone) in Heaven, if only I wasn't so knowledgeable in useless pop-culture trivia, I could be back downstairs, dancing and drinking at the party. (And *now* I could hear a Garbage remix playing. Dammit!) Alex would have determined that I was too drunk to screw without remorse, and she would have left me alone. But no. Now she was taking my pants off tentatively—and I was *letting* her!—and going into her purse for a condom. I couldn't believe it was all happening!

So maybe it was the alcohol. Maybe it was my sudden lack of assertiveness. Or maybe I was just happy to have someone other than Kenny Daniels *want* me for once. It was nice. But I finally decided to throw caution (and gayness) to the wind and go with it. So that is how it happened.

How *I* went to "the center of everything" (for some people, at least) without even asking (or wanting) to.

And just as Alex tentatively took hold of the waistline of my boxer briefs, there was a hard knocking on the door.

I locked eyes with Alex and bugged out my eyes. Like, what a scandal! Then I started laughing at the thought of how my stupid drunk face must look to her. She smiled a little, too, and leaned down to kiss me.

"Hello?" a voice called from the other side of the door. Shit—I'd already forgotten what I was laughing about. "Who's in there?" Double shit! It was Joanna.

"It's Jonathan!" "It's Alex!" we yelled at the same time.

"Uh . . . I've been looking for you, *Jonathan*," she yelled through the door. She was definitely feeling quite the birthday buzz. "'Cause your fucking Marilyn Manson is playing and I thought you'd like to come downstairs and slaughter some kittens or something. Why's the door locked?"

"We're talking in here!" Alex said suddenly to the door.

"So talk out here, *duuuuh!*" was Joanna's brilliant response.

"Uh, no can do," I stammered. "Serious . . . uh . . . serious stuff in here. Thanks for the Manson update, though. I'll see ya later."

"Whatever, dork, I'm skipping the song then," and then she was gone.

We waited a second to make sure she was gone.

Then Alex said, "So, where were we?"

Uh, Cliché Alert!

So, after the clothes came off and the condom went on, I sort of lost track of what was happening. I had no idea what the hell I was doing, but I just let my instincts take over. I mean, biologically speaking, maybe I was meant to do this. To spread my wonderful seed. The world needed more Jonathan Parishes, right?

I'll spare you the dirty details, but let's just say that my heterosexual instincts sucked. It was so awkward. I was bungling everything—knocking over the lamp, accidentally banging Alex's skull against the headboard, and at one point unknowingly humming that freaking Hanson song "MMMBop" to keep some sort of a rhythm going. It was utterly ridiculous. All I could hope was that everyone's first time was this weird, and that I hadn't screwed up everything for Alex. And I could not stop hoping against hope that she wouldn't get completely naked, leaving me to face actual breasts head-on, and thus undoubtedly ending the entire sexual act. That would kind of suck for Alex, too.

"Are you *humming*?" Alex asked me as I stared at Mrs. Marin's floral-patterned guest-bed pillows (who the hell still buys floral, anyway?). "Wait, let me rephrase that—are you humming '*MMMBop*'?"

"Look, just . . . just . . . keep that bra on."

4. Can't Get You Out of My Head

Finally figuring out that you're gay has got nothing on the morning after your gay ass does it with a girl. I woke up the next morning feeling hungover, soaked in alcohol, and—since Alex's side of the bed we'd passed out on was empty—used.

"Cops don't look for drunk drivers at seven thirty in the morning, do they?" I asked Carrie after getting dressed and lumbering around the house to find her.

"I have that T-shirt, I think," Carrie groggily replied to me from her nest of comforters and sleeping bags on the living-room floor. "What the hell are you doing up, anyway?"

"I have to open at Target," I told her. "I can't tell if I'm still drunk or if I'm just hungover."

"Walk the line," she commanded.

"If I stare down at my feet too long I'll get nauseous."

"Then just take your chances. I'm sure you're fine. Now gimme some sugar."

"I'm not sure if there's any logic there, but okay." I knelt down—with great effort—and gave her a kiss on the forehead. "Um . . . you wanna meet me for lunch when I get out at noon? I kinda need to talk to you about something. . . ."

"If I can drag myself up in time, I'll pick you up out front and we'll go somewhere."

"Thanks, sweetie." This time, my "sweetie" wasn't sarcastic. I meant it. I needed her. Carrie was the one who would make me feel better, not just make me feel shittier.

I threw back two Excedrins with a few big gulps of orange juice, put two more in a Ziploc baggie for later, grabbed a Gatorade from the fridge, and shuffled out the front door.

It was overcast, but still unbearably bright. Now I know why people say you can still get sunburned at the beach even if it's cloudy. I should try to save the ozone layer for days like these. I put on my sunglasses and walked up to my car through the hot, humid soupiness.

There wasn't any traffic at the East-West on-ramp in the early Sunday morning haze. Easy on, easy off.

If only my evening had been easy on, easy off.

I still couldn't believe what I'd done the night before. It was so strange, so out of character. For me, someone who plans everything, this was equal to discovering the cure for cancer, wearing plaid in a non-ironic way, or declaring that Mandy Moore had talent. Earth-shattering! Now everything around me looked so . . . *straight*. I saw myself in every happy straight couple on every billboard and in every minivan and parking lot that I drove by. *What have I become?* It was just weird and distressing to have gone from hardly ever *considering* sex with a girl to actually *doing* it. And at nearly eighteen years of age! When I totally knew my sexuality.

Noticing Kylie Minogue singing "Can't Get You Out of My Head" in my stereo, I ejected the CD and replaced it with a Fuel album; I didn't deserve Kylie anymore. Plus, the lyrics to the song weren't helping me forget about what'd happened just a few hours before.

Since it was a Sunday morning, Target was blissfully, predictably slow. Everyone in Orlando was either sleeping or worshipping. Genius that I am (well, *was*), I'd thought of this when I had filled out my availability schedule for work. Since I was only "available" on Sundays from eight until noon, which was when the churchgoers and the lazy-Sundayers (who all think you were put on Earth by God to serve them) started pouring into the store, those are the only Sunday hours that I work. But not a Sunday goes by that I don't get a visit from the store manager, asking me if I'm gonna "stay later and help out." I'll give you one guess what my response always is.

I went about the motions for the day. I went to the display case and spread out the week's new ads. It was Dollar Days again. Hooray. Where every price is an even dollar amount. One-dollar bags of bite-sized Kit Kats. Five-dollar jugs of Tide. Eight-dollar bulk sacks of paper towels. The idiots who think that prices that don't end in a ".99" is a bigger event than the second coming of Christ would be coming in droves this week. I couldn't *wait*.

After crumpling out the ad card, I went back behind the service desk and slumped over my computer. I was achy and wanted to throw up. I vowed to never drink that much again in my life, and to never sleep with a girl after doing so. Alcohol + Vagina = Ugly Sunday.

"Young man?"

I jerked my head up and focused my bleary vision on an overweight middle-aged woman. She was holding a fuchsia tank top and a receipt.

"Any reason why you're sleeping when you should be looking out for customers?" she asked haughtily.

Bitch.

"I just had a really . . . long night," I managed.

"Well, then, maybe you should consider the consequences of your actions before acting," she advised as she handed me the shirt and her receipt.

Fuck it. Let them fire me.

I held up the shirt and pointed to the big red *M* on the tag and said, "I don't think I need to point out the irony in this situation, do I?" I scanned the receipt, pressed a few buttons, and then scanned the shirt's bar code. "Would you like the money back on your card or store credit?"

"Put it back on my card," she huffed. "I'll be taking my business to Wal-Mart."

Like that was a big threat to me. "I'm so sorry you'll be leaving us. The closest Wal-Mart is on Colonial and Alafaya," I told her. "Would you like me to draw you a map?"

She collected her receipts back and stormed off, presumably thinking that I gave two shits about whether she shopped at Target or Wal-Mart. Oh, well, more sleep for me. . . .

"*Girrrrrl*, you can be a *puta*, you know that?"

Juan from electronics was at the counter.

Juan is great. He's twenty-two, goes to UCF, and is about the cattiest, funniest, gayest, Puerto Rican–est guy I've ever met. He's always messing around with me—pinching me behind the service desk, calling me every ten minutes to see if he has any returns—but I loved having him around. He makes the days go by faster.

"Whatever, Juan, *she* was the bitch and I'm hungover and wanting to die," I told him. "She had it coming."

Juan punched in the code for the service-desk door and strutted in all peppy. Didn't he know it was only nine in the morning?

"So, do I have any returns, *mami*?" he asked me.

"At nine on a Sunday? All you have to take back is this Celine Dion CD."

"*Ay, carajo*, I don't blame them." He pinched me as he walked behind me, and I stuck out my leg to trip him. Luckily, he was awake enough to react before he took a spill. We laughed hard, even though it made my head feel like exploding.

"Ohhh, thanks, Juan. I needed that."

Juan stopped laughing and looked at me earnestly. "Honey, is something wrong? You don't seem yourself today."

"You have no idea," I told him, wanting so badly to confide in him. But if I did, I felt like he'd judge me for totally mocking our normality. No, I couldn't. "Maybe I'll tell you later," I continued. "Let's just say for now that I had way too much beer, even more vodka, and way more tequila last night than is necessary for a hundred-and-forty-pound boy."

But Juan seemed to know better. "Okay," he said. "You just tell Juan what you want to when you want to."

"Deal."

• • •

"So . . . Jonathan . . . how's . . . the day going?"

My behemoth of a boss stood in front of me, holding a clip-board and scanning it with a pen like it was some impenetrable code that held the secrets of the universe. He was out of breath—probably from sprinting through the store to catch me before quittin' time—and his forehead had little beads of sweat on it. It must've been close to noon. I glanced down at my watch. 11:57. Praise Jesus. He tapped his pen a few times and looked up at me, awaiting a response. I pulled out my Ziploc of Excedrin and popped the last two, swigging them back with the Diet Coke I'd gotten from the Target café.

"My day's going great, Mr. Ludlow," I replied fakely but not so fakely. "And yours?"

"Fan*tas*tic," he replied transparently. "Look . . . do you think you'll be able to help us out for a few more hours today?"

"Oh, I'm sorry, Mr. Ludlow, but . . . you know my availability."

"Yes, I do, but . . ."

"And I really must get to church," I lied, shifting to the left just slightly in case a bolt of lightning came crashing through the roof.

"Well . . . then . . . I suppose I understand," Ludlow stam-mered. "Have a great rest of the day."

"Will do. Oop! Look at the time. And there's Tameka to relieve me—see you Wednesday night." And I was gone in a flash.

After I clocked out, I ran to the front of the store and searched for Carrie's car. A minute later, up pulled her hot-pink Corsica, lovingly dubbed—by Carrie herself; I'm not this mean—"the Whore-sica," after all the good times she'd had in it.

"Hey, bitch, how much for that fine ass?!" she yelled from the car, tooting the horn a couple times.

I would have laughed if I hadn't already felt like a whore. A whore with a splitting headache.

"Want a date?" she continued.

"You buyin'?" I asked, leaning down into the car.

"As long as you put out." She opened the passenger-side door, since it didn't open from the outside. "Get in."

I got in the Whore-sica and we drove off, hanging a right out of the parking lot toward downtown.

"Is the barbecue place in Thornton Park okay with you?" she asked. "I'm sort of in the mood for something fatty and gas-inducing."

"I couldn't agree more. I should've eaten something on the way to work. I'm dying."

"Excellent. So, why the emergency lunch?"

"My head's splitting in two, and my stomach's been marinating in alcohol all morning. I'll need some food in me before I tell you."

"Bitch bitch bitch, moan moan moan."

Ten minutes later, we were driving around Thornton Park look-ing for a space. Thornton Park is sort of the new up-and-coming neighborhood, and is credited with bringing people back to pre-viously scary downtown Orlando. After just a few years, it's like its own real city, complete with lofts, a gym, a grocery store, some cute little cafés and restaurants, and—of course—a Starbucks. Thornton Park always cheered me up; it made me feel like I was in a real city, rather than the sprawly suburban hell that Orlando—and practically every other city in the country—can be. It was very Sex and the Sorta-City.

The closest space we found was on Lake Eola, which I didn't mind. We strolled along, glancing over at the swan boats that dotted the little lake, and at the real swans that lined the shore. We hung a left on Washington, and a few blocks later we were at the barbecue place.

I got us an emergency order of mozzarella sticks to dull the pain in my head and the toxic churning in my stomach. Thankfully, they arrived in minutes, and I attacked the plate like a starving ape.

"So," I said with my mouth unashamedly full, "how was your night with that Nick kid? How come when I saw you, you were sleeping alone?"

"Turns out little Nicky is a retail slave like you, Jonathan," she replied. "He had to get to his shift at Super Wal-Mart."

"How super! I think I sent a customer his way today."

"He's in produce."

"Sexy. You know, he didn't really seem like your type. I thought for sure you were gonna hook up with that girl—the one in that orangish top . . . that . . . someone brought? God, I don't even remember. Anyway, I was totally getting some bi vibes from her."

"Eh." Carrie shrugged. "I know who you're talking about—and yeah, she was definitely hot. But for some reason I was really feelin' Nick last night. He was just so damn cute."

"So . . . ?"

"So what, dude?"

"Do I have to ask?" I paused.

She sexy-stared me down and lifted one eyebrow. "A lady never speaks of such things," she said, suddenly acting shocked and putting her hand up to cover her mouth.

"Right. But *you* do."

She threw back her head in a dramatic cackle. "Right you are, young sir."

"Get out of character now, please."

"Okay, fine. Let's just say we had a very lovely time and leave it at that."

I yawned as a response.

"And that I popped his cherry!" She laughed and clapped enthusiastically. "Oh, the virgin boys are such terrible lovers, but boy are they sweet!"

I shifted uncomfortably in my seat and started fumbling with my straw wrapper. I wondered how many times I could wrap it around my index finger before it snapped. Three, I found out. Fascinating. I shifted my attention to my glass of Diet Coke, and proceeded to twirl my straw in it, stirring up the ice. I looked up to see Carrie staring at me sympathetically.

"Oh, don't worry, Jonathan," she said. "You'll find someone soon. . . . And you most definitely—despite what you've convinced yourself—will *not* die a virgin."

"Yeah, well . . . I know I won't, because . . . I'm not a virgin anymore."

"*Shit, sweetie!*" she screamed, catching the attention of everyone else on the patio and a gay couple walking by with their pug. "*Who? WHEN? WH—?*"

"Don't scream."

"I promise."

Here goes. "Alex Becker. Last night. The floral guest room. And now I'm in hell."

Carrie, for once, was speechless. She gazed at me, wide-eyed, with what appeared to be a mix of surprise, excitement, confusion, and maybe even a little admiration. She leaned forward slowly, and said very quietly, "You know she's a chick, right?"

"*Of course I do!*" I screamed. I instantly regretted it and grabbed my head. The headache still hadn't gone away.

"Well, that's perfectly fine, honey, but . . . why?"

"I don't know, Carrie, I just . . . I just really liked having someone want me for once, you know? I was really *really* wasted, and then there was 'Like a Virgin,' and then we were dancing, and there was tequila, and then a Britney song came on, and I probably put my face in her cleavage, and I think I totally stepped over the line for appropriate gay-male-on-straight-girl flirting—which I didn't even know *existed!*—and before I know it, we're upstairs and she's telling me about how hot I am and how she doesn't feel like a woman yet and it's probably because she hasn't had sex before and that maybe she could get it over with so she's more comfortable with herself so would I please do her the honor of . . . popping her cherry, as you would say. And I think I told her she was pretty . . . maybe not the best move."

Our food arrived. I dived into my barbecue bacon burger, dying to do something with my mouth besides kiss girls and talk about this insanity.

"Well, baby, I'm shocked," Carrie said. She paused. Then: "Were you any good?"

"Seriously doubtful. I hardly remember. I wonder how I even *found* it."

Carrie busted out laughing. Burger bits everywhere. "I'm sorry," she said through teary eyes. "At least you know you're not a natural at it or anything."

"I don't know, but . . . this whole thing's got me thinking . . ."

"What?" Carrie shot in. "Thinking what?"

"That maybe I'm . . . or I should be . . . straight . . . or something. That I'm not cut out for the gayness thing."

Carrie threw her head back and laughed uncontrollably, and this time, she definitely wasn't acting at all. If she was acting, she deserved an Oscar.

"Not cut out for the gayness thing?" she said through gasps of laughter, her eyes spurting tears. "Jonathan, sweetie, you're the gayest thing to hit Orlando since Neiman Marcus, and I love you for it!"

"You think so? I took out my Kylie CD this morning because it was like I cheated on her or something."

"Oh, Jonny, I *know* so!" she boomed emphatically. "You are a beautiful, wonderful, out-and-proud homosexual, and that's an amazing thing for a high-schooler in this town. You're unapologetic, you have confidence in yourself, and you love your friends."

"Yeah?"

"Of course!" She took a bite of her burger and continued talking. "Just don't have sex with any more of them. Your friendship with Alex is probably fucked now."

"Probably."

She reached across the table and took my hand into hers. "You had a little slipup. You were flattered to have a girl ask you to be her first, and you slipped. It's no big deal. And you sucked at it, anyway!"

This was making sense. "Yeah. You're right, Carrie."

"I always am."

"I'm still gay!" I beamed happily. "I can still listen to Kylie all I want!"

"Of course you can."

"I don't have to have sex with girls to feel good about myself!"

"Of course not."

I felt better already. I knew a lunch with Carrie would solve everything. She was real, she was brutally honest, and she was extremely—sometimes unnervingly—open. I could go on happily now, and pretend the Alex debacle had never happened.

"Hey, Carrie?"

"Yeah?"

"Can we keep this our little secret?"

"Of course, baby," she told me. "No one will ever know."

5. Word Is Out

Everyone found out.

Eventually.

I'm not even kidding.

Strangely enough, though, the day started pretty uneventfully.

I rolled old Aretha (now a quarter of a million miles old—old enough to have driven around the globe ten times, I'd recently figured out) into the senior parking lot and dragged my tired Monday ass out and through the hallways to statistics class. I was feeling very anxious, weirded out by my heightened heterosexual awareness. There was a lot more of that way of thinking, of noticing straight couples that I hadn't noticed before, seeing moms and dads dropping their kids off, stuff like that. And on top of it all, I kept looking at girls. Well, to be more precise, looking at girls looking at *me*. Because of my evening with Alex, I was much more aware of the girls at school checking me out.

It was crazy! I didn't know whether to be flattered or terrified. Because now I was thinking that these girls knew about what'd happened at that party. I mean, Alex was a bit of a blabbermouth.

And Joanna had interrupted us. And we presumably passed out in the same bed . . . together! Maybe someone saw us. Maybe word was out. I could *so* not take this stress . . . and *midterms* were coming up!

Once I was safely in statistics, my class got back our tests from the Friday before (I got a 97—no big surprise there) and we all started a new unit. Then, as I was gathering my stuff to go to Spanish, Laura Schulberg came up to me and plopped her test in front of me, faceup.

"Ninety-one," she declared proudly. "I'm a genius, thanks to you."

"Wow, Laura, that's fantastic!" I exclaimed. "Don't sell yourself short—maybe you've been a genius all along."

I'd used my not-so-shabby math skills to help her through somewhat of a mega study session the week before. She was a math-buddy of mine; we never really hung out outside of school, probably because we didn't hang out with the same crowd. She was way way rich, and hung out with a whole group of people in similar . . . financial situations. Not to say I didn't like her, though. She was actually pretty sweet, and we always had fun in our classes together. Like I said: math-buddy.

But we seemed to have math together every single year. Algebra, geometry, and algebra II she'd done all right with, but something about statistics froze her up. So, naturally I'd been there to help her out, for the price of a meal or two at Denny's.

"Well, thanks, man," Laura said. "But I'd really like to take you out for a proper thank-you, if that's okay with you. I mean, this ninety-one was a fucking miracle!"

"Okay, well . . . sure, why not?" I replied. "I mean, we hardly ever hang out outside of class."

"I know, right? So how about Saturday night? I'll figure it all out."

"I'll pencil you in, darling."

"Great." She paused. "And that was one hell of a party I heard you and Joanna threw on Saturday. I'm sorry I missed it."

Oh. The party.

"Well, yeah, it was fun but . . . I kinda . . . blacked out toward the end of it." Or I screwed a girl. Blacking out. Screwing a girl. Same thing, right?

"Huh" was all Laura said in reply. "Well . . ."

"Okay . . . well, I'll keep Saturday in mind," I said to break the silence. "Bye, Laura."

And then I had to go to Spanish.

And face Alex.

And Joanna, whom I'd been ignoring.

As I made my way through the hallways, I didn't know what was freaking me out more: the various looks from girls I was noticing and wondering if they knew about everything, or the fear of running into Alex Becker before getting to the safety of the classroom. I decided to head to the boys' bathroom—which I *never* do, ick!—to pee, wash my hands very slowly and methodically, and waste as much time as possible before getting to class. I didn't want to see Alex in the hallways or in the classroom until the class had actually *started*.

So I got to class with ten seconds to spare, and Alex was nowhere to be seen. Thank God! Maybe she transferred schools or something. Hey—a boy can dream, right? I planted myself next to Joanna and said hi just as Señora Morales began another lecture on the *subjuntivo*. Then, about ten minutes into the class, in walks—no . . . make that *struts*—Alexandra Becker, wearing a tight black miniskirt, big whorish Ugg boots, and a spaghetti-strap turquoise top. *Way* different from her usual jeans-and-oversized-tee ensemble and coming into class ten minutes early to brush up on the latest verb conjugations.

I caught myself staring, and Joanna staring at me, rolling her eyes.

"Excuse me, Señorita Becker," Señora Morales said, "but is there any reason you're ten minutes late? And strutting into my classroom like it's a runway?"

A few people laughed quietly.

My stomach flip-flopped, and I had to fight back the urge to vomit.

"Uh, no, not really," Alex said flatly. "Guess I lost track of time. I went out for breakfast."

"Do you not have a first-period class?" Señora Morales asked.

"Uh . . . sure, we'll go with that."

A few *more* people laughed at that.

But the teacher totally kept her cool, saying, "Well, I'm afraid I'll need to have someone write you up for that top—you know you're not allowed to wear sleeveless tops. Much less spaghetti straps."

"Yeah, Jonathan might get distracted," Quentin Carmichael, our class clown, blurted out.

Everyone chuckled at that, and I just laughed nervously,

hoping that word hadn't spread as far as *Quentin Carmichael* before lunch, and looked at the teacher and said as sheepishly as I could, "I just love women's shoulders, Señora Morales—they make me *loco*."

She smiled at me, then told the class to settle down and Alex to *sit* down, please, and stop disrupting her class. "You can stay here till the end of class, then I'll have to send you over to the dean's office for that shirt, all right?"

"Sure." And Alex plopped down in her seat, oozing confidence and sexuality. Now I *had* to talk to her after class, as it was feeling more possible by the second that she'd blabbed about our Saturday-night indiscretions. Then again, it could've just been my paranoia. But whatever. I had to talk to her.

"What is your deal, Jonathan?" Joanna whispered to me. "You haven't called since—"

Luckily, Señora Morales resumed class immediately, and I could just bide my time. I could only deal with one person at a time today.

When class was over, I made a beeline for Alex, but just as I was about to get to her, the teacher asked her to stay after for a few minutes. Alex gave me a quick smile and a wink, and I sighed and dragged myself out of the classroom to meet Joanna, waiting for me in the doorway.

"Walk with me," she commanded.

"I can't," I said. "I gotta wait here."

"*What?*" she asked pointedly, then looked over my shoulder at Alex and Señora Morales. "Why do you need to wait here?"

"'Cause I need to talk to Alex," I answered.

"What? About her new fashion statement? I mean, I'm glad she's finally started caring about how she looks, but Ugg boots?!"

"No, I just . . . need to talk to her, all right?"

"Well, why can't I wait with you? You can tell me about the party—I don't remember all of it—"

"Look, I just *can't*, all right? I need to talk to her . . . alone."

"Ever since you two slept together at my party, you've been totally ignoring—"

"Wait! Carrie told you we slept together?!"

A look of pure and utter surprise registered on her face. Not anger, not recognition, but surprise. Crap.

"You . . . what did you say you did?" she asked me. "Did you just say you slept with Alex Becker? At my *party*?!"

"Um . . . yeah, kinda, could we discuss this somewhere else now?" I whispered quickly, wishing I wasn't such a bonehead. "I don't think I need to wait to talk to Alex anymore."

"Yeah, 'cause it seems like you said it all at the party."

"Look, just . . . follow me, okay?" We headed out to the parking lot between the bus ramp and the chorus building.

"I can't believe you did that . . . and didn't even tell me!"

"I wanted to tell you, and I was *going* to, but I thought that maybe Carrie had blabbed to you—"

"You told Carrie and not me?" Her face scrunched up into a mixture of sadness and anger. "Why would you do that? We're best friends!"

"I just . . ." I was sinking, and sinking fast. I didn't know quite how to salvage this one. "I just . . . needed to talk to someone who knew a lot about sex—"

Bad move.

That's when she looked really hurt. And made me feel like a tool.

"Look, Joanna, I'm so sorry, I just . . . Can we talk about this at lunch? I'll fill you and Shauna in on everything, I promise. Okay?"

I don't know if it was my own pathetic-ness or her overwhelming sadness, but she was nice enough to let this one slide. "Okay," she said. "Tell us at lunch." And she walked away slowly, her posture slumped and sad, her steps slow and dragging.

"So did she drug you or something?" Joanna asked me.

She, Shauna, and I were having lunch in our usual spot, and I was glad to see that Joanna was in a much better mood about everything—probably because it was a whole new thing she could rag on me for.

"No, Joanna," I answered, taking a bite of my sandwich. "She basically wanted to lose her virginity that night and thought that I would be a good guy to help her do it."

"Why, because you're so experienced in the ways of pleasing women?" She laughed.

"No, she made it sound like it was because she trusts me and knows I wouldn't do anything to hurt her," I answered. "I guess I should've made sure *she* wasn't gonna go around singing it from the rooftops. I sorta forgot what a big mouth she has." I took a fizzy gulp from my Diet Coke and burped.

"Jonathan, you don't know that she's told anyone," Joanna said.

"Yeah," Shauna said. "I mean, girls check you out all the time. You just don't notice."

"Huh," I grunted. I *had* been noticing, if only for half a day.

"Yeah, you just don't know how cute you are," she said, shifting uncomfortably.

"Yes, he does," Joanna disagreed. "But you're just dense when it comes to picking up on things."

"I'm starting to feel that way," I agreed.

"Finally," Joanna said. "Something intelligent." She actually looked a little bit disgusted now. Less joking, more judgmental.

"Look," I began, pointing my sandwich accusingly at her, "I already gave myself enough shit for this yesterday. I don't want *you* giving me a hard time, too."

"I actually think it's kinda sweet," Shauna said quietly, untying and retying her shoes. "That you'd do that for her."

"Thanks," I said, patting her knee till I got some eye contact. "It *was* kind of ass-backward thinking, but at the time it did make sense. And I was glad to do it for her; I'm surprised I was *able* to." I smiled at her. "And now I have to make sure Alex hasn't and *won't* tell."

"I just wish I could've stopped you," Joanna sighed. "But I'm telling you: this whole thing is all in your head. I don't think she told anyone."

"You probably *could've* stopped me," I told her, "if you hadn't been so drunk when you were looking for me at the party."

Joanna looked perplexed. "What do you . . . ?" she began, looking up to the sky, as if the answer to her confusion lay in the eaves of the auditorium. "Oh my God, I *forgot!*" she screamed suddenly. "You two were about to do it when . . ."

"Yes, indeed-y," I said, smirking, all of a sudden relishing the hell I was putting her through. "I think I was in my underwear at that point." I looked Joanna in the eyes, then screamed, "Oh, *shit* I'm such an idiot! What was I *thinking?*"

"Whatever," Joanna said, cutting me off. "If you're gonna go all straight on us, that's fine. Just don't do it at any more of my parties."

"Uck, I am *so* not going straight on you guys, trust me."

They both nodded, Joanna looking skeptical, Shauna looking like she'd rather be chewing glass.

"Let's change the subject," I suggested.

"Yeah, let's," Joanna said.

"Oh, speaking of the party," Shauna said after a short awkward silence, looking up from her feet and turning toward Joanna, "why don't you tell Jonathan about Trent Kessler?"

Crap! I'd almost forgotten about the Trent situation in all my Alex craziness. Joanna looked as pleased to have the subject changed as I was.

"Oh, yeeeah," I teased her. "Did you pull an Alex Becker on him, too?"

"Actually, no, we didn't even kiss," she said proudly. "But that wasn't the goal, remember? My goal was to just to finally talk to him for real, nothing else yet."

"And to have him lick tequila off your stomach?" I asked.

"Oh, jeez—yeah, I did have him do that, didn't I?" Joanna said, furrowing her brow and obviously trying to remember more of the happenings of Saturday night.

"Well, it was sort of my doing," I told her, silently cursing her for not being sober enough to appreciate it. She is so lucky sometimes and doesn't even know it. "But you didn't seem to mind much."

"No, you didn't," confirmed Shauna. "I would have *died*."

"Well, getting to the point," Joanna said, "sometime during the party, I'd commented on how cute his shirt was, and I asked him where he shopped. He said how he just sort of went to the surf shops and thrift stores, but hadn't gotten much for himself lately."

"Yeah, he does pretty much wear the same thing all the time," I said.

"Right! So, when I asked him if he'd be up for a little shopping excursion, he was all for it!"

"Isn't that great?!" Shauna beamed.

"It is!" I said. "When's it happening?"

"How's Saturday afternoon for you guys?" she asked.

"Good for me," said Shauna.

"Oh . . . so we're coming, too?" I asked.

"Yeah, if that's okay. I'd sort of like some buffers, in case our nonstop conversation on Saturday was just a fortunate side effect of the alcohol." She paused and raised an eyebrow at me. "Hey, if you can devirginize Alex Becker, you can spend a day at Millenia Mall with me," she teased.

I couldn't help but think that there's always some truth in joking, but I bit my tongue this time. But the shopping? I mean, why not? Girlfriends, hot guy, shopping, and playing dress-up? What more could a gay boy ask for? I even had the day off from Target.

"Okay," I said. "I'm in."

Joanna nodded happily and took a bite out of her Little Debbie cake.

"Oh," I said, "I just remembered. You should tell your mom to get rid of those floral sheets in the guest room. They're offensive."

"So you were drunk enough to bone Alex Becker, but you were lucid enough to make note of my mother's taste in sheets?"

"Yes. And yes. Either wash them thoroughly or just buy new ones."

"Ew, you're sick."

"Sorry."

Just then, up walked Brianna "Brie" Brandis. Fiery-redheaded, tall and gorgeous and slutty Brie Brandis. Everyone in school knew—and Brie herself made it clear—that she was out chiefly for one thing when it came to guys. And it wasn't even money. (Lesson in Gay Television Trivia #1: If she were a Golden Girl, she would most definitely be Miss Blanche Deveraux, minus the classy Southern belle niceties.) So imagine my astonishment—and terror!—when she knelt down to me and caressed my arm from wrist to elbow with her finely manicured fingernails, totally ignoring Joanna's and Shauna's presence.

She continued up my arm, ending with a rather forceful grab on my bicep.

I forced out a scared little giggle, and managed to say, "Oh . . . ha-ha . . . hey, Brie. Have a . . . good weekend?"

Not one to be shy or uninformative, Brie's response was, "Totally hot. I got a Brazilian wax."

"Ew," Joanna said.

Wishing I *didn't* actually know what a Brazilian wax was, I nodded awkwardly at these responses, trying to remain cool, but probably acting like a total spaz. I mean, hell if I know how to handle vigorous flirtation with females! I was used to dishing it out for the sake of irony and cuteness, but I definitely couldn't take it—not *this* kind of flirting.

"I heard you had a fun weekend, too," Brie said.

"Yeah—Target, party, hangover, and Target . . . That pretty much sums it up."

"What're you doing *this* weekend?" she asked.

Eek. "Oh, well . . . uh . . . Saturday I have a sort of thank-you date with Laura Schulberg—"

Brianna let out some sort of snorty huff at this under her breath. "Cool," she managed, appearing a little ruffled, but not defeated. "Last I checked, there were more days to the weekend than Saturday."

Well, then. Time for lies.

"Okaaaay," I continued. "And . . . anyway, I think I have plans with . . . Joanna on . . . Friday, and then it's work at Target for Sunday"—until noon—"until closing." I shot Joanna a look that said, *If you rat me out, I'll kill you!*

"Well, just keep me in mind for next weekend," Brie purred. "See you around."

Uh . . . hello! I'm *gay*! I immediately grabbed my hand sanitizer from my bag and dropped a big plop of it on my palms and rubbed vigorously. It just seemed like the right thing to do.

"Could I get some of that?" Joanna asked. "I feel like I might've gotten an STD just from sitting near her."

"Sure." I handed the hand sanitizer to her and Shauna. "Okay, so am I just paranoid now?" I asked. "I think I'd call that some full-contact flirting. And we all know *that's* never happened before."

"Yeah," Joanna said reluctantly. "You might be right."

Shauna just gave me a very telling look. She thought so, too.

6. Come into My World

One o'clock on Saturday afternoon, and Trent, Joanna, Shauna, and I were in Shauna's teal '96 Jetta heading downtown on the East-West. Hers was the only car out of the three of ours that had a reliable A/C, so it was the natural choice for a hot afternoon shopping trip to the Tourist Corridor. In any of our other cars, we might've all melted. The A/C was at full-on arctic blast, and some fun, gay disco-techno-pop music was thumping out the speakers.

"So, what're we listening to?" Trent asked from the backseat. Shit, he was so cute. This was definitely a nice way of distracting myself from the weirdness at school and Joanna's incessant ragging on me. And what better way to remind myself that I was, in fact, gay?!

"Yeah, Jonathan, who is this?" said Joanna, from next to him. "She sounds familiar."

"This is the fabulous Dannii Minogue!" I beamed. "She probably sounds familiar because I put a couple of her songs on the party mixes. . . . And 'cause she's Kylie Minogue's little sister."

"I *love* the Minogues," Shauna said, taking a right off the East-West at the I-4 interchange.

"Who're they?" Trent asked.

I spun around and gasped dramatically.

"Don't get him started," Joanna said. "He'll go on all afternoon. Kylie Minogue sang that 'Can't Get You Out of My Head' song."

"Ohhh, right," Trent said. "She's hot."

There was a short stretch of silence as we merged onto I-4 and headed southwest, away from the downtown skyscrapers. Shauna quickly crossed over three lanes of traffic to the fast lane, and we sped up toward the Merita Bread Factory clock, which read 1:04 p.m. and 92°F (and smelled delicious). Thank God for Shauna's Jetta.

"Windows down!" Shauna called.

Joanna and I rolled down our windows immediately; Trent was a little slow on the uptake.

"Now, breathe in through your nose," I instructed.

We all took deep breaths, savoring the delicious bread smells coming from the factory, and sighed out long, contented "Ahhhhhhhs."

Trent looked a little confused, but I think he got the point.

"So, Trenty," I said, turning around to face him and trying not to stare at his toned, tanned arms, "are you just having the most amazing time with us?"

"Huh? Oh, yeah . . . totally," he said. "Air-conditioning, bread smells, what more could I ask for? And I'm, uh . . . pretty psyched about getting some new clothes."

"I am, too!" Joanna said enthusiastically. "We love playing dress-up."

"Oh, so I'm just entertainment for you guys?" Trent asked.

"No, Trent," Shauna said reassuringly.

"Charity," I stated.

"Yeah—for the poor boy who comes from a town with only one mall," Joanna put in.

"Correction, ladies"—he winked at me: major points!— "Satellite Beach doesn't have a mall—we have to drive to Melbourne . . . or Orlando." He covered his face with his hands in mock-shame.

"Oh, Trent, I just don't know how you *lived*," I said. "My heart goes out to you. Really, it does. Have you been to Millenia?"

"Nah, man. I pretty much stick to Fashion Square and Altamonte."

"Well, you're missing out . . . bro," I said, giggling to myself for having said "bro."

I pumped up Dannii and did a little dance.

"The Holy Land Experience, Shauna!" I screamed. "That's your cue to exit. Pull off here."

Shauna changed to the exit lane, and we whisked by the Jesus-themed theme park, by far the strangest tourist attraction in Orlando.

"Who the hell goes there, anyway?" Trent asked. "Any of you been?"

"Oh my God, no, it creeps me out too much," I said. "Though I *do* think it would be fun to get high and go one day just for shits and giggles."

"Yeah, 'cause *that's* what Jesus wanted," Joanna said.

"Yeah, just like he wanted a fucking *theme park* erected in his honor," I huffed. "Gimme a break."

"You've been, haven't you, Shauna?" Joanna asked.

"Yeah, when my grandmother came down from Alabama, she *insisted*," Shauna said, turning left and heading over I-4 toward the mall. "The place is crazy. They have a replica of Jesus's tomb, they put on shows reenacting stories from the Bible, and there's some Jerusalem street-market thing. It was hell."

"They should have someone dressed as Jesus come through every hour and bust up all the street vendors' tables as one of the Bible shows," I said.

"What?" came all three voices, clearly not getting the Biblical reference.

"Uh, hello . . . I *did* go to Catholic school," I reminded them. "I do know a *few* things."

It's true! My parents did send me to Catholic school from kindergarten through eighth grade. It really wasn't that bad—I had good teachers, who weren't nuns and who didn't hit you with rulers. I mean, yeah, they were strict, but it wasn't anything I couldn't handle. What actually irked me about it the most was the fact that I had to wear a starchy, uncomfortable—not to mention ugly—uniform every "gosh-darn" day.

I think my parents sent me to Catholic school mostly for the education; they weren't religious freaks by any stretch of the imagination. Which is why when I told them I was gay, rather than freak out and send me to some sort of Christian brainwashing facility to convince me I actually *did* like tits and hoohahs, they gave me a simple "What took you so long?"

We don't go to church much anymore. It's not like we lost our faith or anything; we just don't feel like it's necessary to proclaim it on a weekly basis with a couple hundred strangers. . . . It's just not that important to us. Plus, do I really want to be part of an organization that doesn't officially respect gay couples? Or let priests get married . . . or even let *women* be priests? Not really.

"You should take a right here and park by Macy's," I told Shauna. "There's usually some decent spaces there."

We cruised by one of the many MALL AT MILLENIA signs toward Macy's. Seeing the word "millennia" without its second *n* always bugs the shit out of me. I mean, call me anal retentive, but come on—it's just *wrong*. The idiot developers that brought a collection of the world's most exclusive boutiques to Orlando—Gucci, Coach, Louis Vuitton, Jimmy Choo—couldn't spend the few extra dollars to hand over their plans to a copyeditor or English teacher (or me!) and say, "Hey, do me a favor and look at this for thirty seconds and tell me if there's anything blatantly wrong with it?" Oh, well. The mall is *to die for* nonetheless.

We emerged into the bright, climate-controlled, glass-topped mall corridor from Macy's, still shaking our shirts to dry the beads of sweat that had formed on our two-minute walk from Shauna's car to the store. I sneaked a quick glance over at Trent, who'd lifted the corner of his Quicksilver T-shirt to wipe the last few stubborn droplets of sweat from his forehead, and saw a flash of tanned washboard abs.

So hot.

Joanna was looking, too, and we caught each other in the act, and flickered tiny mischievous smiles at each other.

"Aw, hey—there's PacSun!" Trent said semi-excitedly.

I glanced again at his Quicksilver–Rusty ensemble and shook my head.

"Haven't you shopped there enough, kid?" I asked. *"We're dressing you today. . . . Didn't they tell you?"*

"All right, all right—but we're stopping here on the way out, okay?" he said.

"Whatever," I said. "So, ladies . . . first stop, Zara?"

"Oh, yes!" Joanna clapped.

"Absolutely," agreed Shauna. "And then ExpressMen, I think. It's right upstairs."

"Awww, c'mon, guys, I'm gonna look like Euro-trash," Trent whined.

"Never!" I yelled kiddingly. "You're gonna look hot. And *straight.* Don't worry."

"You mean 'metrosexual'?" Trent asked.

"That's an even bigger *never,*" I told him.

"Oh, now you've done it," Joanna said. "You don't know Kylie Minogue and you just said the word 'metrosexual.'"

"Jonathan hates the word 'metrosexual,'" Shauna informed him.

"I just thank God that it's not getting used as much anymore," I said.

"What's so bad about it?" Trent wanted to know.

Here we go. "Well, I'll give you the CliffsNotes version. Basically, I just think the term itself equates fashion sense and *taste* with sexuality. A straight man can't dress well and still be called a heterosexual with good taste; he has to be given a whole new name and be called 'metrosexual.' It just has nothing to do with sexuality, and I think it's moronic."

"You sound so . . . brainy," Joanna said.

"Thanks, I think."

We got to Zara and started thumbing through shirts in the men's section. I held up a stretchy supertight T-shirt with a zipper across its front to show Trent and the girls.

"Okay, Trent's not gonna look metrosexual *or* straight in that shirt," Joanna said.

"Yeah . . . sorry, dude."

"Not for Trent, for *me!*" I said. "Isn't it just fantastically trashy and cute at the same time?"

"Put it away, Jonathan—you have no money and nowhere to wear a banana peel like that," Joanna said.

"Plus, we're here for Trent, remember?" Shauna added.

"Right, right, blah blah blah," I whined.

We blew through Zara and ExpressMen in an hour. We picked out an adorable black-and-teeny-gray-pinstriped dress shirt from Zara that looked amazing on Trent's V-shaped surfer torso, and some tight-in-the-ass Producer slacks, a baby-blue stretchy-fitted oxford shirt, and a cute little graphic tee from ExpressMen. Trent was the perfect dress-up doll; everything looked good on him. Which made me hate him a little, except not really.

Trent and Joanna were being totally flirty—at least from what I could tell. He was so cute and boyish and masculine, but very secure with his sexuality. At one point (it was so cute) he came out of a dressing room in this way-too-tight denim jacket with diamond-looking studs and was all, "How does this look, Joanna?" Where he found that awful piece of trash in the store, I don't know—probably a 90-percent-off rack in the back corner near the socks and underwear or something. But it was totally cute, and Joanna was just eating it up, telling him he looked very "studly." Awwwww.

Bitterness Alert? Oh, yeah. Kinda. But I forced my sad, singleton feeling aside and got excited for Joanna. And I really did want to help out where I could.

Shauna and I were pretty much just hanging back, picking out the occasional item of clothing for the dressing room, and watching the magic unfold, as it were.

Now we were strolling toward the mall's center courtyard, complete with multiple curved jumbo-tron high-definition TV screens broadcasting various advertisements. Trent suggested we take a turn to the right so we could visit the food court, and we did.

Shauna and I were behind Trent and Joanna, and when we all got in line at Chick-fil-A, we gave each other a knowing glance. As soon as Joanna ordered her Kid's Pack and Trent his eight-piece value meal, I blurted out, "You know, Shauna and I aren't really hungry. I think we're gonna go to Forever 21 and pick out something that accentuates her beautiful breasts . . . which in that store is everything."

"Jonathan!" Shauna said, all embarrassed.

"Yeah, so we might be a while." I paused. "Trent, you don't wanna spend the next thirty minutes watching us debate over spaghetti straps or no straps at all, do you?"

Trent looked a little concerned. "Uh . . . no, man, not really."

Joanna gave us an appreciative smirk. "Just go over there and we'll come get you to go to Urban Outfitters and Sisley in a bit."

"Great," I said. "See ya."

Shauna and I turned around and started to walk across the center courtyard to Forever 21. We grinned at each other happily; we were so good to Joanna.

"You realize how fucking smooth we are?" I said.

"Well, I wouldn't necessarily say we were *smooth*, but I think we were slick enough." She laughed, clearly loosening up a bit now that we were away from Joanna and Trent.

"So, I still haven't gotten to talk to Alex yet. She skipped a couple of days this week, I think, and she's just been very elusive. . . . I think she knows I'm upset."

"Uh, yeah, I bet she probably does," Shauna said.

"I wonder how many people she told. . . . It's driving me crazy."

Shauna just kept walking, not really responding.

"Do you want to talk about something else?" I asked her.

"Um . . . sure," she answered, sounding a little happier. "Like what?"

"Like that scorching case of herpes of yours . . . ?" I kidded.

"Oh, you mean that one I got at Bike Week with that pig farmer from Cedar Key?"

"Yeah, what was his name?"

"Jethro. Jed. Judd. I dunno, all my lovers' names start to blend together. But, thanks for askin'—I haven't had a flare-up in weeks."

I loved kidding around with Shauna like this. At times,

usually when there are unfamiliar people around, she's pretty quiet and reserved. Almost achingly so. I often just wanna *shake* her and be like, *Shauna! Please say something! They're not gonna bite!* She's even closed off some of the times when Joanna is around—like she fears the wrath of Joanna's sometimes scathing opinions. But when it was just me and her, she really loosened up. I loved being able to bring that out in Shauna.

"Anyway, back to your problem," she said. "Don't worry about the whole Alex thing. I'm sure it'll all work out soon."

A half an hour later, Joanna and Trent rejoined us. They seemed to be in high spirits. I guess their romantic mid-afternoon meal of crispy chicken did the trick.

After ten minutes in Urban Outfitters, which, of course, reminded us that we could get all their shirts at an *actual* thrift store for a buck or two, I made a suggestion.

"Okay, I've been thinking about it, and Sisley's just far too gay for Trent. I don't think we'll be able to find anything in there right now."

"You just want to keep all the clothes in there for yourself," Joanna accused me.

"*Shut your mouth!*" I screamed. "That's *my* store!"

"Eaaaasy, man," Trent said. "I can skip it."

"Good." I smiled. "So I think we should go down I-Drive and go to Pointe Orlando for Armani Exchange. And then show Trent a *really* good time after."

The girls knew what I meant. Trent didn't.

"Don't look so worried," Joanna said. "Just trust us."

• • •

International Drive is the Times Square of Orlando—an eyesore of tacky tourism, extended into a three-mile stretch of hotter-than-hell asphalt that runs from Sea World north to Universal's two theme parks. There's a haunted house in the shape of a skull, an indoor skydiving wind tunnel, a huge water park, an outlet mall complex made up of *seven* buildings, go-kart tracks, tacky T-shirt emporiums, and the world's largest Checkers. Like in Times Square, the traffic moves at a snail's-pace, allowing you to drink in the sights at a leisurely and, at times, annoyingly slow speed.

Pointe Orlando is at the south end and, for all the tacky shit that surrounds it, has some pretty damn good shopping. We picked out some really hot jeans from Armani Exchange, and a pale yellow short-sleeved collared shirt from a surf shop (we had to give the guy *something*), which looked so cute with Trent's tan skin.

"So, was *that* the really good time you were gonna show me?" Trent asked as we pulled out of the parking garage.

"Oh no, Trent, you're in for a treat," Joanna said.

"I'm assuming that you don't take trips up and down I-Drive, is that right?" I said.

"Uh, no . . . I guess not," Trent answered. "Why would I?"

"Because it's *tacky*!" Shauna exclaimed, getting all cute and giddy now.

"Yeah, you have to drive around it every once in a while to appreciate it for its ridiculousness," I told him. "I mean, where else are you gonna see an upside-down museum?" I pointed at

WonderWorks, where you can experience a 5.3 earthquake.

Trent laughed. He had such a good laugh. Sincere, not forced. "I guess not many places," he said. "What else you got?"

"Oh, all sorts of stuff," Joanna said.

I was actually getting a little concerned at this point that our overzealous attitude toward the irony of International Drive was going to turn Trent off. I mean, it was all well and good for the three of us (and Carrie, too, had she come with us), but it all of a sudden struck me that our weird idea of fun might not be the same as Trent's. I crossed my fingers that we were charming him enough that he wouldn't want to run the other way as soon as we dropped him off at his house.

A while later, after passing a few temples to tastelessness—including the Pac-Man Café and a hotel that looked like a castle—I suggested a stop in a Florida-T-shirts-by-the-pound kind of place to get Trent a souvenir of his day with us. Shauna turned the Jetta out of the crawling I-Drive traffic and parked. We got out and walked across the steaming blacktop lot into the store.

The frigid air-conditioning hit us like an iceberg—and we weren't even at the Titanic museum down the road. Mountains of T-shirts, towels, sweatshirts rose on all sides of us. On hangers, in bins, on shelves. I ran to the girls' section with Shauna and promptly picked out a girls' extra-large Minnie Mouse shirt. That Minnie—she always looked so coy.

"Too small for me?" I asked.

"Not if you wanna look like Walt Disney's personal go-go boy," she replied.

"Sold!"

Whatever doubts I had regarding how Trent was feeling about the whole day went away as soon as I looked over to the men's section to see him and Joanna being very cute and flirty. She kept picking shirts out of piles and off hangers and holding them up to Trent's gorgeous body, then stepping back and assessing while Trent struck various model-like poses. And he was laughing that cute, honest laugh the whole time. It was all very cute and jealousy- and vomit-inducing. They eventually picked out a white Orlando shirt, Minnie Mouse–free. I guess he wasn't *that* secure with his manhood. Then again, maybe he just had more taste than I gave him credit for.

"Well, I think that completes your new wardrobe for a while," Joanna said.

"Shit, I'll say," said Trent. "You guys cleaned me out! But thanks a bunch—I had a lot of fun."

"Well, as an apology for making you spend so much of your hard-earned cash, I think we'll treat you to a gigantic banana split," I said. I looked at Joanna and Shauna for confirmation. They nodded.

"Oh, God, where's that gonna be?" Trent asked me. "In a huge building shaped like a sundae with a cherry helipad on top?"

"No, Trent, nothing as tacky as that," I assured him. "Just up the road at McDonald's—the one with the word's largest Play-Place. It has an ice-cream parlor inside it."

"You're not gonna make me play around in a pit full of balls, are you?" he asked.

I resisted the obvious urge to make an inappropriate joke,

and went for subtlety. "You have no idea how much I want to, Trent, but I think after the sundae, we'll have to take me home. I've got plans."

"Oh, riiiight," Joanna teased. "The hot date."

I rolled my eyes. "Whatever."

"Dress up nice—wear a tie," Laura Schulberg had said. "And I'll pick you up at seven."

Laura's dad owned a big real-estate company. He was one of the first to jump on the high-rise condo building craze downtown and, along with his thirty-story-plus buildings, his already impressive wealth reached for the sky. Rumor had it that he had a multimillion-dollar penthouse in his newest building reserved for him, and that Laura would probably get it when she graduated. A far cry from the dorms at UCF, for sure.

This was going to be a hell of a thank-you date.

I took a nice, long shower to wash all the sweat and stickiness from the hot, humid day off my body. I toweled off and headed into my room to pick the outfit, which ended up being my least plebian collared dress shirt—simple, textured, fitted, and black—my favorite lime-green tie (so exciting, since I never got to wear my ties!), and low-rise tight blue slacks. I decided to go all out and wear my square-toed black dress shoes that made me an inch taller.

I took a look at myself in my full-length mirror.

Decent.

I spent fifteen minutes with my hair wax, getting everything just right. This was a meal with a rich girl that required a tie, after all.

I took another look in the mirror.

Gorgeous.

Then Laura called my cell and said she'd be there in two minutes.

I raced out my door and through the living room.

"Whoa, bud, where're you going all dressed up?" my dad asked from the couch. He was watching his favorite scenes from *The Last Samurai* for the umpteenth time. He paused the movie just as Tom Cruise (with long hair—*so* unfortunate) was about to skewer some Japanese guy. My mom was in her favorite reading chair next to the couch—book in one hand, a cup of coffee in the other—blocking it out.

"Remember, I'm going out on that thank-you date with my friend from statistics?"

"You must've really done something right," my mom said. "You never wear ties."

"Well, that's what happens when you help the richest girl at Winter Park get an A on her stats test."

"When're you coming home?" my dad asked.

"Well, I'm sleeping over at Joanna's afterwards. I'm having Laura drop me off over there after the date."

"That's how you end a date?" my mom wanted to know. "By having one girl drop you off at another girl's house? That's not right."

"Well, I'm not *sleeping* with either of them, so whatever. I'm bending the rules. . . . And it's not even a real date or anything."

Of course, after the week I'd had, I was actually beginning to have my doubts about Laura's intentions. But I really wasn't worried, as I wasn't sure how close Alex and Laura were, and how Laura would've found out.

Just then I saw Laura's black BMW coming down my street.

"Gotta go! My chariot awaits."

"Call and let us know when you're coming home tomorrow," my mom said. "We're cleaning."

"Then I'll be home after that's done. Love you!"

"Are you taking me where I think you're taking me?" I asked Laura as we descended the stairs of the parking garage onto Livingston Street. We were downtown and walking toward Orange Avenue and the main entrance to the Bank of America Building, or whatever it was called these days. At four hundred or so feet, it was one of Orlando's tallest buildings. Not huge by Atlanta or New York standards, but pretty big nonetheless.

"Possibly," Laura said coyly. "I'm really excited about your reaction."

She looked stunning. She was wearing these gorgeous pink-dyed ostrich-skin high-heeled sling-backs and a tight, silky, muted-pink dress she told me her parents got her at the Gucci in Millenia. It was probably worth more than my and Shauna's *cars* put together. Its almost dull color looked fabulous in contrast to her dark, tanned skin and her long, straight, jet-black hair, and it clung to her body perfectly. A six-thousand-dollar dress will do that, I suppose. It had *better* do that.

And I thought *I* was lookin' good. Laura put me to shame.

We walked up to the entrance, and my suspicions were

confirmed: we were heading toward Harvey's Bistro, in the ground level of the Bank of America Building. It was one of downtown's poshest restaurants, and had an incredible menu—duck, lobster, the works. From what I'd heard, at least. I'd always wanted to go, but neither the occasion nor the opportunity had ever really presented itself. This was going to be amazing.

"Oh my God, Laura, this is too much," I said, relieved that she didn't actually do more, because I knew she could. I started to hang a right toward the restaurant.

"Oh, no no no *no*, Jonathan," she said, tugging at my arm and keeping us going in a straight line toward the elevators. "This way."

We walked up to a black podium in front of the elevators, with a woman in a professional chic–looking black dress behind it.

What? I wondered.

"Hello," Laura said. "Schulberg, two. I have a seven thirty reservation."

What the hell?

The podium woman looked into a gold book. "Of course, Miss Schulberg—straight ahead, last elevator. Floor twenty-eight."

What the fuck?!

"Are we really going to—?"

"Manuel's on the 28th?" she finished my question for me. "Of course," she answered it.

"Madonna in Heaven, are you shitting me?"

"I shit you not, Jonathan," she said as we stepped into the elevator. "This evening is special."

Hopefully, I thought, all paranoid, *she doesn't think it's gonna be* Alex-Becker *special. . . .*

• • •

Unbelievable. That's what it was. I was excited, scared, ecstatic, and unbelievably keyed-up all at once, but when the elevator doors opened onto the twenty-eighth floor, all was right with my world for a second. The sun was setting out west, toward Disney, Tampa, and the Gulf of Mexico, casting a breathtaking mix of oranges, pinks, and yellows over downtown Orlando. I could see for miles through the slanted south-facing windows—over the rest of the glistening downtown buildings, out along I-4 toward Millenia and the Tourist Corridor, southwest to the Citrus Bowl, and southeast over Thornton Park and Lake Eola. It was absolutely stunning. I could have ended the evening right there and been a happy boy, but we hadn't even been seated yet.

"Miss Schulberg, I presume?" a maître d' said to Laura. "May I show you to your table?"

"Absolutely. Jonathan?"

I said nothing, only put my arm into hers and got led away from the windows like a dog on a leash.

We were seated at a round table for two in the southeast corner of the restaurant, so we were able to look out over downtown, Thornton Park, and the Orange County Courthouse, which shot skyward twenty-four stories, just across the street. I craned my neck to the northeast and could see the hospital where I was born. Oh, how far I'd come. "So, what do you think?" Laura asked me.

"I think I might shit myself from excitement," I whispered.

"You don't have to whisper . . . well, except when you say things like that."

"Do you have any idea how many hours of taking back used

bras and broken DVD players at Target I'd have to put in to be able to afford a bowl of soup here?"

"Jonathan, I *told* you—this is on me. Don't worry."

As if on cue, a waiter appeared with a bottle of Dom in an ice bucket. He popped the cork and poured a drip of it into a glass for me. I just stared at it, not knowing exactly what was going on.

"Uh . . . I don't think I ordered this," I said.

"Of course we did, sweetie," Laura said.

Sweetie?

The waiter smiled slightly and said, "Would you care to try it, sir?"

"Oh, well . . . yes, I believe I would," I somehow said. I picked up the glass and took a small sip, like I'd seen them do on TV. *Holy crap*, this champagne was amazing! I didn't know much about it, but as far as I was concerned it was flawless. All I'd ever had before were cheap bottles of André or something like that at New Year's parties, and this champagne kind of made me want to jump up and do a gay little jig, but then I remembered that I was not with Carrie or Joanna or Shauna. So, I simply said, in my coolest voice possible, "Perfect."

The waiter proceeded to pour a full glass for Laura, and then for me.

I eyed her suspiciously as the waiter walked off.

"What was that all about?" I asked. "Do you order through telepathy here?"

"No, silly, I had my dad call ahead. He's golfing buddies with the owner."

"Of course he is. But don't you think they could get busted?"

"Right, the cops are gonna come in and bust up the most expensive restaurant in the city. Relax. Let's just toast." She held up her glass; I followed. "To your insurmountable tutoring skills. And to . . . new beginnings. . . ."

Gulp. We clinked glasses, and then I gulped again, but this time it was a gulp of two-hundred-dollar champagne. It was so heavenly. I could actually get used to this.

For the next forty-five minutes or so, over criminally savory appetizers and glass after glass (and eventually another bottle) of champagne, we chatted it up about nothing in particular—my mild obsession with Kylie Minogue, her intense dislike for any article of clothing that incorporated feathers. The champagne was so sublime and the food so incredible that eventually my mind hazed into an almost-high state. The lines dividing my five senses blurred, and all of a sudden I was hearing, seeing, feeling the food in my mouth as much as I was tasting and smelling it. The lights of Orlando twinkled and pulsed, like the thousands of taste buds on my tongue that were bursting to life. Everything was so good, I swear I was seconds away from orgasm.

And that's when I remembered to suspect why I was there in the first place. . . .

"So, Jonathan . . ."

Crap. This sounded familiar. Could she *tell* I was just thinking about my crotch?

Our entrées arrived. Maybe this would distract her.

"So, Jonathan . . ."

Shit. Guess not.

"How're you enjoying your new social status?" she asked me.

"Hmmm?" I mumbled through my mouthful of food. I had no idea where this was going; I just hoped it didn't involve any kind of sex.

"You know what I mean, Jonathan Parish." She took a delicate bite from her rack of lamb. "Haven't you noticed people treating you a little . . . differently than they did before . . . ?"

"Before . . . what?" I asked innocently. "I'm not really sure I know what you're talking about." It was worth a shot.

"Yeah, you do," she said. "I'm talking about the number you did on Alex Becker. Pretty impressive."

"Right." I got quiet for a second. "I guess people obviously *do* know about that. The whole thing was actually a little weird for me. . . . I don't think I'll ever do it again."

"That's funny," she said, refilling my champagne glass. How many glasses was that? I'd lost count. Which was probably the point. Maybe she was hoping I'd drunkenly misplace my penis in her vagina later . . . or something. "Because word has it," she continued as she refilled her own glass, "that that little incident might've made you straight."

"Right," I said sarcastically. "I'd only be straight if women turned into men—and I don't mean in a transsexual kind of way. . . ."

"Jonathan Parish, I believe you're a little tipsy." She smiled, clearly pleased with herself. "I might just have to take advantage of this."

Red flag! Red flag! That did it. . . .

"Look, Laura, I don't know what you're getting at, really," I said, pointing my index finger at her accusingly, "but what're you doing here with me? What about Paul? Your boyfriend?"

Paul Bateman was Laura's star-quarterback trophy-boyfriend, capable of inducing me and my girlfriends to salivate spontaneously. He had this jet-black hair and piercing pale blue eyes that were just beyond gorgeous. To die for. Too bad the jackass had mildly tortured me in ninth grade for being, let's just say, *not* the best in gym class. I know—*so* typical, right?

"Well, actually that's kind of what this is about. . . ."

"What could Paul possibly have to do with my outrageously extravagant thank-you dinner and these double entendres?" I asked her.

"I brought you here to ask you to be my boyfriend."

"Whuh?" *Did I just say "whuh"?*

I noticed a helicopter flying toward the hospital off to the east and wondered if I could dash up the last flight of stairs to the rooftop and wave it over to whisk me away to safety before Laura pounced on me, because I didn't like where this conversation was heading. Actually, I didn't even *know* where it was heading, to tell the truth. Why was she asking me to be her boyfriend? So, yeah . . . that chopper. Safety. Maybe. It was worth a shot. *Holy hell, am I drunk,* I thought.

"I'm not going to have sex with you," I blurted out.

And then she laughed. Hard. So drunkenly and loud that half of Manuel's patrons turned their heads to stare. But I guess this was good; from the looks of it, she didn't want to have sex with me. And *that* was a relief.

"Oh, Jonathan," she said, still giggling, wiping the tears from her eyes. "You *are* a cute one. I'll give you that."

"So, no sex?" I asked hopefully.

"No sex. Honey, I *know* you're gay—I just thought this whole thing could work out to your advantage, if you put a certain spin on it."

"How could this possibly work out to my advantage?" I whispered, a little frantically. "*God*, I screw up *once* and all of a sudden I feel like I've got this . . . this scarlet letter or something. This big scarlet *S* for 'straight'! It's worse than coming out of the closet!"

"I just don't know why you'd want to turn down a chance at real popularity," she said, totally ignoring my rant.

"How do you figure? And what's in it for you, anyway? I hardly think you need more popularity."

"Well, if you date me, you're pretty much popular by association . . . and no girl would even dream of hitting on you if *I* already had you, so you wouldn't have to worry about that. And I'd get to maintain my place on the social hierarchy . . . by dating the newest, hottest guy on the market."

"How do you figure that, genius? You'll be dating a *queer*."

"Ah, you forget something, though," she said, waving her index finger at me. "They'll think you're straight—and you won't do anything to correct them."

"So, let me get this straight, so to speak," I said. "You and me go out . . . Wait, *why* are you breaking up with Paul, anyway?"

Laura made a sound like a sigh and a snort mixed together. "He doesn't do it for me anymore. I'm just way over it, and if people think I'm dating you, I can get what I need elsewhere— other high schools, UCF guys . . . whatever."

"So, you break up with Paul. You and I pretend to go out. You get to sleep with hunky UCF Golden Knights on the side. I get to go back in the closet. All for the sake of maintaining your popularity by dating a hot-item guy, i.e., me. What a deal."

"That about sums it up, yeah." She tilted up her champagne flute, finishing off the contents.

"I'm sorry, but popularity isn't worth going back into the closet for," I told her. "I mean, what would be the point of having more friends if I couldn't be myself?"

"I don't know . . . dinners at amazing restaurants you wouldn't be able to afford otherwise? A night at the Grand Bohemian, just for kicks?"

"The Grand Bohemian?"—Orlando's absolute best hotel—"No, still not worth it."

"So you're gonna make me beg?" she asked coyly.

"Begging won't do any good, either," I informed her. "It'd have to be something huge. Unimaginable. Something even *I* can't think up right now."

"You can't even give me your asking price?"

"You definitely sound like a real-estate mogul's daughter right now."

She paused, smirking a little at my snide remark. I think she was enjoying this. I even sort of was. She was quite the sparring partner, it turned out.

"Hey—how about that Kylie singer you're so into?" she said suddenly.

"'That Kylie singer'? Kylie *Minogue*, you mean? Have some respect!" I sighed. "What about her?"

"I could take you to one of her shows or something. VIP, limo, champagne"—she held up the empty bottle and shook it in my face—"the works."

"No luck there," I said bitterly. "She's never toured the States. And I don't think she ever will. I have a fantastic idea," I said cattily, "why don't you just ship her on over here for my personal entertainment?"

"Well, what is she doing right now?"

"Uh . . . I dunno. Washing her hair? How am I supposed to know?"

"No, you dork, I mean what's she working on? A new album? A tour?"

"Oh . . . well, I think she's recording, and she'll be touring the UK in the spring."

"Feel like taking a trip to London when we gradua—?"

"*Yes!*" I squealed before she could even finish. "Wait . . . are you serious?"

She just smiled wide and kept on talking, not answering my question just yet. "I love London. Gorgeous men. Makes America look like a year-round uglyfest. And I don't think Kylie's all that bad, either. She does do that 'Can't Get You Out of My Head' song, right?"

Ugh. Typical. That was, like, the only Kylie song any American knew. So sad she didn't know the musical amazingness of "Koocachoo," "Too Far," or "Confide in Me." But again, who was I to judge? "So *again* . . . you're saying if I pretend to be your boyfriend, you'll take me to London to see *Kylie Minogue* in *concert*?" I asked skeptically. "Is this a joke? Really?"

"Not at all."

"Really?"

"If you say 'really' one more time, Jonathan, I swear . . ."

Oh my God. This was seriously almost too good to pass up. All I had to do was pretend to be Laura Schulberg's boyfriend, and I'd get to see Kylie Minogue—the queen of pop, the Australian Madonna, one of the loves of my life—in London! And I'd never even been out of the country, unless you count Niagara Falls . . . the Canadian side, obviously. And I knew, unfortunately, in my heart of hearts, that Kylie would probably never grace the United States with her presence (at least not till Americans wised up to her brilliance). She just didn't have the fan base. Unless she wanted to go from selling out seven nights in a row in 18,000-seat arenas in Europe and Australia to do a theater tour in America, she wasn't coming to our side of the pond. I had to do it. *Had* to.

"And I don't have to have sex with you?" I asked, wanting to reconfirm.

"No. We'll have to make out in public every now and then."

"Well, I can handle *that*." I mean, how many times had I *already* made out with my girlfriends in drinking games or bullshit like that, anyway? Plenty. "But, I mean, come on—will anyone believe we're *really* together? In case *you* haven't noticed, I'd make a pretty queeny straight man. I'm no actor; I can't play it straight. I couldn't even play it straight when I *was* straight."

"I don't think that's a problem. You could just be like one of those—"

"If you say 'metrosexual,' I am running through this window and splatting on the pavement."

"I was gonna say 'gay straight men.' Like on *Sex and the City*. Just very open, in touch with your feminine side, and stylish and cultured. It's possible, you know."

"I guess," I said. I thought about it for a solid three more seconds, then squealed, "Oh my God, I'll totally do it! I'm gonna see Kylie!"

"If you hold up your end of the deal," Laura reminded me. "So . . . another toast." We held up our glasses, a little more shakily and clumsily than before. "To maintaining my popularity, to building up yours, and to London."

"And to Miss Minogue, of course," I added. "And to ridiculousness."

We clinked our glasses and downed them in one gulp.

"Oh," Laura said, "I have more in store for our . . . celebration."

I could only imagine.

8. I'm So High

Laura had the best pot I'd ever smoked.

She was also the heaviest sleeper I'd ever encountered.

I looked over at her passed-out body from my side of the king-sized—and incredibly cushy—hotel bed. She'd taken me to the Grand Bohemian—I guess she hadn't been bluffing earlier—and smoked me out in one of their poshest suites, clearly to impress me. Then we stripped to our underwear and went for a dip in the four-foot-deep *gorgeous* pool that overlooked the south end of downtown to discuss some ground rules for our arrangement, which included:

1) No sex or touching of genitals *whatsoever.*
   a) If we were making out in public, though, Laura reserved the right to make me feel her up, to make it believable. (And I promised not to giggle.)
2) A once-a-week Friday- or Saturday-night date, either in a popular Winter Park hangout, or with some of her friends, so we'd be seen together.
   a) One French kiss on said date—in front of people, of course.

b) And Laura would pay for said date, every time (by
   slipping me the cash under the table).

3) I could tell no one except my girlfriends. (This rule
   was nonnegotiable; I told Joanna, Shauna, and Carrie
   everything.) So as far as everyone at Winter Park High
   School was concerned, I was now straight as an arrow.

I took another puff from the joint, which was all mine, since
Laura had passed out after her second hit. She looked happy. Like
she'd accomplished something. Which I guess she had.

My head was kind of a mess, though; I couldn't really sort
out the swirls of emotions looping in and around my brain.
What I was doing definitely seemed way wrong, but so exciting
and fun at the same time. The plush suite's furniture's edges
looked kind of softened, blurring into the wallpaper, the rug, the
windows.

I shuffled unsurely to the window, taking another hit and
tightening the towel around my waist. My face was tingly and
borderline numb. The sound of my own swallowing was all of a
sudden the most intriguing sound I could imagine. It was all I
heard for a minute. So cool . . .

Enough.

I focused, picturing all the distracting thoughts in my brain
to be a big, puffy cloud, and then swept it away, clearing my
head. Mind over . . . mind.

I opened the curtains and looked out onto the view of City
Hall and the asparagus-shaped sculpture in the plaza.

Asparagus. I'm hungry. I could go to that lounge downstairs.

Guess I should call Joanna first.

I headed back over to where my pile of clothes lay on the floor. I took one final drag from the joint and pushed it into the ashtray on the bedside table. I fished my cell out of my pants pocket to call Joanna.

5 MISSED CALLS.

"Shit!" I said aloud, causing Laura to stir a little in the bed. Dammit, I *hated* pot—I'd totally lost track of time. And now Joanna was gonna *kill* me! But, wait—maybe if I put all my concentrative powers into acting normal and sober, I'd totally fool her. Totally.

"What the hell, Jonathan?" Joanna answered after one ring.

"Heeeeey, sweetie . . ." Suddenly, my mind went blank. Why was I calling her? This was funny. I started to giggle. Laugh. Hysterically. Laura stayed asleep, of course. Her snoring sounded like a buzz saw.

"Are you drunk?"

I managed to stop my choking laughter. "Yeah. But not so much anymore." I wiped the tears from my eyes.

"Drunk on what? Where'd she take you?"

"Where'd *who* take me?"

"*Laura*, dumbass!" She sounded pretty annoyed; I guess she was entitled. "Are you high, too? Where'd she take you? It's way later than I thought you'd be calling. . . . I've been trying you for two hours!"

"Uh . . . that's a lot of questions right there, but I'll answer the first one you asked: Yes, Joanna, I indeed am high."

"What kind of a thank-you-for-tutoring-me date was this?"

"Um, the kind where she took me to Manuel's on top of that Bank of Whatever building then took me to the Grand Bohemian."

"*What?* Jonathan, what are you doing at a hotel with her? Did you and her—?"

"No, nothing quite like that. I'll explain it to you tonight."

"So you still want to spend the night with me or do you have some more hymens to bust or *weed* to smoke?"

"I'm *telling* you—we didn't have sex! But, yeah! Of course I wanna still hang out tonight—maybe we can make some . . . some cheese dip or something! Or a cake! And we have to gab about our day with Trent! Anyways . . . Laura's sort of . . . dead-asleep and unconscious right now, and I don't have a car—"

"Okay, okay, I'll just come pick you up. Where is it exactly?"

"On Orange and . . ." And then I started laughing again. "Hey, I could just flag down one of those rickshaw guys. They're cute—maybe they'd take me to your house. It's not that far."

"Oh my God," Joanna muttered under her breath. "I swear. *Jonathan*, listen to me: I live, like, twenty miles from there—you are *not* flagging down a rickshaw. Now where is this hote—? No, wait. Fuck it. I'll just Google it, okay?"

"Ah, thank you, Al Gore, for the Internet."

This actually got a little laugh from Joanna. "Okay, dipshit, I'll be there in, like, forty-five minutes."

"Thanks, duuuuude. Hey, did that sound straight?"

"You're welcome. *And* you're an idiot. And you'll never sound straight."

We said good-bye and I pushed END.

I crawled onto the bed and shook Laura awake. Well, some version of awake.

"Heeeey," she moaned sleepily. "My new boyfriend . . ."

"Yeah, good morning, honey. You sorta passed out. So, thanks for the dinner . . . and the hotel . . . and the pot."

"Yeah, no. No problem. I should be thanking you. . . ."

"All in a day's work."

"Charming. So, I guess we'll each get what we want."

"In a nutshell."

I got off the bed and pulled on my pants under my towel. No point in wearing the pool water–soaked underwear. "Well, since you're kind of stoned and drunk and I'm supposed to be at Joanna's now, she's gonna come pick me up."

"Oh. Okay."

"So, I'm gonna wait for her down in that Bösendorfer Lounge and get something to eat."

"Yeah, just . . . charge it to the room."

"Really? Wow, uh . . . you're a doll. See ya in class on Monday."

"Mmm-hmmm . . ."

And she was out again. I tied my shoes and headed out the door, into the elevator, and down to the lobby level.

I walked into the lounge. It was kind of dark. The lighting was very dim, and the bar was made of black marble. Rich crimson curtains hung from the ceiling, and there were some large paintings on the walls. One was a very dark painting of a lion, and it sort of freaked me out. It was beautiful, though, but the lion's face was the brightest section in the painting, and it seemed to be leaping, roaring out of it.

I found a small table by the window and sat down. I lay back in the thickly cushioned chair and took a deep breath. There was a DJ playing some ambient techno lounge-y music I didn't recognize, and I had a view of the whole bar and the adjacent room with the Imperial Grand Bösendorfer piano, allegedly one of only two in the world. In my altered state, I kept picturing Tori Amos sauntering into the lounge, taking a seat at the piano, and playing a little ditty to sooth me further.

I wonder why people couldn't always be in this relaxed state of mind. I guess because there'd be too many car accidents or something. And nothing would get done. And all the McDonald's restaurants would be so overcrowded with people satisfying their munchies that they'd have to open up on every corner like Starbucks. And then Americans would be even more unhealthy than they are now. But, still. It'd be nice.

"Good evening," a voice said to me.

I sat up and looked to my left and greeted a black-clad waitress. She had a really cool outfit on—actually, all the waitresses had it—that was like a formal dress but with pants, too.

"Do you know what you'd like?"

"Um . . ." I hadn't looked at the menu. I didn't want to. Nothing else this evening was ordinary, so why do something as simple and pedestrian as open a menu? "Something . . . chocolatey?" Speaking of simple and pedestrian.

"We have a sort of death-by-chocolate kind of cake. How 'bout that?"

"That sounds great." Really great. Really *really* great.

"Will this be charged to a room or will you be paying some other way?"

"Oh—Laura Schulberg's room," I said, a little loudly to be heard over the music. I gave her the room number. Maybe I said it a little too loudly, 'cause this girl at the table in front of me turned around and gave me a weird look. Of course, I was stoned, so maybe I was just being paranoid about the look.

"Oh, yes of course, Miss Schulberg's room." Of course. Why *wouldn't* she know? "Will you be wanting one of our signature martinis to go with your cake? Maybe the Soprano? It has espresso—"

"Sold! That sounds awesome. Thanks."

And then she was off. And she hadn't even IDed me.

Again, that girl turned around. She looked kinda familiar, actually—she might've gone to Winter Park. Anyway, maybe I wasn't being paranoid; maybe she was just totally checking me out. I loved this whole being-hyper-aware-of-my-cuteness thing. Pretty cool.

I leaned back into the chair and thought about my evening. My first thought was, obviously, that it was entirely insane. But then again, I'd had the most mind-boggling dinner and champagne in the most gorgeous restaurant overlooking my most beautiful, sparkly hometown. I got to spend a few hours in a suite in Orlando's best hotel, and now—the waitress returned and put my post-pot choco-fest in front of me—*now* I was sipping on the most silky, delicate, and . . . poetic (that's the best word I could think of, and for some reason it made sense to me) espresso-chocolate martini and eating the moistest, richest, most delicious piece of cake this side of the Mason-Dixon Line. Not to mention the fact that on Monday, I was gonna be the toast of Winter Park.

I was a fucking rock star.

9. Put Yourself in My Place

"It is, without a doubt, the worst idea I've ever heard,"
Joanna said to me, dipping her spring roll in fish sauce.

The first time I tried to explain my little situation to
Joanna—the night before when she'd picked me up from the
hotel—hadn't gone too well. Well, of course it was gonna get off
to a rocky start when she told me she'd been circling the hotel
for twenty minutes, because I hadn't told her I'd be in the
lounge. Then, from what I can remember, it went something
like this:

Joanna: "Thanks for showin' up, jerk." *(turns down music)*

Me: "Sorry. I thought you knew I was in the lounge." *(turns up
music louder)* "Yay, Madonna!" *(starts vogueing)*

Joanna: "Why the hell would I know that?!" *(ejects CD and
throws in backseat)*

Me: "Because there's *chocolate* there!"

Joanna: "Sure. So what was this date about?"

Me: "I agreed to pretend to be Laura's boyfriend and as pay-
ment she's gonna take me to London to see Kylie Minogue. And
so, yeah, I'm straight now. Ta-daaa!" *(does a kind of ballerina flourish
with arms and hands)*

Joanna: "Real straight. Especially that little dance move. You'll really fool 'em."

Me: "I will. And you guys will have to, too. I'm back to hetero, baby. Bring on the poon!"

Joanna: *(yells)* "You're kidding me, right?"

Me: "Nope." *(giggles)*

Joanna: *(stony silence and stewing anger)*

Me: "I want Vietnamese. Don't you?"

So after lecturing me about how selfish I was being and about how no, the Vietnamese places were *closed* and that it was Taco Bell or nothing (which I, of course, accepted), we went back to her house so she could talk about herself and the whole Trent thing. I pretty much kept my mouth shut since, yeah, I was being sort of a stoned moron, and I didn't want her to lose it and leave me off to ride a bus home from East Colonial Drive. Then we slept in and I called in sick to Target and we met up with everyone for lunch.

Joanna had called it an emergency gathering to discuss my— what she called "idiotic"—situation. We'd met at Little Saigon, one of those Vietnamese restaurants with a menu the size of a bridal magazine. Who needs three hundred choices, anyway? It was one of our favorite restaurants in what we called Little Vietnam, a teeny area near downtown Orlando with Vietnamese *everything*—gift shops, restaurants, music stores, and boutiques. I still had to satisfy my craving from the night before.

"Well, I'm all for it, hotshot!" Carrie countered. "Well, not *all* all for it, but I totally support it and think it'll be sorta fun."

"I'm jealous," Shauna said, stirring her beef-ball soup.

"Of what?" I asked.

"Well . . . that you get to see Kylie, jerkface!" Shauna exclaimed.

"I just think it's awful that you're going back in the closet for some stupid concert," Joanna said. She was kind of being especially mean today, for some reason. Maybe I'd been *really* annoying the night before.

"It's not just 'some stupid concert,' it's Kylie Minogue!" I screeched. "I'll *never* get the chance to see her here!"

"Well, let's face it," Carrie said to Joanna, "there's no going back in the closet for our little Jonathan. It's not like he's gonna show up to school on Monday all decked out in American Eagle or something. Are you?"

"Never," I stated emphatically.

"But, *Jonathan!*" Joanna said. "You're still gonna be telling everyone at school that you *are* straight, Timberlands or no Timberlands—"

"Ew, stop it, I can't take it!" I joked, putting my hands to my ears.

"I'm serious," Joanna continued. "Telling people you're straight is the same as going back in the closet. For shit's sake, that's what you did when you thought you *were* straight! You've always been kind of a little flamer, you know."

"*Hooooo,*" I said, flipping my hair Cher-style to prove her point. "Look, what's really the difference? It'll be just like before I came out: whoever wants to think I'm gay will think I'm still gay, Laura Schulberg at my side or not. And whoever wants to think I'm straight will think I'm straight."

"I can't believe you're doing this for Laura, though," Shauna said. "You hardly even know her."

"I'm not doing it for *Laura*, I'm doing it for *me*," I said. "For Kylie," I reiterated.

"I guess," Shauna said quietly. "But she's still getting something out of it—and it seems like a lot to do for someone who isn't even like a best friend."

"So you're only doing it to see Kylie, not because you want to become this big popular studhorse?" Joanna asked accusingly. "'Cause we all know that as soon as Laura Schulberg gets a new boyfriend, he, like, instantly becomes as popular as her."

"*No*, I'm not doing it for that at all," I insisted. "In fact, that was the first thing she even *offered* me—just the popularity. And I even told her that changing who I am just for the sake of being 'cool' isn't worth it."

"But then she mentioned Kylie," Joanna said flatly.

"Well, yeah."

"I guess everyone has their price."

"Well, I'll say it again," Carrie said, slamming her big soup spoon on the table like a gavel, breaking up the impending volatile argument. "I think it's a great idea. Who the hell cares what everyone thinks if you're just going to college next year, anyway? As long as all of us still know you're gay, why should it matter?"

"Exactly," I said. "And I can't reiterate this enough: I'm going—"

"Right, right," Joanna interrupted me, "Kylie, London, girl-friends, dates, blah blah blaaaaah."

"Thanks for the support," I said sarcastically, rolling my eyes. I was really getting annoyed with this bullshit.

"I'm sorry, I just can't give it to you." And that seemed like her final answer.

"Shauna?" I asked. "What about you?"

Shauna looked from me to Joanna, and then at Carrie, and then sort of averted all eye contact, saying, "I just . . . don't know. Do we really have to keep talking about it?"

"You don't *know*?" Joanna said. "How could you not know? It's pretty cut-and-dry."

"Maybe for you," Carrie said. "And it is for me. But leave Shauna alone—like she said, she just doesn't know."

"Yeah," Shauna said quietly. "Exactly."

Joanna rolled her eyes and said to me, "Look, I'm sorry. I just don't think it's the best idea. There's just something *off* about it." Now she turned to Carrie and Shauna. "And you know *we're* gonna have to cover for him, right? He's going back in the closet and he's dragging us all with him."

"That's a good point, I guess," Shauna agreed.

"Hey, I don't mind," Carrie said. "All you have to do is say, 'No, he's straight now.' See? Not so hard."

Shauna said nothing.

Joanna tapped the table with her chopsticks.

Carrie just smiled and said again, "Not hard at all." Then suddenly, her eyes got really wide and she bellowed, "Oh my *freaking God*, I *completely* forgot!"

"What? What?" I asked desperately, so happy to have something interesting and tidbit-y to distract me from the previous conversation.

"What's Laura saying she's gonna do about Paul Bateman?"

Oh, well. The reprieve was fun while it lasted. "She said she's gonna dump him."

"Well, that's interesting," Carrie said scandalously, "because I heard yesterday that she broke up with him after school on *Friday*."

I nearly choked on my mouthful of pork.

"You've been together twelve hours, and she's already lying to you?" Joanna asked all-knowingly.

"Fuckin' women," Carrie laughed.

"So, she'd already broken up with him be*fore* she had dinner with you?" Shauna asked, all of a sudden coming into the conversation. "That's kind of awful."

"Guess she knew she'd buy you off *somehow*," Joanna put in.

"Well . . . whatever," I said. "I just hope Paul Bateman doesn't pull some quarterback choke-hold move on me or something. . . ."

"Mmm, I wouldn't mind it," Carrie purred. "That boy is smokin'."

"Yeah, but he's kind of a dick," Shauna said.

"I'd still tap that," Carrie said. "If he just didn't talk." Then, turning to me, she said, "But don't worry about him—he wouldn't do anything to you, especially in school."

"Naah, I think I'll be fine," I told her. "I'd just fight dirty. Did you know how easy it is to rip off someone's outer ear? I think I saw it on TV or something. . . ."

Carrie, Joanna, and Shauna all cringed.

Then Joanna spoke up and said, "See what you've already gotten yourself into. You're talking about a possible fight with our starting quarterback, and you can hardly kill a cockroach."

That did it for me. "Well, let's end this discussion, now that we all know how *eee*veryone feels about it," I told them. "Because I'm starting to get bored."

"Fine," Joanna said. "What do we talk about now?"

Maybe about how bitchy you're being about all this? I wanted to say.

"Joanna, baby!" Carrie said. "I almost forgot! Tell me about the day with Trent! I'm sad I didn't get to see it firsthand."

"Yeah, I just didn't want to overwhelm him or anything," Joanna said, eyeing me but perking up just a bit. "Sorry I didn't invite you."

"You think *I* would over*whelm* him?" Carrie said jokingly, stroking her Afro. "I totally don't care. Now spill."

"Okay," Joanna said, finally relaxing a bit more. "Well, it was really great. He had such a good time—"

"And they were totally flirting it up," Shauna interrupted. "It was cute."

"Oh, yeah," I said, smiling slightly in an attempt to get less pissy, "and Shauna and I left them alone to talk about love and the stars and marriage over Chick-fil-A." I tried to keep the mild bitterness out of my voice.

"Yeah, well . . ." Joanna trailed off. "We didn't talk about too much, though—just kind of bullshitting around. But he's so cute."

"I know, I know, we've heard—so, when're you gonna slam him up against a wall, baby?!" Carrie said excitedly. "I wouldn't mind doing it myself, actually. Right after Paul Bateman." She laughed.

I kept my mouth shut for the moment.

"I dunno," Joanna said. "I did the whole talking-to-him thing, but getting us to be more than friends is a whole 'nother thing. . . ."

I sighed. "Just go with the flow, I guess," I told her. "Hang out with him a little more . . . but keep flirting! Lord knows you're closer to getting him than *I've* ever been."

"Yeah," Shauna said, "I'm sure it'll work itself out, and before you know it, you'll be Mrs. Trent Surfer-God Kessler."

"I wonder who'll get married first," Joanna said sarcastically. "Me or Jonathan?"

"Let's discuss Halloween!" I said, ignoring Joanna's last comment completely.

Halloween's our favorite holiday, and the four of us had been planning for months—many months—to be different versions of Madonna. It'd actually been in the works for years. We'd wanted to do it since freshman year, but for some reason we could just never get our shit together. And finally this year, we were gonna do it. And we had to start doing some serious shopping.

"Oh, yeah!" Shauna said, getting happy and animated again. "Let's go sometime next week."

"Yeah, we'll figure it out," I said. "I can't believe we're finally doing this! I'm so excited!"

"I call 'Like a Virgin'!" Carrie exclaimed.

"You called that months ago, dork," I said. "Just like I called 'Vogue' Madonna while in the womb."

"Hey, Jonathan," Joanna asked me, "what's your girlfriend

gonna say when you tell her you want to dress in drag for
Halloween?"

"Well . . . I'll just have to find out when it happens," I said.
"'Cause we've been planning this for too long."

"Good answer," Joanna said.

And so it was, on Monday morning, that I made my big debut at
Winter Park High School as Laura's boyfriend.

Laura wasted no time in staking her claim on me, walking
right into our first-period statistics class and planting a big, wet
kiss on my lips. Any inkling that she might've instituted a
"mourning period" for the end of her relationship with Paul
Bateman was gone immediately. The kiss actually sort of caught
me off guard at first, and then it registered, and I returned it.
No tongue. Just a typical boyfriend-girlfriend morning hello
kiss. Or what I imagined one would be like.

"Morning, sweets," she said.

"Hey," I said. "Beautiful day, isn't it?"

"Absolutely."

After stats, we walked hand in hand to my Spanish class, getting looks the entire time. People poked each other, whispered
into ears, or just flat-out stared, subtly and not-so-subtly. It had
been a week since the Alex Becker affair, and now I was dating
one of the hottest, most glamorous girls in school.

We stopped in front of the door to Señora Morales's room.

"So," Laura said to me, "I guess I'll see you at lunch."

"Lunch? But I'm gonna eat with Shauna and—"

"*Jonathan, if we're going to have anyone believe us, we have to* at least *eat* together on our first day . . . together," she said, looking into my eyes only every few seconds. She was looking over my shoulder sort of frantically.

"What are you looking at?" I asked.

"No one—nothing. Just . . . meet me out by the flagpole at lunchtime."

"Fine, but I'm not gonna eat with you every—"

Laura interrupted me by grabbing my face and pulling it into hers, giving me a fierce French kiss good-bye. Again, I was caught off guard, but sort of let myself go with the flow and melt into it, closing my eyes and trying to make it look believable. (Picturing Ashton Kutcher helped.) I opened my eyes for a split second to see Alex Becker walk into class, staring at the two of us, looking very confused.

"Bye, luvah," Laura said to me.

"Bye. So, like I was saying," I whispered, "I was gonna eat with—"

"Yeah, yeah, yeah, so do you think she saw it?"

"Who saw what what who?" I asked.

"Alex, *stupid*. Do you think Alex saw us kissing?"

"Actually, yeah, she did."

"Perfect." She smiled. "The whole school will know by lunchtime."

"Bitchin'," I said, mocking her.

"Don't get all sassy with me, honey," Laura told me. "I'll see you at lunch."

Jeez, she was fierce. And I kind of liked it.

I said bye and walked into class and plopped down in my seat next to Joanna. She leaned over to me and whispered, "Quite a display, *breeder*."

"Hey, shut up," I said back, "*I'm* the one who says 'breeder' around here."

"Not anymore, dude—you're straight." And with that, she kind of shrugged and leaned back into her desk.

After class, Alex immediately came up to me—such a change from the past week of complete avoidance!—and asked, "So, Jonathan . . . is Laura your new girlfriend or something?"

"Um . . . actually, yeah, she is," I answered. "It just sorta happened this weekend."

"Really?" she asked as we walked into the hallway, sounding confused. "But aren't you gay?"

"Um, well . . . I guess that night with you might've done the trick, so to speak."

"Are you for real?"

"Sure, well . . . uh, I don't mean to completely change the subject, but would you mind telling me how so many people know about *us*?"

"Look, I really didn't mean for that to happen, it just . . . totally got out of hand," she said, seeming genuinely upset. "What we had that night was really special, and I really didn't mean for it to get out."

"Well, what happened?"

"I just told Veronica—and I totally thought she was my best friend, which she is, I guess . . . but I know she blabbed it to the wrong people, and it just sort of escalated from there." She looked like she was about to cry all of a sudden.

"Yeah," I said, nodding, "that does tend to happen around

here, I guess. . . . But don't worry about it, okay? You look like you're about to break down."

And then she did. I'm talking major waterworks—tears, snot, gasping for air, the whole deal. I totally didn't know what to do. Except get us the hell out of the hallway.

"Here, let's uh . . . go somewhere more private."

"Ohhh," she howled, "*that* sounds familiar!"

"Seriously," I pleaded, taking hold of her arm and leading us to the door at the end of the hallway that led out to the bus area. Not too many kids hung out there, so it was semiprivate. God, this was, like, the second time in two weeks I'd gone running out that door from Spanish class.

"Look," I said when we got to a quiet corner, "what gives? What's wrong here?"

"N-n-n-nothing," she sputtered. "J-j-just you tell me you're gay at Joanna's party, and th-th-then we h-h-have *sex* and you're so sweet and wonderful and beautiful and I just . . . n-n-*never* felt so good in my life!"

"Oh, God," I said frantically, wondering where the off button was to all the hysterics. I really couldn't take crying like this. I swear, I could never have kids, 'cause I'd just give them anything they wanted to shut them up. Crying freaked me the hell out. "I mean, you told me you didn't . . . or *wouldn't* have feelings for me."

"Well, you can't blame a girl for *trying*, Jonathan!" she screamed, easing up on the crying a bit, now able to get out full sentences without struggling for air. "It's just that I *never* get the guy, y'know? I don't know what it is, but I can just never follow through. And sometimes I just feel so ugly and *gross* and totally unwanted, and you were looking so hot last Saturday, and you were dancing all sexy with me, and I just thought that maybe . . . maybe you might've liked me."

"Uh-huh? Go on."

"And then I figure that it's all right that you don't like me, 'cause you're gay, and now you tell me that now that you've taken a girl out on a test drive, you've decided you like it and now you're with *Laura Schulberg*!" And then the crying recommenced.

"I—I—I don't know what to—"

"And when I heard that rumor about you two, I didn't believe it, 'cause Whitney Bronski is such a drama queen, and then I come into school and see you and Laura totally making out—"

"Whoa, whoa, wait. . . . Rumor?" Now I was worried.

"Whitney told, like, a *thousand* people this weekend about how she saw you at some hotel downtown ordering drinks and charging it to Laura's room, and that Laura'd only broken up with Paul the day before, and I didn't believe it 'cause I thought—"

"—that I was gay."

"Yeah!" she sobbed. "And now I just feel like such a frumpy, stupid *idiot*! Why does *Laura Schulberg* ALWAYS get what she wants?! No guys ever even *look* at me!"

"No, no, that's not true," I assured her frantically, trying to come up with good stuff to say. I really had to stop the crying; I could not take it any longer. "I mean, maybe you just don't *notice*, you know? Maybe you're not looking around you—"

"Oh, I'm lookin'!" she yelled. "But no one's lookin' back."

I felt so bad for her, because she was totally echoing how I felt most of the time. I just wanted to make it better. So this is gonna sound bad, and like I'm a total tool, but understand that I was under some major damage-control pressure.

"Look," I told her, "maybe it's okay if I tell you this . . . but I'm actually not . . ." And here's where my Kylie-conscience kicked in, singsonging, *Don't you want to see me, luv?* in an adorable Aussie accent. I couldn't spill the beans on the *first* day, because if I did that, how could I possibly last till graduation? I scrambled for something to say, *anything*, and all I could come up with—as it popped randomly in my head—was, "I'm actually not sure you noticed Trent staring at us dancing at the party—he kind of looked jealous or something."

As quickly as I'd remembered and said it, I wanted to take it back immediately. Because for all I could tell, Trent didn't like Alex. It was just a weird look. But as soon as I said it, it seemed more likely to be true. Of course, I'd been a paranoid mess for a while lately. Regardless, at least she'd stopped crying.

"Yeah?" she said, wiping off her face, and the very faint beginnings of a smile spreading across her face. "You think so?"

"Um . . . totally," I said, hoping I was wrong. "Maybe that's something to think about."

"Yeah. Maybe. It'd be kind of weird, since we've been friends forever . . . but a lot of relationships start out that way, right?"

Oh, God, Joanna would kill me for this. "Sure they do. That's what I hear. . . ."

"Well, um . . . maybe I'll just let that . . ."

"Marinate?"

"Sure, that's the word." She looked a little happier now and a lot more embarrassed. "I'm really sorry about all that."

"No problem," I said, relieved that it was over. "Just don't let it happen again," I joked.

"No, not at all. I *do* like you, Jonathan. You're a catch for any girl. I'm . . . I'm just happy for you and Laura. Sorry about my spaz-attack."

"Don't mention it. Look, I'm gonna run to class, okay?"

"Okay. Well, bye." And she leaned into me and got on her tip-toes to give me a hug. "Thanks again. Oh, and one more thing."

"Mm-hmm?"

"You don't think that maybe I . . . might've . . ."

"Turned me straight?" I ventured.

"Yeah."

Hmmm. No. You didn't turn me straight. In fact, it was your and your friend Veronica's big mouths that made me the hot topic at Winter Park, thus attracting the scheming mind of Laura Schulberg and sending me ironically screaming, "I'm gonna see Kylie! I'm gonna see Kylie!" all the way back into the closet.

But that's not what I said. (Duh!)

"You know, Alex," I said, a little dreamily, "I don't think you did. I think on some level I always knew I was really straight. . . . And now, I'm . . . I'm happy." (Ew, I was seriously starting to creep myself out—and it was only day one.)

"That's great," Alex said. "Like I said, I'm happy *for* you. So . . . bye."

She went up the stairwell and I headed back into the now-empty hallways.

So, it looked like by day one, I was already screwed. I just hoped that (a) Alex completely disregarded what I'd told her and then maybe Trent and Joanna could live happily ever after, and (b) that Paul Bateman didn't explode with jealousy at the thought of his ex-girlfriend getting it on with a formerly gay guy only twenty-four hours after he'd gotten dumped by her. But, hey—maybe he'll just think that she and I were doing it way *before* we'd been found out at that hotel. Yeah . . . that'd be *so* much better.

Oh, and maybe (c) should be considered: WWJD. Meaning, What Would Joanna Do if she found out what I'd blabbed. I just pictured her huffing and puffing with pure, burning anger, and transforming into a hideous, green-skinned Hulk-Joanna, bursting through her purple tank top (somehow her enviable hair is still intact) and flattening me with one swat.

But maybe she wouldn't have to find out. . . .

Correction: She *couldn't.*

All the stress from those little worries was nothing compared to lunch with Laura's girlfriends, Tiffani and Tina, and Tiffani's boyfriend, Chad. It was pure hell on earth.

First off, all that the girls talked about was clothes. Which, granted, I love to talk about—but when I talked about clothes with *my* girlfriends, it was more along the lines of: *Hey, you'll never guess the bargain I got at Express this weekend.* With Laura, Tiffani, and Tina, it was more like:

"Oh my God, I am *so* over the Banana Republic on Park Avenue—I am so *never* going anywhere in Winter Park now except for Nicole Miller."

Or:

"Oh my God, you will *never* guess how much I paid for this bullshit pink bag that I could've gotten at Target for twenty bucks but got at Millenia instead." (I'm paraphrasing, of course.)

"I *know*, Tiff," Tina said, looking online on her BlackBerry for how many calories were in a green apple. "Thank *God* for Millenia; now I don't have to go to Miami or Atlanta any time I need a new Louis."

Vuitton, that is. Louis Vuitton. Give me a fucking break. Get a fake one online.

"What about you, Jonathan?" Tiffani asked. "Where do you shop?"

"Uh . . . pretty much wherever. Sisley's my favorite, though."

"Sisley," she repeated. "Yeah, Sisley's okay. Kinda gay and Euro-trashy sometimes."

"Yeah, well, I don't really care if I look gay, so . . ."

"So, dude," Chad said, "since you brought it up . . ."

There was an awkward pause, which I decided to let Chad fill by finishing his sentence.

". . . you're not gay after all?"

"How *could* he be, Chad?" Laura interrupted. "He's with *me*." She smiled and wrapped her arms around me.

"Yeah, I guess things sorta changed for me two weekends ago," I said. "When me and—"

"Yeah, bro! I know what you're talkin' about!" Chad exclaimed, holding up his hand for a high five. "Had one taste of the poon and he's *hooked!*"

"Uh-huh, that's definitely it," I said. I stuck my hand up to meet his high five, hoping that it would connect. I was never too good at high fives. I never got the point of them. Miraculously, it was a direct hit. *Fuckin' A!*

All of a sudden, I was longing for more clothing talk. Or something other than the image of poon. It just sounded so *dirty!*

The girls rolled their eyes. I wanted to, too, but I decided to stick with my role as best I could.

"Hey, hey, hey," Laura scolded. "No high-fiving over that little . . . ex-girlfriend or whatever she is. Like I said, you're with me now, unlike that lame-ass Paul. . . ." She pulled me over for a kiss, and then sort of chuckled, looking over my shoulder at something. "Speaking of which . . ." she said, clucking her tongue.

I turned around and saw . . .

"Paul, hey!" Chad called. "What is *up?*"

Paul Bateman had arrived at the flagpole where we were eating lunch. He looked big, bad, and bloodthirsty. And did I mention big? Oh, yeah—and hot? (Hey, I can't help it.)

"What's up, guys?" Paul asked everyone while his eyes bored into mine.

Everyone, including me since he was staring right at me, mumbled their "nothing much"es.

With that, he walked up to me and poked a finger to my chest, saying, "I'm not talkin' to you, Parish. I don't have anything to say to you." The guy was clearly looking for a fight.

"Well, in that case, I'll just back up a few steps, then," I said. "I'm just getting over this nasty cold, and I don't wanna give it to you."

"Why not, baby, you already gave it to me," Laura said. Then to Paul, "What the fuck're you doing here? Didn't I say we were through?"

"I was just comin' to find out a couple—"

"What?" she interrupted him. "If that whole hotel rumor thing that Whitney Bronski started was true? Yeah. It was. I took him to the hotel for a little . . . celebration."

"For what?!" Paul yelled.

"To celebrate my dumping your ass and moving on to something way cooler"—she put her arm around me—"way hotter"—and leaned over to my cheek—"and way better"—and kissed me—"than you ever were."

I really thought Paul was going to explode. I could see veins popping out of his neck and the color rising in his face. He was cracking his knuckles with one hand and making a fist with the other.

"And if you ever try to fuck with me or him," Laura continued, "I'll have your balls for my charm bracelet. And they're the *perfect* size."

And with that, Paul stormed off, looking completely devastated. I would've felt kind of bad for him, if he wasn't such a fuckwad usually.

"That was *so* fab," Tina said. "You just totally *reamed* him!"

"Yeah, well . . . you gotta let 'em down easy, right?" Laura laughed.

"So, Laura, are you still having that Halloween party?" Tiffani asked. (*Shit!* I thought.) "Me and *this* guy"—she leaned into Chad—"have to come up with a costume."

"Yeah, I definitely am," Laura answered. "And me and Jonathan are gonna be Barbie and Ken. I bought this totally amazing wig already."

What?!

Joanna and Shauna and Carrie (especially Joanna) would beat me senseless if I dressed up as Ken. *Kill* me, even.

"Um . . . Laura? . . . I was kinda planning on doing a costume with—"

"Well, you'll just have to call it off," she said sweetly, shooting me a subtle yet piercing look. "I'd really like to do a couple's costume." She batted her eyes, then leaned into my ear and whispered, "Here's a secret: I like my fun," into my ear—a Kylie reference.

The all-of-a-sudden Kylie-reminder ("Kylieminder" for short, shall we say) took me by surprise, but I boldly continued, "But, *sweetie*, in all fairness, you only came along this weekend. . . . *They've* been with me for—"

"Jonathan, we can talk about this later, okay?" she interrupted me.

"Awwww, shit bro, you're in for it!" Chad howled.

"Oh, baby, leave 'em alone," Tiffani cooed. "It's their first fight."

"Sure," I managed. "We'll talk later."

And so I sat there and thought for the next twenty minutes—listening to Laura and the two Ts drone on about "fashion," caloric intake, and workout routines, while Chad pretty much just sat there and made bad jokes—about how the hell I was going to make Ken look like Madonna, or Madonna look like Ken.

• • •

At the end of the day, I was out by my car, telling Carrie, Joanna, and Shauna all about the lunch happenings (except Halloween stuff, of course—no need to piss them off yet), when Laura sauntered up, interrupting the conversation.

"Can I borrow my boyfriend for a minute?"

Joanna said nothing.

Shauna said, "Um . . . sure."

Carrie, uncharacteristically bitchy, said, "Hi, by the way."

"Oh, right, sorry," Laura said. "Hi, everyone."

"Laura, you know Carrie, Joanna, and Shauna, right?" I said. "Guys, this is Laura."

"We know," Joanna said, breaking her stony silence. "And sure, go right ahead and take him away."

"Thaaanks," Laura replied. "Oh—I'm sure Jonathan would like you there, so I'm officially inviting you to my Halloween party, okay?"

"Thaaanks," Joanna mimicked.

"Me and Jonathan are going as Barbie and Ken—"

"Um, don't we have to have that conversation?" I asked, interrupting her and leading her away from my friends. "I'll be back in a minute," I called over my shoulder, noticing that even Carrie was looking annoyed with me.

"What was that about?" I asked Laura when we were at a safe distance. "You can't just tear me away from my friends."

"It kinda seems like you were the one who just ran away," she told me.

"Yeah, maybe 'cause you were about to tell them about our

'couple's costume,' which I totally don't want to do. I'm supposed to dress up with them—"

"Hate to break it to you, dear, but you're dressing up as Ken, and that's that."

"What're you gonna do, take my allowance away?" I asked pointedly, suddenly put off by her bitchiness. I guess I'd never been on its receiving end. "What can you do, anyway?"

"I'll pull out."

"Not so fast—there was nothing in our agreement about my having to do this with you."

"Yeah? Well, then I'm counting it as our date for the week. And you *do* have to have one public date with me a week, and I call the shots on the dates. Remember *that* part of the deal?"

"I do, but it's not reasonable. Halloween's our favorite holiday of the—"

"Boo-hoo, Parish, you'll just have to live with it. That is, if you still wanna go to London in the spring."

"Fine," I said grudgingly, avoiding eye contact. She was definitely a tough one. I had to hand it to her: she knew what she was doing. But so did I. I'd think of something. At least, I hoped I would. "Hey, nice Kylie reference at lunch, by the way." I smiled a little, hoping to relieve the tension a wee bit.

"Thanks," she replied, a little nicer. "I'm doing my research—she's actually pretty great."

"Tell me about it!" I beamed. "And, listen . . . thanks for inviting my friends."

"The more the merrier."

"And this is the last surprise you pull on me, get it?"

"Oh, and just so we don't have to have these little fights anymore," she said, disregarding my last comment, "just let the Kylie references remind you of what we're doing here. If I have to break up with you, it's no Kylie trip. I'm telling you, Jonathan, do not make this difficult for me. I don't wanna be fucked with."

"Are you, like, some angry mother-in-law from *Passions* or something? I feel like I'm watching a soap opera. . . ."

She laughed a little. "Just you wait, baby." Then she winked at me and was gone.

I turned around to go back to my friends. But they were gone, too.

10. I Guess I Like It Like That

That Friday, Laura and I went on our first date. For maximum visibility, she decided we'd go to Winter Park Village and eat at Seito Sushi.

Winter Park Village is sort of a miniature mock-city where the old and decrepit Winter Park Mall used to be. I guess that people decided that the mall was getting too ghetto and outdated, so what else to do but completely demolish it and build a fake city, complete with a megaplex, restaurants, shops, condos, some major parking lots, and of course a Cheesecake Factory. No Starbucks, though—that was across the street.

Seito Sushi was right next to the movie theater, where multitudes of Winter Park students gathered before spending eight bucks to go see the latest Steven Spielberg–Tom Hanks gagfest.

Okay, my pissiness reading: high to very high.

Why?

Who the hell knows? I mean, getting to see Kylie would be amazing and all, but I was already getting shit from Joanna about having to keep my self closeted, I *hated* having to eat lunch with Laura and the Idiot Crew, and Laura was sabotaging my Halloween!

But, whatever. I'd made an arrangement and I was gonna stick to it.

I was listening to *Impossible Princess*, Kylie's masterpiece of an album, as I drove Aretha down Palmer to pick up Laura in her fucking mansion. Palmer was where some of Winter Park's richest lived, including the old Magic player Horace Grant—I remember loving his blue goggles as a kid.

"You *are* kidding me, aren't you, sweetie?" Laura said as I pulled into her gigantic circular driveway. "You expect me to get into that Swedish armored car?"

"Jeez, talk about Impossible Princess!" I moaned, leaning over to unlock her door—the automatic locks had puttered out years before.

"What's *that* supposed to mean?" she demanded.

"Nothing. You ready?"

"Yeah, but my dad wants to meet you first."

Thunk.

That's the sound my jaw makes when it drops to Aretha's floor. Her *dad*?

"What? Why? I mean . . . when, like, now?"

"Yes. Now. You have any more *W* questions for me there, champ?" She paused. "Didn't think so. C'mon, let's get this over with. Just be cool."

Be cool, be cool, be cool. . . .

I was actually pleased when the very large, very rotund, very imposing and intimidating Mr. Schulberg sauntered out the colossal oak doors that led into his castle. At least all I had to deal with now was an enormous *person*, not the enormous house as well. I think I could have very well shit my pants if I'd had to go through that.

"Well, well, is this the Jonathan Parish who's taking my daughter out tonight?" he said jovially.

Jovially?

Yeah, jovially—I could deal with this.

"Uh . . . yeah"—I cleared my throat—"I mean, uh . . . yes, sir, I'm Jonathan." I stuck my hand out to give him a firm, manly, hetero handshake.

"Yes, I said that," Mr. Schulberg teased. "I'm Lou, nice to meet you."

I stifled a giggle at the rhyme.

"You, too," I said. "I'm excited about our date."

"Oh, are you taking me out?" Mr. Schulberg—I mean Lou— said. "I'm sorry, my shoes don't match my purse." He did a little impression of what I can only guess was this nasty man's idea of how gay men walk.

Good-bye jovial, hello homophobe.

"All right, Dad, we're goin'," Laura said, interrupting his comedy routine.

"Now, Jonathan," Lou said, getting all serious, "what are your intentions for my daughter?"

"*Dad*, could you *please* get out of the fifties? You're embarrass—"

"Oh, no, Laura, it's all right," I interrupted her, giving her a little half smile. "Mr. Schulberg, I want to assure you that my intentions regarding Laura are nothing but virtuous—"

"God, *kill* me!" Laura groaned. "I'm about to go on this date by myself—"

"No, Laura, Jonathan here's a gentleman," Lou said. "Have her home by eleven. You were out all night with the girls that night *last* weekend, so . . ."

I gave Laura a subtle, knowing glance.

"Twelve!" Laura demanded, ignoring me.

"Eleven!" Lou insisted.

"Tw—"

"I can do eleven," I told him, shooting a playfully mean look at Laura as I turned my back on her jackass father.

"Primo, son! See you at eleven, princess."

And we were off.

"Fuck you," Laura said as we pulled out of the driveway.

"Now, now . . . you know our agreement: no sex," I said innocently. "Here, wanna hear an amazing song?"

"No." Laura was looking at the car surrounding her, pouting. "You're gonna have to park, like, way far away. I'm talking Albertson's parking lot, Jonathan."

"Here. Listen to this," I told her, skipping ahead to the sixth track. It's one of my favorites—delicate, breathy vocals and a warm, trance-y beat. It sounded like no other Kylie song I could think of, which was one of the reasons I liked it so much—it was original.

"Did you hear what I said about the par—?"

"*Yes!*" I cried. "You're not even listening to the song!"

"Sure I am—'Say Hey,' right? I really like this one."

"Wow, you really *are* doing your research!" I commended her, impressed with how much she already knew. "You're branching out past the obvious albums."

"Yeah, this one's not bad. . . ." She gazed out the window as I turned us onto Park Avenue.

"Not *bad*?" I squeaked incredulously. "It's amazing!"

"Yeah, yeah, I hear ya. Let's just get to dinner."

After parking Aretha in the Albertson's grocery store parking lot and walking the extra five minutes it took to get to the Village, we sat down at our outdoor table at Seito Sushi. After all, what was the point of eating at Seito if no one in front of the movie theater could see you?

It was a nice night, anyway. For once, the Central Florida humidity seemed to be giving it a rest. There was even a light breeze. Summer was finally transitioning into fall. I couldn't help but think that had this date been with a guy, everything would be perfect.

Dream Date would be handsome, with a gorgeously chiseled face and dazzling green eyes. We'd sit down, exchange sad-but-oh-so-humorous food-poisoning stories as we looked over the restaurant's raw-fish selection. Then we'd promise each other that if we got sick that night, we'd keep each other company, holding back each other's hair, preparing warm chicken-noodle soup, and arranging saltines in the shape of a heart on a big plate. Okay, yeah, I know: weird fantasy. But it's just something my mind cooked up as we opened our menus, and I kind of liked it.

"What're you *grinning* about, Jonathan?" Laura asked curtly, shocking me back into reality. She leaned over the table, cutting down the space between us to a mere few inches. "You thinking you're gonna score tonight or something?" she whispered sultrily.

I couldn't help but burst out laughing. The whole thing was so ridiculous I just had to. Laura laughed, too, reaching over and patting my hands, then taking them into hers and looking dreamily into my eyes. Star couple George Fisher (varsity basketball stud) and Rachel Tanner (student-body president) glanced backward at us as they walked hand in hand to the movie theater.

Laura gently released her grip on my hands and gave me a little wink.

"You're *far* too good at this," I said, smiling. "I'll bet you get your charm from your dad, don't you?"

"Ugh, don't mention my parents, *please*," she moaned. "I'm so not in the mood."

"Well, what should we talk about?" I asked. "This *is* a date, you know."

"Let's talk about ordering," she said, nodding her head toward our incoming waiter. "This *is* a restaurant, you know." She smirked. Impossible Princess.

Our waiter was this kind of sleazier older gay guy who served me my sushi with a side of innuendo every time I went to Seito, which wasn't often, but often enough. He was kind of what I pictured Kenny Daniels would grow up to be. Not that I was one of those obnoxious kids who thought *all* older guys were nasty—I enjoyed checking out *many* an older man—but I was not this waiter's biggest fan. I rolled my eyes in anticipation, and wondered how I could play it off.

"Hel*looo*," he said, lengthening the *oh* sound unnecessarily and giving it a sort of Valley-Girl inflection. "Wh-*at* can I give you, darling?" he asked me, completely disregarding Laura.

I was about to politely ask for more time to look at the menu—what else was I supposed to do?—when Laura spoke up.

"Um, you can *not* call my boyfriend 'darling' and give *us* some more time to look over the menu, thanks." And she just looked back down at her menu. That's it. End of discussion.

Our waiter huffed and scuttled away, taken aback to say the least. For the first time in a week, I was pretty glad to be Laura's boyfriend.

"So where were we?" Laura said to me. "Ah, yes, conversation topics."

"You're insane," I told her.

"Don't mention it," she replied, clearly taking what I'd just said to be a thank-you. "Now—give us a topic."

"College?" I asked. "I'm thinking I'm gonna go to UF—Gainesville. Maybe something relating to urban planning or sociology or something like—"

"Could we switch the topic to something that's *not* gonna make me snore into my miso soup?" Laura asked all fake-politely.

Now that's something Dream Date would never have said.

"Okay, then . . ." I pretended to search around in the air for a topic, to Laura's apparent amusement. "How about we talk about why you've been such a raging bitch since we started dating?"

"Or about why you love it so much," she shot back.

I laughed again, and so did she. When she smiled, she actually lit up the place. She had a gorgeous set of perfect white teeth. I *did* like her spunk, her nastiness—usually when it wasn't directed at *me*. And the nice thing was that she could dish it out, and she definitely seemed like she could take it right back.

"Okay, seriously now," she said, calming down a bit. "I'll be nice."

"*Finally!*" I yelled good-naturedly. Another few people I recognized from our school looked over at us from in front of the movie theater and smiled.

"Nice work, baby," Laura said happily. "So. Now. College . . ."

"Yeah."

"Well, basically . . . I dunno. Haven't thought about it much except for the fact that I'm getting a condo on top of one of my dad's buildings."

"So that *is* true?" I asked. "I'm so jealous!"

"You knew about that?"

"Well, yeah . . . people talk."

"Ah, you're clearly learning."

I grinned at her. "I guess."

We spent the next hour or so discussing a bunch of random stuff: her past boyfriends, my past lack of boyfriends, her vacations to villas in Tuscany, my family road trips to Tennessee, her growing love of Kylie, my growing respect for her musical sensibilities. It was actually pretty pleasant, and by the time we got the check and she slipped me some cash under the table, her bitchy sarcasm had totally grown on me (though I wouldn't ever *tell* her that—it'd ruin the fun) and I wasn't even thinking about Halloween (which I'd sort of been seething about for the first part of the date). In fact, I was thinking about how, oddly, she could turn out to be a kinda fun friend.

"Hey," she said as I was counting out the tip. "I'm sorry about my dad earlier . . . just so you know."

I was touched. Truly and unexpectedly touched. "No problem," I told her. "Thanks. And, hey, I meant to ask you—what's he think of you dating me only a week after you and Paul broke up?"

"Oh, he couldn't be happier—he always thought Paul was an asshole."

"Seems to be the consensus . . ."

"Are you scared of him?" she asked teasingly.

"Well, aren't I allowed to be?" I whispered. "I mean, it's not like I'm your *real* boyfriend or anything, and I didn't think getting my ass beat was part of the deal. I'd like to make it to Kylie in one piece!"

"Awww, is Pauly Wauly being mean to Jonny?" she asked in baby speak.

"*Shut up!*" I said excitedly. "The guy's been giving me mean looks all week and—"

"What, mean looks? You should get a restraining order!"

"Laura, I'm just worried that—"

Laura put her finger to my lips to shush me. "Jonathan," she said calmly. "Trust me—the guy wouldn't lay a finger on you. He's all talk and no action, *believe* me." She smirked at me. "I told him to lay off you, and he will. I swear."

"Yeah?"

"Trust me. You're free and clear." Her eyes flickered to the parking lot behind me. "Incoming," she muttered, then smiled and leaned in for a kiss, which I gave her, closing my eyes and picturing Dream Date. It was nice and warm, lasting a few seconds. Had my brain not flashed back to reality so soon after the kiss began, we might've been making out forever.

"Not bad," she said, leaning back into her chair. "Leave fifteen percent," she instructed me. "That fag was slow."

I gave her a look, and she blushed.

"Sorry," she said. "I guess I am my father's daughter."

"Yeah, well, lose it, okay?" I said. "Anyway, he was not *that* slow—he was nice. Gross and *forty*, but nice. I don't think he'll mess with me again. And it's not his fault the kitchen took too long with the food. He gets twenty."

"Fifteen."

"Twenty," I said, not even bothering to look at her as I laid down another couple of ones. "It's my money, after all. Remember, sweetie?" Looks like Laura had met her match.

The right corner of Laura's mouth curled up into a little sneer. "That's true, honey muffin." She pinched my cheek. "You're a good guy."

It was only when we stood up to leave that I saw the couple that'd walked by us as we had our "magical" kiss. It was Trent and Alex, and they were about to go into the theater. I couldn't tell if they were on a date or not, but it was only the two of them, and Trent was dressed up pretty nice, and Alex, still sporting her new look, was looking pretty hottish herself. But actually, Trent was in one of the outfits we'd gotten for him the weekend before—maybe he was only showing it off. I kept searching for an indication of what his "intentions" were for her (or Alex's for him, more accurately), but found nothing conclusive. He held the door open for her and followed her in. He was carrying the tickets.

"So how was your *date*?" Joanna asked when I picked up the phone on my way home.

"Uh . . . actually, not too bad," I said haltingly. "It was actually kind of okay, actually." I'd wanted to say it was fun, but after seeing what might have been Alex and Trent's first date—*Think only happy thoughts, Jonathan, only happy thoughts!*—how could I?

"Say 'actually' one more time and I'm outing you."

I coughed out a nervous chuckle. "Sorry, I'll, uh . . . I'll have a prepared speech next time."

"I'm serious, though, Jonathan," she said. "I'm getting pretty sick of having to tell everyone who asks about you that you're straight. I swear sometimes it makes me wanna puke."

"I'm sorry, I'm sorry, I'm sure it'll die down soon as word gets around," I assured her.

"It had better. And Shauna's not liking it too much, either. But of course she's being all close-lipped about it."

"Did you have a reason for calling or did you simply want to give me yet *another* lecture?" I asked impatiently. Wow. Laura must've been rubbing off on me.

"Easy, lady," she said. "I was just seeing if you wanted to go to Thriftko to Madonna-shop with us tomorrow. You know—to find some *Ken* bullshit?"

"Oh, *right*, well . . . I'm working, anyway, so . . ." I said, hoping she wouldn't press the issue.

"Well, what about Sunday after work?" she said, pressing the issue. "At noon, y'know?"

"Yeah. Well, truth be told, I already got my costume," I lied.

"I'm not surprised," she said. She didn't sound angry. Just hurt. I was such a dickwad! But, shit—wait'll she hears about Alex and Trent. Of course, there *could* be nothing to tell, after all! Right? *Happy thoughts, Jonathan! Happy thoughts . . .*

"Fine. Whatever." She sighed. "What's with you, anyway? You sound strange. . . . Did something happen on the date? I swear, if you pull any more weird shit on me, I'll flip out."

I weighed my options. And it was no contest. I *could not* tell her yet about Trent and Alex. Because I think telling her the crush of her life was possibly now dating Alex Becker was definitely "weird shit," and I kind of felt like living at least long enough to see Kylie Minogue in concert. I felt awful, but I dared not say a word. I mean, I was responsible. This was way shittier than abandoning them for Halloween. If I'd kept it zipped up and left the room to get some water, Alex might still have been the sweet, shy, understated girl that she once was, without the confidence to go after hot, hunky Trent Kessler. (And I would've felt a *lot* less crappy the next day, I'm sure.) Not that I thought she wasn't hot enough for Trent in the first place—I just don't think she would've had it in her. And if *only* I had kept my mouth shut about Trent's possible feelings for her, she would've stayed away. And I wouldn't have been sitting there in Aretha at a red light, sweating bullets through my favorite button-down dress shirt.

So my natural answer was: "Me? No—nothing weird here. . . . Have fun at Thriftko tomorrow. And don't worry about Halloween—it's gonna be super-fun, no matter what happens."

I crossed my fingers and hoped I was right.

11. Shocked

A couple weeks, another great date, and some rather annoying-Laura days at lunch later, it was Halloween time. It was most definitely about time for my favorite holiday, as I'd been getting kind of annoyed with Laura at school—mostly at lunch, like I just said. It was sucky, because after our first couple of dates I thought we'd really been hitting it off. Unfortunately, Laura seemed to need to exert as much power over me as possible in front of her friends. And, for the sake of the perceived integrity of our relationship, I mostly had to oblige.

Three times a week now, I was being subjected to the inane Tiffani-Tina-Laura chitchat ("How much do you think Nancy Fischer's parents spent on her nose-job, because they *so* need a partial refund!") and the idiotic drone of macho-man Chad ("Aww, c'mon, Parish—how much can you bench?"), and when the talking wasn't about pointless bullshit, Laura often felt the need to complain about how I spent more time with my friends than I did with her.

"Per our agreement, bitch, you get only one date a weekend!" is what I wanted to scream at her, but of course I couldn't.

"You're lucky I'm even agreeing to sit with you at lunch for more

than a day a week!" is another thing I felt like yelling in her face. But again, I couldn't so I didn't.

And if those dumb ho-bags commented *one more time* on what I ate—as if I *needed* the advice, hello!—I was gonna be like, "Yeah, bitches, tell it to my almost-washboard abs." But would I really? Yeah . . . you guessed it.

Uck.

If that's what being rich and popular was all about, I didn't want a goddamn part of it.

And then there was the issue of having to say over and over again that I was straight. I could tell why Joanna and Shauna were upset about it, because for a few days there I had to say to every girl that came up to me for a date or non-date or "drive" (and it was definitely adding up—*so* weird) that: yes, I *was* straight but that sorry, I was taken by a Miss Laura Schulberg. Regardless of how often I had to do it, it never failed to freak me out just a little.

Then of course there was Kylie, which got me through it all.

But regardless of how happy the Kylie Wall made me each time I came home, how reassured I was every time I admired her fabulously coy-yet-sexy poses, I still needed this party. I needed it bad. I needed it to be so fun that it mended things a bit with the girls and reassured me of Laura's overall goodness.

But with the question of Alex and Trent still in the air, and how everyone would react to my costume situation, I didn't exactly know *what* to expect from the evening.

Twenty minutes before Joanna, Shauna, Carrie, and I were supposed to leave for the big bash, I walked up the stairs to Joanna's bedroom in a black hoodie and long trench coat. When I walked in the room to find them already all dressed up, Joanna greeted me with:

"Jonathan, what *took* you so long? And you're not even dressed yet! How hard is it to dress up like Ken, anyway . . . ? Wait. Are you wearing eyeliner?"

And with that, I pushed PLAY on the little boom box I had under my coat, tore down the hood from my sweatshirt, and threw off my coat to reveal my actual costume:

"*American Life Madonna!*" Shauna cried over the blasting music as I gyrated and lip-synched. "It looks great!"

"Fabulous," Carrie said. "Absolutely fabulous."

"Could I ever be anything *but?*" I yelled, rubbing my hands over my G.I. Joe–style camo outfit, shortish dark brown wig, and beret. I looked at Joanna and waited for her reaction.

And then, smiling (surprise!), she said, "So, no Ken? How're you getting away with this?"

"I just told her how it is," I lied. "And I would've been Vogue Madonna, but you have *no* idea how hard it is to find pointed bras! Anyway, you guys are way more important to me than Laura is—especially on this, the holiest of days."

And then we all hugged, and Joanna (surprise again!) whispered in my ear so no one else could hear, "I'm sorry I'm impossible sometimes. You know I love you."

• *Convince your best friends that you changed costumes just for them.* CHECK.

I pictured my karmic worth plummeting as she said this, scolding myself for being such a coward. I hadn't told Laura anything, except that I'd be there by nine. When I got there, I planned on telling her I was dressed as G.I. Joe (or some form of him) and hoping that she wouldn't go ape-shit.

Hoping I wouldn't come back as a toilet brush in my next life, I whispered back to Joanna, "Love you, too," and got our little group-hug circle to dance and shake around to the stuttering beats of "American Life."

After dancing to the song and laughing our asses off, we went to the mirror to put the finishing touches on our makeup. Me in my camo gear and Che Guevara–style beret, Joanna in her pink dress and elbow-length pink gloves, Shauna in her tight plaid shirt and cowboy hat, Carrie in God-knows-what-kind-of-fishnet-ripped-T-shirt-crimped-hair clusterfuck: American Life Madonna, Material Girl Madonna, Cowgirl Madonna, and Like a Virgin Madonna.

We were dazzling.

"I gotta pee," Joanna said. "Be right back."

As soon as she was out of the room and I heard the bathroom door close, I grabbed the opportunity.

"You guys," I whispered, "I never told you this, but on my first date with Laura, I think I might've seen Alex and Trent on a date. But they're not acting like a couple at school, and I haven't heard if they're official or anything yet. . . . What the hell should I do?"

"Why would you think they were on a date?" Carrie whispered back. "I mean, they've been friends for a while now, you know."

Shit. I'd forgotten about that minor detail.

Shauna just stayed silent, focusing intently on her makeup.

"No reason . . ." I said. "Just that . . . I'm a scandalously horrible friend and I might've accidentally told Alex that I thought I saw Trent checking her out at Joanna's party to get her to stop crying."

"You *what*?" Carrie gasped.

"*Shhh!*" I urged her. "I'm really, really sorry, but you heard me right. So, yeah—I'm an idiot."

For once, Carrie had nothing cute or witty to say. She just shook her head disappointedly.

"Look," I pleaded with them, "she was crying and you know how I can't handle that and she was thinking she was gross and too unattractive for a boyfriend so I remembered how I saw Trent looking at her at the party kind of weirdly—"

"Wait, so you weren't making it up?" Carrie asked.

"Well, I sort of thought I was. It's just something that popped in my head that I thought might get her to stop with the boo-hoos so I just . . . blurted it out." I paused. "Should I tell Joanna?" I glanced to the bathroom door, hoping she'd be in there just a few seconds longer. I could feel my scalp starting to bead up with sweat around the wig line. "Shauna, should I?"

"I dunno," she said, looking only at herself as she adjusted her eye makeup. "Just . . . don't ask me about this stuff, okay?"

"The answer is *no fuckin' way!*" Carrie told me emphatically. "Don't tell her shit till there's something to tell. Things are on kind of delicate balance with her lately, if you haven't noticed—"

"Hey, guys!" Joanna called from the bathroom. I heard water running. "I'm thinking tonight's the night."

"For me to go insane?" I said quietly to Shauna and Carrie.

"For what?" Shauna called back, looking away from me.

"For me to put the moves on Trent."

"Oh, yeah?" Carrie said, shooting me a wide-eyed look. "That's . . . Are you sure that's the best idea? I mean, you've only hung out a couple times."

"Yeah, but I don't wanna sink into that whole 'friends' thing and never get out," she replied. "Plus . . . it's time . . . you know?"

"Uh . . . yeah," I said. "I'm super-excited."

"Good," she said, opening the door and walking back into the room. "I think I'm gonna wrap my arms around him and tell him that I wanna be his Material Girl," she laughed as she adjusted her long pink gloves.

Shauna sighed almost inaudibly, but I caught it. Luckily, Joanna hadn't.

"So you're *sure* your brother's chauffeuring us tonight, right?" Shauna asked me, expertly changing the subject.

"Yeah, I'm positive. He hates Halloween, and if we each give him five bucks, it'll be enough to buy him some beer or something and he'll be plenty happy."

"How can *anyone* hate Halloween?" Carrie gasped. "It's the one time of year I can dress up like the slut I pretend not to be!"

"You don't pretend very hard, hon," I said playfully.

"Ha," said Carrie.

"Okay, so let's finish our makeup and get ready. My brother'll be here any minute. Then he's picking us up from the party and dropping us all here for our little sleepover."

"I'm gonna kiss the spit out of Trent tonight," Joanna declared determinedly. Clearly, she had only one thing on her mind tonight. How fantastic.

After a quick ride in the car—during which we made our traditional detour to check out a certain former *NSYNC member's mansion to see if he was watering the plants or something (he wasn't; he never was)—the four Madonnas made their grand entrance into Laura Schulberg's even grander entryway. We pushed open the two heavy oak front doors, each twelve feet tall, and walked into a foyer fit for royalty. It was cavernous, and we were faced with twin limestone staircases that led up to a wall-less second-floor walkway that looked down over the entire foyer/living room. Throngs of costumed Winter Parkers crowded the house, and a hired DJ was spinning some remixed Top 40.

"Holy shit," Carrie said. "Bitch can throw a party."

"Seriously!" I gawked.

"Okay, ladies, let's go freshen up," Joanna declared.

"Wait, wait, can we *please* just dance to this song first?" I pleaded over Kelly Clarkson's booming voice. "It's 'Since U Been Gone'!"

Joanna rolled her eyes like she hated the song and was doing me a favor, but then shot me an "of course" kind of look.

We all ran to the cleared-out portion of the living room where there was a small group of cool people dancing around crazily to the infectious chorus. By the end of the song (which I think the DJ extended because of our uninhibited dance-antics), we were properly pumped full of happy endorphins and even more ready for a great time than when we'd been dancing around getting dressed. The song segued into some Mariah, and we promptly left the area.

- *Start out the evening in a fun way with best friends.* CHECK.

"All right, so now we're *definitely* gonna go freshen up," Joanna panted. "You comin'?"

"Nah, I better go find Laura and tell her we're here. I'll find you all soon."

I walked back up toward the foyer, where I ran into Laura (Barbie) and Tina, who was dressed as Christina Aguilera à la "Dirrty" video. I had to bite my tongue to keep it from giving her a lashing. She had it all wrong: the blonde wig was straight, with no knots or black streaks to speak of, and she had hardly *any* eye makeup on. I could've done it so much better. Amateur.

"Heeeey . . . *Ken*?" Laura said to me, coming up and giving me a kiss. She paused, then stepped back, and gave me an appraising look. "What the fuck is this?"

"Didn't you say you were gonna be Barbie and Ken?" Tina asked Laura, shifting her weight from slut-booted foot to slut-booted foot. She was definitely already a little sloshed. "What's with this camouflage-makeup thing?"

I could see Laura's eyes flicker almost imperceptibly with concern over losing her alpha-female status for not having control over her man, at which point I spoke up and said, "Yeah, don't you remember, baby? I told you I couldn't find any appropriate Ken garb, so I went with G.I. Joe instead. . . . Figured that was a cute couple-y thing to do, too."

"Oh, yeah—totally slipped my mind," Laura replied, picking up on me right away.

Tina tilted her head and looked at me inquisitively, scrunching up her face and squinting her eyes. "Why does G.I. Joe have long hair and makeup?"

"Well, I couldn't just go as G.I. Joe," I explained to her. I'd thought this whole thing out when I'd gone costume shopping. If all went well, Laura wouldn't pick up on the fact that I had dressed as Madonna, and my girlfriends wouldn't even *conceive of* who I was telling Laura and her friends I was dressed as. "So I tried to go for a sort of Italian-looking, smoldering version. Say, Giuseppe Joe."

"You're weird," Tina informed me, stirring her drink with her index finger.

"Whatever, Tina," Laura said, coming to my (and our) defense. "I think it's hot. Guys should totally be allowed to wear eye makeup all the time."

"Uh . . . yeah. Yeah, I can sorta see that," Tina said, adjusting her crotchless chaps (at least she got *that* detail from the video right). "You really like that Italian thing, don't you? The costume, how much you love Sisley—"

"Definitely," I said, hoping Laura was buying all of this. "Actually, I—"

"So where're your friends?" Laura interrupted.

• *Convince faux-girlfriend that new costume was assembled with only her in mind.* STATUS PENDING.

"I'm not sure, they just left to—"

"*Hmph,*" Laura hmphed. "That's a first." She turned to Tina. "I feel like they own him sometimes." She looked at me and raised one eyebrow, seemingly daring me to say something. I really don't think she completely meant it—she was probably just fucking with me.

So I ignored the comment.

• *Have faith that faux-girlfriend is human and has feelings.* STATUS PENDING.

Kylie Kylie Kylie, London London LONDON! I thought to myself furiously, keeping my ultimate goal in mind.

"Can't a soldier get a drink around here?" I asked, changing the subject.

"Oh," Laura said, "drinks are over by the kitchen. Just tell one of the bartenders. Whatever you want . . . just *don't* fucking tip them; they're already getting paid a crapload."

"Thanks," I said, composing myself and getting my anger under control. "I'll go get a drink and find you later."

I headed toward the kitchen, looking frantically all around me for Alex; I *had* to find out about her and Trent. If they were in fact together and I was officially the Worst Best Friend in the World, someone would have to warn Joanna about it.

And that's when the other Madonnas bumped into me.

"I'm looking for Trent," Joanna said. "Help us."

"What?" I asked incredulously. "You're already looking for him?" I shot looks at Cowgirl Madonna and Like a Virgin Madonna. "You're *all* already looking for him?"

"There's no stopping her," Carrie said.

"Well . . ." I said. "I'm gonna just mingle for a bit. I'm sure you girls can find him. Just . . . let me know when the wedding is, okay?"

"Cute," Joanna said. "Wish me luck?"

"Wish *me* luck," I muttered.

"Huh?"

"Nothing—good luck!"

"Thanks. See ya."

As soon as I could, I scrambled through the party—through the Golden Girls, Foxy Cleopatra, Paris Hilton, and a few random werewolves and vampires—looking for any sign of Alex. I didn't find Alex right away, but what I did find was a bunch of lazy-ass guys. What is it about some guys and the absolute *refusal* to compose a decent Halloween costume?! I'm sorry, boys, but a cowboy hat or a sailor's cap or a set of vampire teeth are *so* not gonna do it. And the funny thing is, these guys I was noticing were cute—and could *totally* get a girl's attention if they just played into their fantasies with a little more effort. Get a hot gladiator getup or a *complete* cowboy costume, complete with way-too-tight-in-the-crotch jeans and a dusty plaid shirt, and they'd be beating the girls off with a stick instead of beating them*selves* off at the end of the night.

But I digress clearly, as I was snapped back into attention by Adam Fitch snapping at me: "What're you *staring* at, Parish?"

"Nothing," I said, resuming my search for Alex. "Just your shitty excuse for a cowboy costume."

"Well, what the hell're *you* supposed to be?"

"Don't ask," I told him, and continued my survey of the house.

Madonna's "Express Yourself" came on, probably played by the DJ in honor of the four lovely Madges that'd just walked in ten minutes before, and I really wanted to dance—"Express Yourself" was a personal favorite—but I had to find Alex. Because if Joanna found Trent and started hitting on him and he was already taken, then Joanna was gonna make an ass of herself and so I had to find Alex or maybe even Trent—

Or both of them at the same time.

Right in the middle of the staircase.

As Britney Spears and Kevin "FedEx" Federline.

Reunited and expressing themselves all over each other's faces, locked in a drunken, lovey-dovey lip-lock. Tongues swirling, lips dancing, teeth biting, hands feeling, pelvises grinding to the beat—the whole deal.

I guess that answered my question.

My next question was how to let Joanna know.

And that was answered, too, when I spotted her, Shauna, and Carrie at the top of the staircase, looking down on Alex and Trent . . . and me. It was too much for Joanna. I turned to see her jaw drop and eyes well up, her lips quivering. I felt like shit. No, worse than shit. Whatever that is. Diarrhea? Ew, that's just gross.

Joanna ran away, Shauna and Carrie in tow. I flew past Alex and Trent, taking the stairs two at a time, probably looking like a total idiot, to catch up with them. I got to them on the landing overlooking the living room, amid a crowd of dancing party-goers.

"Joanna, wait," I said, grabbing hold of her elbow.

"*What?*" she snapped, tears in her eyes. "What do you want? To *gloat?*"

"Gloat?" I asked. "About what?"

"About how I shouldn't have . . . counted my *fucking* chickens or whatever? Why does this shit *always* happen to me?!"

This must've looked weird to everyone: a quadruple Madonna-drama clan, with our own fucking song playing in the background.

Joanna seemed to notice the attention we were getting, so she leaned in to whisper to me, "And you knew. I can tell. I saw you looking at them and you hardly even looked *shocked*."

"Joanna . . . I—"

"Don't try to lie. I might've known Shauna for longer, but you're my best friend," she continued in my ear. "You knew. I don't know how you knew, but you did. So thanks for the heads-up."

"Joanna—"

"And nice try with the costume," she continued, the tears now rolling down her cheeks. "I overheard everything; you should be more careful."

And with that, she whispered something to Carrie, took Shauna's arm, and was off.

"What was *that*?!" I said to Carrie.

"She just wants to be with Shauna now," Carrie told me. "I think she's a little overwhelmed."

"I'm such a shit," I said. "No. Worse than shit. But I'm not gonna go there."

"No, you're not. You just slipped up . . . again. You know we all love you. Especially for this." She straightened my costume and wig, smiling, then sighed. "Even if you *didn't* tell Laura to shove her Ken costume up her non-defined Barbie-vagina . . . you're still a good friend." She gave me a hug and took a deep breath. "Thank God Jesse's picking us up. 'Cause now I wanna get fucked up. This might be a long night."

"And I guess it's safe to say that Jesse's dropping me off at home, not Joanna's," I said.

"Yeah, probably. Let's go."

We made our way down another staircase toward the bar. As we approached, I noticed that one of the bartenders—a twenty-something black-haired indie rock–looking guy who seemed like he had better things to do—was pretty damn hot.

"Mmm," Carrie said. "He could fix my mood any day."

I laughed. "Why don't you go take a cold shower?"

"Nah . . . but I *am* gonna leave you for just a few. I see Heather from my calc class over there dressed as Avril Lavigne and I wanna go slap her upside the head. And tug on her tie with my teeth." She smiled really big, as if asking permission.

"Of course," I said. "I'm really okay. I need a second to unwind, anyway. Have fun." I gave her a kiss on the cheek and she was gone.

So I walked up to Hottie-Hot Bartender and ordered a dirty martini. . . . "No, actually, make it a dirty *Grey Goose* martini," I told him. "And do you have those bleu cheese–stuffed olives?" I asked him hopefully. This was, after all, a Laura Schulberg party.

"We certainly do, sir," he answered.

"Awesome. Thanks. And *please* don't call me 'sir'—it's so embarrassing!"

"No problem," he said, smiling a little. He started making my drink. As he was spearing my olives, he looked up at me and asked, "So what're you supposed to be, if you don't mind my asking."

"Giuseppe Joe," I said as he handed me the drink.

He laughed a little. "What?"

I looked around and leaned closer to him conspiratorially, whispering, "Actually my girlfriends and I are supposed to be different versions of Madonna—"

"Aaaah," he whispered back. "So you're from the 'American Life' video."

"Exactly," I answered. "But my . . . *girlfriend* girlfriend"—*still* not used to saying that—"thinks that I'm G.I. Joe, so I'm trying to fool her enough to not get my ass kicked. She originally wanted me to go as Ken. She's Barbie."

"Girlfriend?" he asked, seeming both surprised and slightly disappointed. I had no idea he was gay, but as soon as he asked that, I couldn't *believe* I'd missed it. Was I *losing* my gaydar?

"Well, actually, I . . . uh"—I looked around the house at all my fellow Winter Parkers, catching a glimpse of Laura in her long, blonde wig—"yeah . . . girlfriend. She's the one who's throwing this party. Barbie, like I said."

"Ooooh," he said to me, giving me a look I couldn't decipher. Pity? Condescension? Confusion? "She's . . . uh . . . pretty."

"Uh, yeah . . . she sure is—"

"Hey, man, could I get a Corona?" someone interrupted.

I glanced over and who else would it be but Trent Kessler, all dressed up (or down, really) in a wife-beater and stupid hat as Kevin Fucking Fedora-line. God, even as a wannabe wannabe-gangsta (and a lazy-boy attitude toward Halloween costumes), he was adorable.

"Here you go, sir," Cutie Bartender said, handing Trent his

Corona with a lime inside and turning his attention to the next customer.

"Thanks." He took a swig of his beer and turned to face me. "Oh! 'Sup, Jonathan?" he asked me. "I hardly recognized you."

"Oooh, in my army gear?" I said. "Well, I figured, if I'm gonna be straight now, I might as well go all the way."

"But you've got on eye makeup."

"Well . . . *almost* all the way," I laughed. "Old habits die hard."

"I hear ya. . . . So, uh . . . congrats on you and Laura."

"What?" I asked, distracted by the bartender's ass as he shook up a cosmo for some girl in a Catwoman costume. "*Oh*, yeah, right—thanks. . . . and same to you and Alex. That's pretty great. She's, uh . . . she's just great."

Trent gave me an appraising look—which I for a split second fantasized was him checking me out.

"Well, she'd have to be to turn you on to girls, right?"

Whoa. That was so unexpected. I coughed and vodka sort of came out of my nose, which burns like you can only imagine!

"I'm sorry, bro," Trent laughed. "Didn't mean to scare you."

"No, no, it's all right. . . . I figured everyone at school knew, anyway." I grabbed a cocktail napkin and dabbed at my nose. "I'm glad to see you're not weird about it."

"Nah, man, you can't control a girl's history, you know?"

"I suppose."

"I just hope I can rise to the challenge."

Ugh. Mental image. *Hot!* "I'm sure you can, Trent, don't worry about that. . . . I've only liked girls for a few weeks—you've liked them your whole life."

"Damn straight."

"That you are." I nodded, then coughed the last few stubborn vodka droplets from my throat and smiled shyly, my face feeling pretty red. He was still kind of staring at me . . . sizing me up, maybe? "So have you guys been friends awhile?" I asked, breaking the silence. "You two came to"—I paused for emphasis—"*Joanna's* party together, after all."

"Yeah, a couple years, actually," he answered. "It was just, like, all of a sudden, *bam!* she was there. I can't believe I hadn't thought about it before."

"You'd never thought about it?" I found it hard to believe.

"Well, I'd sorta thought about it, but not really seriously. But now . . . who knows? You know?"

Not exactly. "Sure."

This was sort of nice. If not for the obvious treason I was committing against Joanna, I was actually having a pretty nice time. Trent's a sweet guy. It was obvious that he cared about Alex, and if it took my dancing nastily with her and then having awkward sex with her to get his attention, then so be it. And the fact that he seemed cool with everything that'd happened between me and Alex was just testament to the fact that Trent was great. Great guy. Great face, great ass, great—

"Jonathan, *baby*, can I show you off a little?" Laura cooed. Where the hell had she come from, anyway?

"Hey!" I said, surprised. "Well, actually, Trent and I were—"

"Pleeease, sweetie." She leaned in to give me a kiss on the neck and whispered, "What do I have to do?" Great. Kylieminder #2. And one of my favorite songs.

"Oh! Yeah! Sure!" I said. I downed my drink and turned to the bartender and said, "Could I just get an Absolut Mandarin and Sprite, please?" I turned back to face Laura, who looked a little pissy for being kept waiting. "Sorry, babe," I said sweetly.

"All right," she said.

Hottie-Hot Bartender handed me my drink with a smile. "Enjoy."

And then, feeling some effects of the alcohol and suddenly wanting to piss Laura off, I reached into one of my cargo pockets and pulled out a five-dollar bill and gave it to him.

He looked at Laura and said, "Oh, sir, I . . . uh . . . I couldn't—"

"Oh, shut up, you can and will," I said. "In fact, we'll use this cup right here and start a little tip jar for you. You make a mean drink. Ouch!" I felt Laura trying to squeeze the life out of me through my fingers. I looked back to the bartender, who was giving me a weird look, and said, "Ouch! *Real* mean drinks." Then, to Trent, "Nice talking to you. I'll see you later." Then I turned to the bartender and said, "And I'll be back . . . trust me."

And I was carted off.

For the next hour or so, I was moved around the party from friend to friend of Laura's like a goddamn pinball. But I played along, being ever the good boyfriend by putting on the charm, making people laugh, and getting everyone (myself included) lots of refills. This meant lots of quick runs to my bartender— who was a UCF psychology student named Dade, I found out— for drinks and flirting. I mean, mingling is one thing. But being shown off like some number-one-popular-guy trophy-boyfriend was another. I needed the breaks. And I sure as hell didn't mind the flirtatious intermissions, which, along with my blood-alcohol level, started to add up. Plus, it was fun noticing Laura catching on to me, but not being able to say anything at the risk of showing everyone her true colors. She'd look like a total bitch yelling at me for getting her girlfriends more drinks, and she knew it. It was sweet.

On my, like, twenty-seventh trip (not *really*—I'd be *dead!*) back from the bar, I put my arm around Laura and spotted Paul Bateman nearby, dressed as—guess what!—a Winter Park football player. So original.

"What's he doing here?" I whispered to Laura frantically, not wanting her newest batch of friends to hear. "I thought you told him not to fuck with you!"

"I said for him not to fuck with *you*, not me," she said quickly, trying not to cause a scene in front of her friends. She adjusted her wig and took a dainty sip from her Bacardi and Diet. "Clay asked if it was okay if he came with him—and you *know* they're best friends—and I can't be a *total* bitch twenty-four/seven." She winked at me and gave me a kiss. "Besides, nothing's gonna happen. And *shit* you're drunk, by the way."

So a few minutes later, I found myself standing-swaying behind Laura, with my arms hugged around her, as my drinking caught up with me and I started getting punchy and Clay Evans asked us (rather suspiciously) how we decided to get together. To which I replied, not giving a damn that Paul was right there, "Well, she took me out to celebrate getting an A on her stats test and when I saw her I just *had* to have that fine, *fine* ass!" as I smacked her on the butt and got two handfuls.

This sent Clay and his buds—except Paul, of course—into hysterics, and Laura just smiled bashfully, saying, "That's my rabid animal," and she turned around and gave me a peck on the cheek. "Just don't go blabbing to all the boys in the locker room about your little conquests."

"I don't have gym this year, babe, and we both know that my *conquests* are *faaaaar* from little—"

More hoots and hollers from the football boys.

Laura gave me one of her signature rapid-quick death glares, and I took it down a notch, and for some reason decided to try and make conversation with Paul.

"So, Paul—that's a pretty . . . cool costume."

Even more uproarious laughter, this time with all the girls who were holding on to their football-player boyfriends joining in. They were eating it all up. And I, perhaps seeking revenge for the freshman-year gym-class taunting, continued on, thinking I was invincible:

"What's up, man? I'd think that a football player who dresses up as a football player for Halloween would have a remarkable sense of humor!"

And the laughing just kept going.

Laura dug her nails into my arm. I laughed and pointed at her fingers, saying, "Whoa-ho-hoooh, *this* brings back memories!"

I had the crowd practically pissing their pants.

"Thank you, folks, I'll be here all week!" I said, comedian-like. "Oh, c'mon, Paul, laugh! Release some endorphins! I'm *totally* kidding, anyway—"

That was when Carrie ran up to me, panting and out of breath.

"Act casual and walk with me," she whispered to me. Then to Laura: "Can I borrow him a minute? *Thaaanks*," before Laura could protest.

I excused myself from the group and walked outside to the pool area with Carrie. She led me down a walkway flanked by palm trees clad in white lights to a semiprivate area behind a fountain that fed into the pool.

"Problems?" I asked.

"That Nick guy from Joanna's party is chasing after me. . . . I mean, I have nothing against doing it more than once with a guy, but he's dressed up like some eighties hair-band singer or something and the pink leopard-print spandex pants and gigantic blond wig just aren't doing it for me. It ain't happenin'."

"I totally understand." I sighed. "But how's Joanna? Is she never gonna talk to me again?"

"I think she'll be fine by the end of the night," Carrie said. "She and Shauna are mingling and getting drinks. She'll end up having fun in about"—she looked at her watch—"two margaritas. Just hang back for a while and let her drown her sorrows for a bit."

"Just make sure she . . . uh . . . drinks some *water*," I said, hiccuping. "It's good for you. When you're drunk."

"Uh, Jonathan . . . how drunk are *you*?" she said, laughing a bit. "Do *you* need some water?"

I reached out and pulled her in by the fishnets for a hug. I kept my hands in the air, though, so not to spill my precious drink. "Thanks, Madonna, I owe you one. You're the best."

"Bitch, I'm not *fetching* the water for you," she said to me. "Those days ended with Abraham Lincoln."

"Then let's both go. *Road trip!*"

"Just keep that Nick kid away from me and I'm down."

"No one messes with *this* version of Madonna," I said, flexing my muscles. "You know I do yoga and Pilates. You have nothing to worry about. And about me being drunk—don't worry. I'm just really buzzed; I'm not about to get sick on you."

"Good." She held out her arm. "Shall we?"

We walked in and were headed toward the bar for some water when we saw Shauna and Joanna leaning over the bar, making conversation with Dade. Shauna appeared to be a little inebriated already, constantly touching her cowboy hat like it was a prop. Joanna had further to go. . . .

"Forget it," I said. "I don't wanna face her yet. I'll drink out of a sink somewhere."

"No can do on that one," Carrie said. "At least at the downstairs bathroom—it's currently being guarded by someone resembling the singer from Mötley Crüe."

"Who's dressed as Mötley Crüe?" I asked excitedly.

"*Nick* is, you dork," she laughed. "God, you're ridiculous. . . . So what do you wanna do? We can't stay down here, and I don't really feel like dancing on that walkway thing."

I thought about it for a second. And then my mind flashed back to the Grand Bohemian and my first date with Laura. Perfect!

"Let's find Laura," I said with determination.

"Why?"

"'Cause I've got an idea."

"Fuckin' tell me!"

"Fine, I will. She just . . . She's got . . . She'll . . . If we . . . We could . . . *pot!*"

Carrie's eyes lit up devilishly. "Why didn't you just say so?! Wait . . . are you gonna be okay to smoke?"

"Sure, I'll be fine," I assured her. "I just won't smoke that much."

"You weren't shittin' me with that I'm-only-buzzed talk?"

"No, not at all—trust me, I don't feel like barfing tonight."

"Well, cool!" She looked around for a few seconds. "There she is!" she said, pointing upstairs. She grabbed hold of me and strong-armed me up the stairs, past Trent and Alex, and through the throng of dancing, sweaty bodies to Laura. She was dancing with Tina and a couple other girls.

"Craaaap, I don't wanna smoke with those girls," I slurred into Carrie's ear. "I don't wanna say it to *the girlfriend*, though."

"Just leave it to me," Carrie answered confidently.

"What? What're you gonna say?"

"Trust me, Jonathan. Remember: I know everything."

"All right, fine." She'd proven herself so far. "Go for it."

I stood back and watched Carrie walk up to the group of girls and work her way through to Laura. She leaned in and whispered something in her ear—something funny or charming, I guess, because Laura sort of giggled. Carrie could truly charm the pants off anyone. She looked up briefly and gave me a cute little mischievous look. We were in business.

• • •

Thirty minutes later Carrie, Laura, and I were sitting Indian-style in Laura's walk-in closet, high and happy, passing around a joint. We'd snuck in unnoticed and locked the door behind us, stuffed a towel at the base of the door, and then gone to her closet for good measure. We didn't want anyone joining us; anyone trying to get into her room would just assume that she and I were getting it on. (*God*, I hate that saying.)

It was a nice high—kind of giggly, kind of talkative, and kind of hazy. Nothing too gross at all. In fact, after two hits, I stopped so I wouldn't get sick. I just needed to relax. Not throw up.

"So, thanks for smoking us out," Carrie said. "This stuff is really good. Isn't it?" She laughed.

"Only the best," Laura replied. "I'm sorta glad to be away from that party for a while, anyway. My friends can be so lame sometimes."

"Tell me about it," I said. "I *swear*, if I have to meet any more people—"

"You do your part and I'll do mine, darling," Laura said, leaning affectionately in to me. "I need to show you off, remember? Just lay off the sauce, okay? You're acting like a jackass out there."

"Did you just refer to alcoholic beverages as 'sauce'?" I asked with a shocked look on my face.

"Bite me, Parish."

I bit her arm. She laughed and slapped me playfully.

"Awwww, you two are such a cute couple," Carrie laughed. "I wish I had what you have. . . ."

"Yes, Carrie, it's like I always say: When you find true love, you know it. When the right girl comes along"—*what* was I *babbling* about?—"you just know it's time to settle down and commit. Laura here has given me the best few weeks of my life"—how messed up *was* I?—"and I love her for it. . . ." I looked at Carrie and Laura, who were giving me the you're-so-fucked-up-and-cute look. Then I finished my thought-slash-monologue-slash . . . whatever: "The only thing she's missing is a penis."

Carrie and Laura erupted in laughter. And then I did. For what reason, I don't really know. What I'd said wasn't that funny—but watching Carrie and Laura laughing until their faces turned beet-red and their eyes watered so much that it actually looked like they were bawling and not crying just made *me* laugh, too. We slowly calmed down and regained our composure, such as it was.

"Anyway, *boyfriend*," Laura said to me as she finished off the joint, "I like your *Madonna* costume."

"Madonna?" I asked innocently. "No, baby, I'm your real American hero—well, real *Italian*-American hero."

"What, do you think I'm an idiot? It didn't take two seconds for me to see through it."

"Watch it, Jonathan, don't let yo bitch get outta line!" Carrie said, snapping her fingers.

"Are you mad?" I asked Laura. "Did I fuck up the deal? Are you canceling on me? . . . Are you . . . How long have we *been* in here?"

"Actually, no," Laura answered. "I'm not mad. As long as everyone else buys it, whatever. I'm not a bitch for bitchiness' sake. Plus, your loyalty to your friends touches me," she added sarcastically.

REASSESS:

• *Have faith that faux-girlfriend is human and has feelings.* CHECK.

Then she leaned in and kissed me.

Um, *okay,* I was about to give her a penalty for unnecessary kissing. . . .

"Well, thanks, then," I said calmly, realizing there really wasn't anything to get all worked up about. "I think people bought it."

"Yeah, it's cool."

"So, Laura," Carrie said, changing the subject, "I've seen you two makin' out a few times; I'm very convinced."

"Well, Jonathan here's a good kisser," Laura said, seeming oddly proud.

"Eh, you're not so bad yourself," I said. "But you're no match for Carrie."

"How do you know?!" Laura screeched, laughing and hitting me on the shoulder. "How many girls are bribing you, kid?"

"No bribes," Carrie said.

"Yeah, just a few drunken drinking games," I told Laura. "Ha-ha—*drunken* drinking games. That's a bit redundant redundant."

"The word you're thinking of is repetitive repetitive," Carrie said.

"Whatever whatever," Laura said. "So you don't get weirded out? I mean, you guys are, like, best friends."

"It's all in good fun," Carrie emphasized. "And it's not like we do it regularly. Consider it practice, for when Jonathan finds his man. And you know as well as I do that Jonathan is *beyond* safely gay."

"Amen," I said.

"So you really think Carrie's a better kisser than me?"

Uh . . . hello, Jealousy, how're you today?

"Hate to break it to you, girl, but yeah," I told her.

"No way!"

"See for yourself," I challenged. I looked at my watch. "*Man,* how long *have* we been here?"

"You think I'm scared or somethin'?" she asked, all John Wayne–like.

"I'm not," Carrie said, actually looking a little excited. "I dig brunettes in blonde wigs."

"And I'll pretend to be turned on like a straight boyfriend would!" I said, clapping my hands, then caught myself and got back in character. "Fuckin' lesbians are *hot*, bro! *Yeah!*"

Laura considered it for a moment. "All right," she said. "Let's do it. I mean, I gotta please my man."

I leaned back against the wall and watched as Laura nervously leaned forward from her sitting position to crawl on the ground toward Carrie. Carrie got onto her hands and knees, too, to meet Laura halfway. After a moment's hesitation—or maybe just a moment to observe each other—they both leaned forward to kiss. Carrie lifted her hands from the ground to place them on either side of Laura's face, as their tongues danced around each other, making sweet, slurpy noises. It was actually sort of cool. And funny, too, of course, considering I was basically watching Barbie and an early-eighties version of Madonna going at it in a walk-in closet. . . .

But it was beautiful all the same. They pulled apart from each other after a few seconds—which, in my highness, felt like five minutes—and laughed.

"I think you *are* better than me," Laura giggled.

"I appreciate that," Carrie said coolly.

All of a sudden I was jealous. Pissed, even. And a little sad. Why did Carrie and Laura get to kiss, but I had still never kissed a boy? I mean, one of the things I'd learned in the past few weeks was that I was indeed cute. It wasn't just my affected narcissistic charm anymore; I knew that people thought I was hot. So why not put it to use? Why not get out there and *meet* some people? It'd been long enough. I had to get out of that closet right then and there. I didn't know exactly what I was going to do, but I had to get out of that smoky little cave.

"See you guys later," I said, getting up quickly, "and thanks for the pot."

"Awwww, c'mon, sweetie," Laura laughed. "Two girls kissing can't be *that* disgusting!"

It wasn't. But I had something to do.

12. Spinning Around

"Where's Dade?" I asked one of the other bartenders breathlessly.

"In the wine cellar, sir, getting—"

"Hi, Dade."

"Uh . . . hi, Jonathan."

The air temperature in the wine cellar was kind of cool, I guess to keep the bottles at just the right temperature. I didn't know what'd come over me, but all of a sudden I'd just *had* to find Dade. My mind was sort of a jumbled mess, but I'd gone with my instinct.

Dade looked a little confused as to why I'd barged into the wine cellar, but after a few seconds of silence he actually cracked a little smile. He was so hot, oh my God—about my height, a little more muscular, and he had this amazing black hair that fell over half his face, leaving only one sparkling emerald eye completely visible. And then there was that cute, crooked smile.

That was it.

I stepped toward him, slipped off my wig and beret, and

kissed him. Actually . . . *kissed* him! Turns out, it was a lot like kissing a girl (tongues are tongues, I guess), but the difference was that when our mouths met and started kissing intensely, wetly, as if they were *made* to do it, it felt thick, heavy, electric. His lips and tongue against mine sent miniature shock waves through my body, down my entire frame, to even my toes. It was amazing. My first kiss with a boy.

He pulled away for a second and said, chuckling, "What about your girlfriend?"

I smirked and said, "Oh please, honey," and, emboldened, grabbed a handful of that beautiful hair at the back of his head and pulled him into my face for more. I could have done this forever—I hardly knew the guy, but I just all of a sudden *needed* that first kiss. I didn't want to make him my boyfriend. I just wanted him to kiss me, dammit. Maybe it was the alcohol or the pot. Maybe it was watching Laura and Carrie kiss. Or maybe it was a little act of rebellion against my fake girlfriend/sometimes-dictator Laura. But I just had to do it.

I don't know how long we kissed—a minute? two? ten?—until I heard:

"Love . . . at first sight." Kylieminder #3.

I spun around to face Laura, a little embarrassed, a bit giddy, and a lot turned on. But even more disappointed.

"Hey, Laura," I said.

"Miss Schulberg," said Dade.

"Don't you have some wine to bring upstairs?" Laura asked Dade pointedly.

"Yes, ma'am," he said, then grabbed the box at his feet and

quickly walked off. When he passed Laura, he turned around and gave me a little wink.

Laura stormed up to me, looking intensely furious, and practically foaming at the mouth. "Just what the *fuck* do you think you're doing? *Huh?*"

I was through with this shit. I'd just kissed a guy. I could do anything! "What did it look like I was doing, *Barbie*? Are you blind? Blind Barbie?"

"Where do you get off pulling that crap on me? We have a *deal*."

"There is *no rule* stating that I can't make out with guys," I answered defiantly.

"Well, moron, I think that it's implied that if we're supposed to act like we're together, you don't *suck face* with some other guy at *my party!*"

"Why not? You kissed another girl—"

"Shut up. I call the shots around here. And if I catch you doing this again, I'll—"

"You'll *what?*" I spat. I was so fucking angry; it all just started coming out. I wasn't controlling it. "You gonna call off the bet? You don't have the guts."

"I will," Laura said angrily. "Don't test it."

"Well, why don't you just do it now?" I challenged.

"Because I'm giving you one more chance," she said. "One more."

"You're not ending it now because right now you *need* me. You need me so much right now it's not even funny."

"You think my life depends on whether or not people think we're together?" she laughed. "Because if you think that, you are way delusional. But if you want to end it all right now and not get a chance to go to London to see your favorite pop diva, we'll fucking end it."

"Fine!" I screamed.

She paused from her rant and smiled devilishly.

"Oh, and I was just chatting with my dad recently about my new favorite pop star, and guess what?" she said.

"What."

"Turns out her tour manager has a penthouse in one of Daddy's buildings. I'm sure I could finagle a meeting with Ms. Minogue after one of her shows. . . ."

"You're pulling my leg."

"I'm not pulling anything, Jonathan. I'm dead fucking serious."

Fuck her! She totally had me. In all the adrenaline-fed arguing with her, I'd forgotten why I was putting up with this situation in the first place. I mean, really, she hadn't done anything *totally* wrong to me. Right? And I guess it did make sense that I wasn't allowed to make out with a guy *literally* right under her nose. I guess if I kissed any guys, no one at the school, including Laura, could know about it. That little charade wouldn't be that hard to keep up, would it? It's not exactly like I'd been fighting off the boys anyway. So, really, what choice did I have?

Especially now that I might get to *meet* Kylie.

"Fine," I grumbled. "It's still on."

"I can't hear you," she said patronizingly.

"It's still on!" I practically shrieked at her, then pushed my way out of the room, wanting to be anywhere else.

• • •

I found Shauna outside an upstairs bathroom door, beer in hand. Truth be told, I was hoping for Carrie at that point, since Shauna hadn't exactly been all that, well, *anything* about my Kylie/Laura arrangement, but she'd have to do.

"Joanna's in there crying," she said slowly, a little slurred. "She was okay for a while, but . . . whatever. Carrie's in there with her now, giving me a break."

"Well, you're about to go back on duty," I said, my eyes stinging. "We need to find somewhere to go."

"Oh, there's a free guest room right over there," she said with purpose, snapping into action. "Let's go."

She led me into a nearby room, closed the door, and joined me on the bed. An old black-and-white movie was playing on the TV set.

"What is it?" she asked.

And that's when I just broke down sobbing. It was all too much. Too many emotions. Too many substances. Too much excitement all in the space of a few hours. I didn't know what to make of my jumbled emotions, so I guess my body just decided that I had to cry some of them out to get a clearer head.

And Shauna was great, rubbing my back and letting me just cry and cry. Of course she was pretty drunk, so maybe she was just kinda zoning out, but I'll give her the benefit of the doubt.

"I'm sorry I'm talking about all this," I said through my diminishing sobs. "I know you've been kind of pissed at me this week."

"Pissed?"

"Yeah, for having to tell people I'm straight and all . . ."

"Oh well, yeah, that's sort of it, I guess," she said.

"I just wish that I could take it all back at this point," I said, surprising myself. "But I'm so excited about that trip that I'm finding it impossible to say no. Does that make me a masochist or something?"

"Does it hurt?" she asked suddenly.

"What, being a masochist?"

"No."

"Then does *what* hurt?"

"You know . . ." she said shyly. "When you and Alex *did* it . . . did it hurt her?"

"Oh, um . . ." I was kind of taken aback. "It seemed to hurt her a little at first, but eventually she got more comfortable."

"Oh." She picked up the TV remote and started fumbling around with it, turning the volume up two notches, down two notches. Up two, down two.

"Why do you ask?" I said, not really sure if I wanted to hear the answer.

"Just . . . you know . . . curious." She paused, looked at her beer bottle, then finished off its contents in one big gulp.

"Okay . . . You know, we can talk about this stuff if you want to," I said. "Maybe even Carrie would be better to talk to about it. But I have no problem with it . . . if you have any questions."

"Then why Alex?" she blurted out. "When she's not even a really good friend? And now you're doing this other ridiculous favor for some other girl you hardly know?"

"Shauna, I know them both pretty well—"

"Yeah, but not as well as you know me!" I'd never really seen her this drunk or bold. Something was clearly in the air on this All Hallows' Eve.

"Shauna, are you trying to tell me something?"

"I didn't want to bring it up . . . honestly. This wasn't some sort of setup or something. And I never planned to give you a trip to London or a fancy dinner or take you anywhere or whatever—I shouldn't have to. But I do have to know—why them and not me?"

"What do you mean?" I asked, getting a little antsy. "Be specific."

"Do I have to be?" she asked, averting her eyes.

"*Yes!*" I yelled. My already bad mood was deteriorating rapidly.

"Well, I can't—"

"Shauna, are you asking me to have *sex* with you?"

"Well . . . I don't know what I want." But her look said it all.

All of a sudden my mood was just shit. No more deteriorating. Just shit.

"Are you *fucking kidding me*?!" was all I could think—or not think, rather—to say. "Now not only have Alex and Laura used me, but now you want to, too?! This is, like, the last straw. I mean, where the fuck is this coming from? I did *not* sign up for this . . . this *fucked-upness* . . . at all!"

"Jonathan"—now *she's* starting to cry—"I just wanted to—to—ask you because I—I—trust you."

"Well, you *fucking* shouldn't have, okay?" I yelled. For some reason, Shauna's crying was having the opposite effect on me that Alex's crying did. It just set something off in me, and I was going crazy. "Don't you think I've been dealing with enough tonight? And now you want to add to the mess and screw me up even *more*?! No way. No *way*!"

Now she was really crying, streams of tears pouring down her cheeks. But I'd completely shut off. The anger would not stop mounting. A small part of me wanted to comfort her. Then I realized that I'd come to *her* for comforting not five minutes before, and all she did was fuck things up more! But I took a deep breath and contained myself. She'd fucked up, but she was fucked up herself. I needed to remain just a little calm.

"Everyone who's come up to me for the past few weeks has been at me for *something*," I said quietly. "They all want me to do *something* for them. They want a date or a pretend relationship or popularity or to get fucked, and I want to fucking *punch* some of them in the face because"—I was stammering now, getting more worked up, shaking with anger and frustration, my stomach acids churning and rolling—"because it's hard for *me*, too! It's hard for me to *know* what I want and *know* what I like but not have a choice about it. I don't have *any* gay friends, much less a boyfriend of my own, and it's *fucking HARD*! And even if I *did* have a boyfriend, I couldn't date him in public because that would screw up this whole Laura thing. And I can't *deal* with it anymore, Shauna. I just can't! This whole thing is just too . . ."

I couldn't even finish. It was too everything. Too weird. Too wrong. Too confused. Too draining. Too . . . everything. Wait, I already said that. There isn't a word that could sum up all the "too"s that this situation was.

So I left.

Shauna was crying her eyes out.

And I left.

I was gone. So, *so* gone.

As I stormed out the guest room of horror, Carrie was emerging from consoling Joanna.

"What is *wrong* with you, Jonathan?" she asked me. "You look . . . crazed."

"I'm getting out of here," I said, continuing to storm down the stairs.

"Well, what the hell just happened?" she asked, trying to keep up with me.

"Shauna just asked me to have *sex* with her!" I spat out. "What is *with* tonight? *I hate Halloween!*"

"Shit," was all she could muster.

"I'm just gonna go out front and find a ride."

"Well, let me help you," she offered as we opened the front doors and headed out. "Maybe we can—"

"Wuddup, pussy," someone said. I looked up from the asphalt to see Paul Bateman—extraordinarily clever costume and all—standing at the center of a semicircle comprised of all his football friends. The hottest, most popular guys in school staring me down, probably out for blood. I felt my stomach churn with dread.

"Who're you calling a pussy?" Carrie said defiantly, not an iota of nervousness in her voice. "Him or me?"

"I was talkin' to Parish, not you," Paul said.

"Shit," I mumbled, really starting to freak out a little. Some people were moseying out of the party now, getting a good spot for the viewing. I felt like I was in the Colosseum, about to be devoured by lions to the delight of drunken Roman spectators. But you know what? After all the crazy shit I'd been through lately, this wasn't looking so horrible. In fact, it was mostly looking interesting.

"I said I was talkin' to *you!*" he yelled.

"This pussy's fine," I managed.

"You thought you were a funny guy tonight, huh?" he said.

The crowd oohed.

"Still am."

The crowd aahed.

"Well, I'll show you funny," he said, walking up to me.

"What, are you gonna pull your dick out?"

The crowd drew in a collective breath.

Carrie stepped in front of me, taking off her wig to let her big 'fro bounce out. "You'll have to show *me* first," she said. "I'm always up for a laugh."

"C'mon, bi-girl, let the pussy take care of himself."

My insides were roiling. It was either the adrenaline or the vodka.

"Did you *really* just say that, Bateman?" she asked.

"Damn straight I did, bi-girl," he said, taking a step closer. "What, you can't decide whether you like dick or pussy just like you can't decide if you're black or Asian?"

The crowd—even Paul's cronies—gasped. Mutterings of "oh, shit" and "no, he didn't" hung in the air.

The next five seconds seemed to happen in slow motion. I saw Carrie's face darken into the expression of some primordial predator, about to zero in on its kill. The muscles in her wrist twitched as she balled up her fist and brought back her right arm, to release a mean right hook on Paul Bateman's jaw. But just as she was about to connect, I watched Paul feint to the left, then with all his strength throw Carrie to the ground with a painful thud. Quivering with rage, a lightning-quick slide show of gym-class taunting flashing through my brain, and my blood pressure skyrocketing, sending blood inundated with adrenaline coursing through my entire body at rapid speed, I balled up my own fist, and released a wallop on Paul's stunned face.

That was when it all came out of slow motion, into fast-forward, and to the part where Paul retaliated with a cheap punch to my gut and I—

Threw up.

Puked.

Vomited.

Spewed.

I'm talking Linda Blair in *The Exorcist*-type of yakking.

All over his face.

Miraculously, he drew back immediately, screaming various obscenities. His "friends" started laughing hysterically. The crowd cheered. Carrie patted me on the back. Someone dressed as Spider-Man came up and gave me a bottle of water.

"You are *fucked up*, Parish!" Paul screamed, wiping my dinner off his face. *"Fucked up!"*

"That's how we do it in the O.C., bitch," I deadpanned, quoting one of my favorite shows (Orange County, Florida, but Orange County nonetheless).

Everyone continued laughing and cheering, sending Paul on his way down the driveway.

"*Paul!*" someone screamed from the front door. I turned around. It was Laura, arms crossed across her chest. "*What* did I tell you about fucking with my boyfriend?"

"Your boyfriend just hurled *all over me!*" he yelled back. "He's a goddamn *freak!*"

"That did not answer my question. What did I tell you about—?"

"*You said not to, all right?!*"

"Or I'd have your balls for my charm bracelet," she reminded him. "Well, let me warn you again. If you so much as come within five *feet* of him, I'll sic my mom on you." (She was only a partner in one of the biggest law firms in the county. Go, Laura!) "You'll wish you never met me."

"I already do," he said, looking to his friends for support. They held their hands up in a no-way-man sort of way. Paul looked all around him, searching for an ally, but finding none. "I'm outta here," he managed. And then he was off.

The crowd sort of dispersed and headed back into the party, Carrie and Laura and Paul's buddies (or former buddies, I guess) hanging back with me.

"Be sure to drink that water," Carrie said, laughing. "That was insane!"

"Yeah, well . . . I read somewhere that that's how vultures get rid of danger—they just puke on them."

"So you did that on *purpose*?!"

"Oh, no way!" I said. "It just sort of happened. So are you okay?"

"Don't worry about me—just a little scrape and some runs in my arm-stockings. No biggie."

"Sorry about Paul," Laura said to us. "I think it's safe to say now that he's *definitely* never gonna mess with you now."

"Comforting. Really." I took a swig of water and burped.

"So, you goin' home?" Carrie asked. "Did you need a ride from someone?"

"We'll take 'im," Paul's friend Clay said. "As long as he doesn't puke in my truck!"

"Yeah?" Laura said. "You'll take good care of my guy? No bull-shit?"

"Hell yeah, man!" another one yelled. "Parish is the *shit*, kid! Fuck Paul!"

There was a chorus of "yeah, bro"s and "yeah, dude"s from the group.

Carrie and Laura laughed.

"All right," Laura said, "you can take him home."

"Home?!" Clay said. "We're goin' to this kegger out by Edgewater! You in, man?"

"Dude," I said, wiping my mouth, "I just puked."

"So what?" someone called. "Room for more, right?! C'mon, J!"

More cheers and chants. Jesus, I felt like I was in a freakin' *locker room*. And I was starting to like it. And "J"? I guess I was offi-cially cool enough to have my name abbreviated to a single let-ter. The goal of my life, really.

"Uh . . . sure. Kegger. Rock on." I looked at Carrie. "Thanks for everything, sweetie. You were stellar. You got my brother's number?"

"Yeah, I got it." She winked. "Call me about everything, okay? And get some ice for that right hook."

"And drink some more water," Laura said, hugging me. "Don't let these guys do anything stupid."

"Hey, can we quit with this couples bullshit and get outta here?!" one of the guys yelled. "C'mon, Parish!"

I waved bye to the girls as Ryan Andopolis—slightly baby-faced, olive-skinned, Greek god—esque (literally—he was wearing a toga . . . mmm!) fullback or wingback or whatever-back—drunkenly ran up to me and slung me over his shoulder and threw me in the bed of someone's pickup, laughing good-naturedly the whole way.

"Kegger! Kegger! Kegger!"

13. Kids

When will I ever learn that partying till the wee hours of the morning will have a direct effect on how I feel in the early hours of Sunday mornings at Target? Between my second and third bottle of water, just as the lazy-Sundayers were starting to trickle into the store, I got a weird name popping up on my cell phone.

R.A. MUTHAFUCKA! CALLING

"What the hell?" I muttered to myself as I groggily flipped open the phone to take the call, dropping discreetly to the floor so I wouldn't be spotted. Had I met a vulgar R.A. from UCF or something last night?

"Yeah?"

"Wuddup, man!" a loud voice boomed into my ear. "We still picking you up at noon?"

"Who is this?"

The voice on the other line roared with laughter. "'Who is this?' That's good, J, that's good."

"Seriously. I'm at work. I don't have much time. Who. Is. This?"

"Ryan Andopolis, bitch!" he said. "You *were* ripped last night, weren't you? You were a freakin' maniac!" He made a hurling sound. "'That's how we do it in the O.C., bitch!' Classic!"

I had only a few clear memories of what happened after I threw up in Paul Bateman's face: Ryan Andopolis putting me in the bed of a pickup truck. Me wondering to myself if he'd just write it off as a drunken accident if I accidentally undid his toga. Ending up at some random senior from Edgewater's keg party. Lots of laughing. Lots of water and refusing politely to drink more. And then funneling one beer. And ending up back at my car in the morning. Somehow.

Now with Ryan Andopolis's call, I had one more pop up in my brain: Ryan taking my phone from my hand—"You're way too drunk man, let me do it"—and storing his number. But why?

"So, dude? Noon?"

Before I could think of anything else to say—and because I could hear Mr. Ludlow making the rounds—I blurted out, "Sure, gotta go," and hung up.

I stood back up too fast and got a head-rush, and came face-to-face with a smiling Juan.

"So? Your boyfriend?" he teased.

"I have no idea."

"Mmm. I know just what you mean, *chica*."

At 12:05, I was lying down on the bench outside work, waiting for Ryan to show up and take me God-knows-where to do God-knows-what. I was too hungover even to fantasize, so I just contented myself to lie on the bench and get some much-needed rest. Of course, it was impossible *not* to let my mind wander to the series of happenings last night—and wonder about how the hell things would ever get back to normal. Joanna hated me, Shauna hated me, and if Joanna forgave me for the first reason she hated me, she'd probably hate me even *more* because of what I did to Shauna. But it had only been a few hours, and I tried to put it behind me for the time being. I'd figure out what to do as soon as I could think about the word "vodka" without dry-heaving.

"Excuse me?" someone said. "Are you still having that sale on the Bounty rolls or did that end yesterday?"

With difficulty, I looked up into the sunlight to whatever jackassed, inconsiderate, inbred *idiot* was asking me a question when I wasn't even *in* the store (much less *sitting upright*) to simply say, "You're kidding me, right? This is a joke?"

"Well, no, it's not a joke. It's a question."

"Then here's your answer: I don't know. Ask someone *in there*." I pointed to the store and lay back down, putting the ice pack I'd bought that morning back on my head. Even the customer's footsteps hurt as they stomped off.

Suddenly, I couldn't *wait* for Ryan to show up. And just as I realized I had no idea what kind of car he drove, my answer came to me in the form of a gigantic black gas-guzzling Suburban, blasting some quasi-gangsta rap. The window rolled down, and Ryan yelled over Clay Evans in the passenger seat for me to get in the back.

I heaved myself off the bench and made my way up to the car. I got in and noticed my backseat buddy was George Gordon, the token fat guy on the football team. Just the sight of the poor guy made me want to feed him some celery or carrots or something—

he was rosy-cheeked and sweaty, looking like he was desperately in need of some healthy, juicy vegetables.

"Yo, Parish!" he greeted me, clapping me on the back like we'd known each other forever. "Damn," he said, pointing to the ice pack, "you still messed up?"

"Huh? Well . . . yeah," I said. "How the hell are you guys so damn chipper?"

"Hey, Andopolis," George said to Ryan, "turn that shit down, Parish's head's gonna blow."

He did, and I thanked them.

"Anyway," George continued, "I guess we're just bigger partiers than you. More used to it, I guess. You eaten?"

"Uh, no, actually. I just sort of ended up here . . . more or less on time. You?"

"Yeah," Ryan said. "But we'll do a drive-through for you. Want some—?"

"McDonald's?" I said. "Yes. Like, stat."

Ryan turned the Suburban off Colonial into the closest McDonald's, which thankfully was only a block away. After I'd ordered and was wolfing down my first of two cheeseburgers, I decided to find out what this was all about.

"So, guys," I said, "I'm sorry to say I have *no* idea where we're going. Did you tell me at the party last night?"

They all laughed, and I had another flashback: me making fun of their clothes (since, naturally, they weren't all dressed up) and saying they'd get more play if they'd let me take them to Millenia and dress them . . . and them laughing and agreeing.

Oh, Christ.

"Never mind," I said. "I just remembered."

"You at least remember what you did to Paul last night, don't you, Parish?" Clay asked me.

Shit. This was no shopping spree. This was an abduction-slash-beat-the-crap-out-of-me road trip. Who knew where I'd end up—Winter Garden? Winter Springs? Winter Haven? Kissimmee? (Ew!)—and in what condition!

I must've looked suddenly terrified, because Clay assured me, "Relax, man, don't worry. Paul had that comin'. And after that shit he said to your friend, he's no friend of mine."

"He's got no respect for the women," George said.

"None," Ryan agreed.

"And you know what else, Parish?" Clay continued. "We've never really seen Laura so . . . I don't wanna say *happy*, but . . ."

"Not so bitchy?" Ryan offered.

"Yeah, sure," Clay said. "She's never been so not bitchy before. She must really like you, man, so you gotta be cool."

Yikes. I was the man making Laura—gulp—"not bitchy"? That sounded scary. Almost as scary as that random kiss she'd planted on me in the closet the night before. But I decided not to think about it—didn't I already have *enough* to think about?—and just said, "Well, thanks, guys. Let's do this shit!"

"You look *awesome!*" I cheered for George Gordon. "Black is thinning."

"It's no miracle color or something, Parish," he said, unsure.

"Don't question me," I told him. "That black dress shirt is

perfect for you. And the khakis with it—classic. Not really my *personal* favorite combo, but for you it's—"

"Perfect," Ryan finished for me. "We get it. Now what about me?" he whined, coming out of the adjacent dressing room. "Does this say trying too hard to be metro—?"

I cleared my throat.

"Right. Sorry. Ix-nay on the etrosexual-may," he said. "So? You really think pink?"

"Um, *yeah*! With your dark hair and complexion? It's a wonder your mother didn't *make* you wear pink as a child." I paused. "But those were different times back then, I guess. But, totally—guys with darker skin can pull off brighter colors. You don't want to *not* get girls' attention, do you?"

He laughed. "You've got a point." He turned around and checked himself out in the mirror. "Aw, yeah, man—I'd do me, right?" He looked over to George. "Would you, big boy? I'd say you're slimmed down almost enough for a cheerleader's uniform!"

"Fuck you, man!" George said, laughing. "All right, so, a little less jerseys and gigantic T-shirts—"

"And a little more dark-colored, slightly tighter-fitting collared shirts . . . and don't forget thin, vertical stripes!"

"Right, right. Thin, vertical stripes are my friend," he said like a mantra.

"And there's a step two, 'cause it's not all about clothes. You should eat a little less grease and a little more raw vegetables."

"C'mon, man!"

"They're good, I *swear*!" I said. "And celery actually *burns* calories when you eat it. Oh, and there's another thing about the shirts—you should be sure to get the extra-long ones, so the bottoms of the shirts go over your stomach and down to your waistline and don't just hang out in the air."

"That's cool, man!" George exclaimed, getting kind of excited. "Anything else?"

"Well, shirts with patterns aren't a bad thing, either, because they sort of distract the eye. . . ."

Just then, Clay walked out of the next dressing room. "I dunno, dude—purple? I look like an Easter egg."

"No!" I cried. "That was for Ryan! You were supposed to try on the burgundy and dark blue stuff. You're too pale for purple. Go back in."

I looked over at Ryan, who was still admiring himself in the mirror. I glanced at his face and noticed a day's worth of facial hair.

"Hey, Ryan—I have another little piece of advice for you," I said.

"Yeah?"

"I think you shouldn't shave so much—you look pretty good with some stubble."

"I dunno, man—I kinda like the clean-cut thing."

"Really?" I persisted. "'Cause you don't want girls to think you haven't gone through puberty."

He chuckled, all hotlike. "Trust me, dude, they're not gonna think I haven't been through puberty."

"Okay, I'll say it, Ryan—you've got a baby face!" I blurted out.

He looked at me with a horrified expression. "What does that mean?"

"It means you have *soft features!*" I said, probably making it worse. "You need to compensate with a little ruggedness."

"They'll fuckin' eat it up," Clay called from his dressing room. "Parish knows his shit." He opened the door and emerged wearing the dark blue graphic tee and khaki cargo shorts I'd picked out for him. "So?" he asked us.

"Excellent!" I said. "Stick with those kind of dark, hard colors, and you'll be great. You're a little pale for anything much brighter. And textures, too!"

"Hey, man," Ryan said, "you look pretty good."

"Why don't you two just go get a room somewhere?" George teased Ryan and Clay.

"Hey," I said. "If your friends can't tell you that you look good, who can? Don't do that bullshit, all right?"

A gorgeous saleswoman with shimmering black hair appeared and stopped in her tracks. "Wow," she said. "Did you boys pick out these outfits yourselves?"

There was an awkward and bashful chorus of "no, he did"s from the football boys.

"Well, you're in good hands then. You all look hot. Lemme know if you need anything else." And she walked off.

"See?" I said. "*Always* listen to a . . . well, never mind."

As the guys paid for their clothes, I thought back to the day Joanna, Shauna, and I took Trent out shopping. It was such a fun day, and we were all so happy. I really hoped I could straighten things out, but I just couldn't do it yet. I needed a few days to cool off, I think. And this educating-the-straight-boys shopping trip was a really fun distraction (thanks in part to Mickey D's for soaking up some of the remaining alcohol in my system). Because not only was I making them look better; I feel like I was doing a little tiny something to make them better guys in general.

"So, great," I said, looking at my guys. "We're off to a good start."

"*Start?*" George gasped. "We're not *done?*"

"Oh, far from it, G," I said, smiling. "If I could make it through that kegger, you guys can make it through another couple hours here. Trust me. You'll thank me later."

14. Too Far

Ever since the Halloween party, Laura had been consistently sweet to me. It was like our blowup in the wine cellar had never happened. Which was one of the reasons why I was eating lunch with her and her crew every day. The other obvious reason was that I was not gonna sit with Joanna and Shauna—at least not for a little while.

And lunch wasn't that horrid these days, with the addition of my new boys Clay, Ryan, and George, who I was actually enjoying hanging out with. Still not the most stimulating conversation, but then again, what lunch conversations with Joanna and Shauna had ever been that groundbreaking? We just talked about what we thought was cool; these guys talked about what *they* thought was cool.

"Seems you're making quite an impression on these boys. I've never seen them looking so good," Laura said.

"Oh, stop or you'll make me jealous," I replied.

"Cute. So what's up with your *other* friends—your girlfriends? I haven't heard you mention them for a couple days."

"Oh, uh . . . Carrie's got this big paper due and . . ." I was cornered, unable to come up with a decent excuse, so I just opted for the truth. Or most of it, anyway. "Well, things are weird with

Joanna and Shauna right now. I'm just hanging back awhile."

"Hm." Another silence. Then Laura started to say something, but stopped herself.

"What?" I prompted her.

"Nothing, it's just . . . I'm surprised you guys hang out so much as it is. There seem to be some . . . I dunno, communication issues."

"What? Who? What does that mean?"

"Well—"

"Actually, why don't you just stop while you're ahead?" I snapped, cutting her off. I didn't want to hear it. "We might be hanging out a lot lately, but I don't need you second-guessing my friendships that, for the record, didn't start with a bribe."

She recoiled, looking a bit surprised and hurt, and said softly, "Fine. Forget I said anything."

I mean, what the hell was *that* about? I felt like an ass, but I wasn't about to take that.

"I'm sorry, Laura," I said. "I'm just wound-up, I guess. . . . You still wanna hang out tonight?"

She let out a small chuckle and said, "Sure. I'll call you."

Tonight would be, like, the third night in a row we'd hung out. Laura'd been sweet to me, and it was becoming easier to just chill with her, do homework with her, grab some chips and salsa after school with her—and I was actually really liking it.

Oh, but there were also some random displays of affection, like sometimes kissing me good-bye when no one was really around—those I was actually *not* liking. Well, not so much not liking, but not *getting*.

Regardless of those random weirdnesses, I had to make the relationship last for as long as Laura deemed necessary, and lately that wasn't really an issue. I felt like I was making new friends in her and the boys, and I was getting to be myself . . . mostly. And at this point anything was better than having to deal with all the stuff I'd fucked up.

Shauna had obviously told Joanna about our little Halloween incident, too, because things between Joanna and me were pretty strained. Not to mention the fact that Joanna hadn't brought up exploding at me at the Halloween party herself, but I sure as hell wasn't ready to mention it, considering I'd then have to talk about *everything* that had gone on that night. She hadn't really been outwardly mean, but I could tell that her overall silence in Spanish class wasn't just because of her depression over Alex and Trent or jealousy at how well I could conjugate the *subjuntivo*. And with my afternoons taken up by Target, my new boyfriends, and Laura, I hadn't even gotten the chance to call her. Then again, she hadn't called me, either.

On Friday, Carrie and I skipped first period and went to Einstein's for breakfast. She was giving me some sweet advice on how I should handle the Joanna/Shauna thing, since it had been nearly a week.

"Jonathan, *stop* being such a pussy and talk to Joanna about it," Carrie said to me. "I'm sure she'll know how to handle Shauna's feelings or whatever. Plus, you guys have to talk about your own little drama."

"Uck." I sipped my soda. "Why do you have to always tell it like it is? Can't you just bullshit me once in a while?"

"One of these days . . ." She smiled. "My best advice is to start with Joanna. Because she'll help you figure out how to talk to Shauna, who's probably way too mortified to even speak to you. And both your friendships are gonna fizzle out quick if you don't step up."

"Well, don't *you* know what to do about Shauna?" I asked. "Have you even talked to her?"

"No, and none of them have talked to me much, either," she said, crumpling up her wrapper and stuffing it in her empty coffee cup. "I think they think we're allies or something. . . . Partners in crime."

"Well *that's* bullshit."

"Well, I dunno—I'm not taking it personal or anything. We're the ones who've had sex and everything. . . . Maybe it's easier for her to talk to another virgin."

"Someone like . . . Joanna, I guess."

"Oh, baby, you're just too good." She laughed and slapped my thigh. "At least that's what I've heard from Alex Becker!"

"Fuck off, Carrie," I said, laughing back. "And, you know, I still consider myself a virgin."

"Oh, you mean you need to lose your *guy* virginity in order to consider yourself not a virgin."

"Bingo. Sounds mean, but that's how I feel."

"No, I get what you mean—I mean, I don't totally relate since I like girls *and* guys, so there's no one real virginity I picked to lose." She gave me a cute, self-satisfied little smirk.

"Well, I *do* have a virginity I want to lose eventually, and it has nothing to do with . . . It's too early for the V-word, actually. . . ."

"You're such a little baby sometimes," Carrie told me. "So what's up with you and Laura? You've been hanging out a lot this week."

"Yeah, we're actually having a pretty good time. . . ."

"Yeah?" Carrie gave me one of her signature suggestive winks.

"No, no, not like that," I said, then thought for a minute. "But she *has* kissed me a few times when she definitely didn't have to. And there was that random kiss in the closet on Halloween. . . . You don't think she's—?"

"What? Got the hots for you?"

I laughed, all of a sudden a little flustered. "Maybe?"

"I wouldn't sweat it, Jonathan. She's probably just being friendly. It's sort of a switch from her normal bitchiness, though, huh?"

"Who's bein' a bitch?" someone asked from behind us. I turned around to see George standing there, smiling.

"Who do you think?" I said, relieved to see him smiling. He must have walked in on the conversation just then. I let out a big mock-sigh. "Women. I think I'm ready to go back to guys."

He laughed. "No way, man!"

"Yeah, Laura—she's . . . way too hot," I said. "So whatcha got there?" I asked, pointing to his bag.

"Egg white on whole wheat toast, man," he declared proudly.

"Nice shirt, George," Carrie said. "It looks good on you."

George looked pleased.

"I'll probably see you at lunch," I told him. "I gotta finish talking shit about my girlfriend. Don't tell her, all right?"

"Cool. See ya."

Carrie waited till he got out the front door before she put her face down into her hands and started laughing maniacally. When she was physically able to speak, she said, "What. The hell. Was *that*? That was am*azing*!" She put her arm around me. "If you can make George Gordon eat whole wheat and shop at Express, you can talk to Joanna. 'Cause the sooner you do, the sooner we can all get back together and back to normal. I need to watch some *Strangers with Candy* and bake some of those crazy cookies with my girls again soon, okay?"

"Okay," I sighed. "I will."

I really did miss those dark chocolate macadamia nut surprise cookies. And my old life.

I waited outside Señora Morales's room for Joanna to show up for Spanish. I was sort of nervous. I mean, the major issue was what'd gone down with Shauna, not the whole Joanna/Trent/Alex thing.

But I guessed that was screwed up enough. It was Shauna. One of our best friends. And by screwing up that friendship, I'd screwed up mine and Joanna's further. So maybe I did have a reason to be nervous. Like, what if she didn't want to talk to me ever again? What if she decided that my Kylie charade had been despicable enough to cancel me out as a friend who mattered? What if she was tired of keeping me closeted and had simply had enough? What if—?

"Hey, sexy."

"Huh?" My eyes refocused after having blurred up during my mini-panic attack, and I looked down to face Brie Brandis. "Oh, hey Brie. How's tricks?"

"You tell me, stud. Have you cleared a slot in your—?"

"Look, Brie, I'm totally *not* in the mood right now to—"

"I didn't mean right *now*, you dirty boy! I was thinking about maybe Saturday."

"No, Brie, you're not getting it. I'm not in the mood to *discuss* this right now, not have sex. . . . Well, I'm not in the mood for *that*, either, anyway, so just . . ." I let out a sigh. "I'm taken now anyway, in case you haven't heard."

"You are such a *prude!*" she accused.

"Um, excuse *me* for believing in love!" I said passionately.

"'Scuse me." Joanna worked her way between Brie and me and into the classroom.

"Joanna!" I called.

She spun around. "Yeah?"

"Could you come here for a sec?" I turned to Brie. "And could you leave us?"

Brie let out a huff of air and sashayed into the classroom.

"Break another heart, Jonathan?" Joanna asked me as she walked out into the hallway.

"No, I'm . . . Look, do you think we could—?"

"Talk? Yeah, I think we need to. You can come by tonight if you want. My mom's in London. You working?"

"Yeah, till ten."

"Just come by after work."

Just then, Alex Becker breezed by us and bounced into class, looking sickeningly happy. I swear she was practically skipping.

Joanna sighed and skulked off dejectedly.

• • •

Juan was looking at me, smiling and shaking his head from side to side, his arms crossed across his chest, as I dealt with a customer call on my red Target phone.

"Okay, let me tell you what I can do for you," I said, trying to keep my frustration in check. "It's very simple. We're gonna pretend like you don't have that expired receipt."

"But I *got* a receipt!" the woman on the phone yelled.

"Just read me the set of numbers under the bar code, please," I said. She did, and I told her what her refund was gonna be. She wasn't happy.

"But since I'm entering the return without a receipt," I explained. "I can only give you what the clearance price is, which is eighteen forty. . . . Now, you're lucky I'm pretending that you don't have a receipt, because even *with* a ninety-day-old receipt, we can't take anything back—"

"Whah not?!"

"Because your receipt is useless!" I screamed. Juan burst out laughing. I continued on. "Your *receipt*—since you've made it abundantly clear that you *have* it—*clearly* states that all returns must be made within ninety days. It even gives you a deadline date *on the receipt*, and you've passed it. So for all intents and purposes, for *your* benefit, that receipt doesn't exist to me."

All I heard from rude-ass-bitch-slash-bane-of-my-existence was heavy breathing.

"So eighteen forty," I said. "Store voucher. Take it or leave it."

"Whuht *tahm* you workin' till?" she asked threateningly.

"I'm closin' the store!" I yelled. "Come on over!" And I slammed the phone down.

"*Mami*, you are *loca!*" Juan gushed. "Crazy! How do you still work here?"

"Because I know what the fuck I'm doing. I just couldn't take any more of that crap. If she comes in here, I swear I'll cut off her mullet and make her *eat* it!"

"Violence! But I hear you, girl. So what're you up to after work tonight?" Juan asked me.

"Just going to my girlfriend Joanna's house . . . to talk."

"This the girlfriend who won't let you out of her sight?" he asked.

"*No!*" I said emphatically. "Joanna's, like, one of my best friends. Well, at least I hope she still is. . . ."

"*Cálmate*, baby, *cálmate*," Juan said. "I didn't mean anything by it."

"I know, I know, I'm sorry," I moaned. "I'm just really sensitive about this whole thing. It's kinda been driving me nuts lately." I sighed. "I'm talking to Joanna about what happened at that party—she's pretty much been ignoring me all week."

I'd decided to spill it all to Juan a couple days before, because I really was needing someone to talk to. He'd been great—even if he *was* treating me like my life was a daytime soap for him. But it was all in good fun. He cared.

"Don't you have any gay friends, baby?" Juan asked me out of the blue. "Or am I the only queer ear that gets to hear about all this?"

"No—just the girlfriends. . . . Wait, why? I mean, it's sort of the same thing."

"Hate to break it to you, but it's not," he told me.

"How?"

"I dunno, *mami*, it's just different." He paused and thought about it a second. "No matter how much your straight girlfriends love you, they just don't always . . . get it, y'know?"

"Well, I'm sorry, Juan, but short of you, I don't really have much contact with any *out* gay guys . . . other than the few at school, who just *bug* me. Which actually kinda sucks, but I'm used to it." I looked down and shuffled through some receipts, organizing them into neat, clean piles.

"Well, at least you got a little slice of that hot bartender at your girlfriend's party," Juan laughed. "But, girrrl, I gotta take you out with my crew and show you a good time. We gotta *educate* you!"

"I'm only seventeen, remember? Options are kinda limited in this town."

"When you turn eighteen?"

"Next Saturday, actually."

"There you go!" Juan cried enthusiastically. He reached into the electronics returns box and started pulling out his go-backs. "You just say the word and I'll set it up."

"Thanks, Juan. Maybe I will."

But I probably wouldn't. I may not be shy, but meeting a bunch of gay guys and leaving my comfortable little girlfriend-shell kind of weirded me out. Not that I'm scared of gay guys—after all, I *was* still quite the out-and-proud Kylie-loving queen who made out with his first boy last weekend—but I was scared of mixing up my life too much more. It was crazy enough as is, thank you.

• • •

"Hey," I said when Joanna opened her front door.

"Hey," she said back.

Awkward three-second silence that seemed to last three minutes. Great start.

"Hey, where's you car?" she asked. Okay, progress.

"Oh, typical Aretha—she wasn't feeling too good, so she's getting towed from Target in the morning. I had someone from work drive me out here."

"Oh."

I looked around anxiously. I glanced down the street; every house was practically identical to the next. I hated that about this neighborhood.

"Um, Joanna? Can I come in or do I have to chill on your front porch all night?"

"Oh! Yeah, yeah, yeah. Come in."

I followed Joanna into the house, and she got us glasses of Diet Coke. We sipped from them and tried not to look at each other directly at the same time.

Joanna broke the uncomfortable silence. "Any Target stories?"

"Ummm . . . some imbecile tried to return a supersize bag of chips and said he wanted a price adjustment because they were on sale at Wal-Mart for a dollar cheaper."

"Ha! Did you give it to him?"

"Nope. Not without our competitor's ad." We both laughed at this. "Oh, the joys that the little power I have bring to me."

Joanna sighed uncomfortably and excused herself to get us something to nibble on. I looked around the room at all the memories. The floor we spread our sleeping bags on to watch

Zoolander for the first time. That same night, when we got our cookie recipe just right. The little cabinet filled with board games that we used to play for hours on end. Near-fistfights over Monopoly; dictionary-challenges during Scrabble; bullshit answers for Trivial Pursuit. The couch where, on that hot, rainy evening in June, I came out to Joanna, sweat, rain, and tears of relief and fear soaking my T-shirt.

I wasn't thinking that I was going to lose Joanna anymore, since things seemed to be going all right. I mean, she did suggest that I come over, right? And she wasn't being hateful or mean. If she despised me, it's not like she'd have had me over to talk. If she hated me, she would've told me off in the hallway at school, maybe even slapped me. Joanna and I always had this secret fantasy about having a reason to slap someone—real hard—right across the face. We thought it would be like a big, orgasmic rush to just let out all your anger *smack* on somebody's face.

"Two more Diet Cokes," Joanna announced as she reentered the room. "And Triscuits."

"Thanks."

"So let's get to it," Joanna said suddenly, about half a second after putting the Triscuits box and soda cans on the coffee table. I saw that her face was a little flushed. She seemed to be bracing herself up for the awkward conversation sure to follow. "I'll make the first part easy on us, because I was psychotic on Saturday. So, I'm sorry I flipped out about the whole Trent deal."

"Oh, I'm sorry I didn't tell you," I said. "But I just didn't want to hurt your feelings before they had to be hurt. I wasn't sure if they were together."

"Why did you think that, anyway, though?"

"Just 'cause . . . I saw them together at the movies and they . . . they just looked kind of couple-y and I was skeptical."

No *way* was I gonna tell her about my little conversation with Alex that day after Laura and I "got together." So that was good: one down, one to go. . . .

"Okay, then," Joanna continued. "Part two: Why . . . what . . . what the *fuck* was going through your head, Jonathan?" And there it was.

"*I know, I know, I know!*" I replied at rapid pace. "I don't know what the hell came over me. It was just a weird night and everything was just going to hell at that point and when she asked me to have sex with her I just . . . I just lost it. Big-time."

"I know, Shauna told me everything—all the embarrassing stuff. She's actually really pissed off with herself that she'd even brought it up with you. She doesn't know what got into her, either, actually. . . ."

Oh. This was good.

"Well . . . that makes me sorta happy," I said. "I mean, I was afraid that you and her were thinking that *I* was the jackass."

"Well, you still are one, Jonathan." She sighed. "You shouldn't have yelled at her like that. Even if you thought you were in the right. And she even thinks you *were* right. But she's still humiliated."

"I'm sorry."

"You can't tell *me* that; you have to tell her."

"So you guys don't hate me? 'Cause I've been wanting to talk about this all week—I was just waiting a little bit till things cooled off. But I've been missing you. Carrie has, too."

"Well, at first I think Shauna didn't want to see you ever again. . . . But I think that was 'cause she was embarrassed . . . and pretty drunk. . . ."

"She shouldn't be embarrassed. . . . It was just a lapse in judgment."

"Well, she misses you. And so do I."

I let out a gasp of breath I'd been holding since I'd arrived. "Oh, thank God. That's such a relief. I'm really, really sorry things got so awful."

"It's okay, dude." She punched my arm and then held up her glass. "A toast?"

"Sure," I said. "What to?"

"To you apologizing to Shauna and to things getting back to normal . . . or as normal as they *can* get, with you having a girlfriend and all."

"Amen!"

We clinked glasses and sipped our drinks. I popped open the Triscuits at last.

"And while we're on the sorrys," Joanna said, "I might as well apologize for sort of avoiding you. I was kinda dealing with Shauna and it was just . . . strange to think about dealing with you yet. And I figured I'd wait to apologize about *our* Halloween deal till we talked about Shauna stuff."

"It's okay, I get it," I said. "Shauna probably needed you more than I did."

"Oh, I almost forgot!" Joanna said. "I wanna show you something."

She got up and led me through the living room into the kitchen and up the stairs. We went into the infamous guest room, where all the craziness had begun. But something was different. I couldn't quite put my finger on it, but something was . . . THE BEDSPREAD!!!!

"Your mom bought new sheets!" I screamed excitedly.

"That's right, bucko—no more floral."

"Ohhh, this is so exciting!" I put my drink on the bedside table and clapped my hands. "At least *one* good thing came out of it. What made your mom do it?"

"You did."

"What?"

"I just told her you didn't like them, and no one values a gay man's opinion more than my mom. That's what all her little Park Avenue girlfriends taught her, at least."

"I find that a little offensive, but whatever." I smiled and winked. "They're great!"

"Thanks."

We both plopped down onto the bed and let out long, content sighs as we lay back against the cushy pillows. We turned and looked at each other and grinned.

"Oh, shit, but that was a fun party," I said.

"I know! It was!"

"I can't believe *I'll* be eighteen soon, too."

"We should go out somewhere—like Tabu or Cairo or something. I hear they're fun."

"Definitely. . . . God, I can't believe I'll be an adult soon, too."

We gave each other our cringe look and smiled. I missed messing around with her. It'd only been a week, but it had felt like an eternity.

"No," Joanna said. "I refuse to acknowledge that we're adults when it was just, like, six months ago that we had that Cinco de Mayo party with sombreros and a piñata—"

"And when I had to puke from all those margaritas and the bathroom was taken so I threw up in the empty husk of that poor piñata donkey!"

"And then that night I took a pair of your boxers and—"

"Soaked them in water and put them in the freezer and the next day I had no underwear?" I said, finishing her sentence for her. She looked at me and shook her head from side to side, laughing her ass off. *"Yeah,"* I said curtly. "I remember that crap. Sooooo clever of you."

"It *was!*" Joanna laughed. "You never expected it!"

"That's because I was passed out on your back porch holding a puke-filled piñata!" I yelled. "I wasn't expecting to sleep with a papier-mâché donkey, much less wake up with frozen underwear."

"Boooo-hoooo!"

"Shut up." I snatched my drink from the table to finish it off. "Can you believe all the dumb stuff we did, and here I am, almost eighteen, and I did the craziest, stupidest thing right here in this very bed?"

"Ew, you're creeping me out. Don't remind me about you and Alex," she said uncomfortably.

"I'm sorry, it's just . . . bizarre when you think about it."

"I don't even have to think about it to know it was bizarre. Why the hell would you do it, anyway? I *still* don't get it."

"I mean, it just sort of happened, I guess. . . ."

"What, like stuff like that just *happens?* That's lame, Jonathan. . . . And you know what else is lame?"

"What?"

"That you didn't tell me about it at first. It really hurt me."

I sighed gently. "Yeah, I know that was lame. It's just that you can be a little . . . judgmental about stuff. I love you, but sometimes it's not that easy to tell you everything."

"I guess so," Joanna mumbled sadly, looking a little hurt. "But I can see what you mean. . . . Why don't we just start being totally honest with each other? Starting now."

"Yeah?"

"Yeah. I mean it, Jonathan. No more secrets. I think it's so much better that way."

"I do, too . . . mostly."

"Mostly?" She looked intrigued, like she was about to get a hot piece of gossip served up to her.

"Look, are you serious about this no-secrets thing?" I asked, aching to get you-know-what off my chest. "Even if it might hurt one of us?" I ventured.

"If it's secrets that have screwed us up for the past few weeks, then the only way to avoid it in the future is by not having any." She paused, seeming to think about it for a minute, then said, "So let's have it. What's up? I'm totally here for you."

I crossed my fingers mentally and got on with it. I told her the whole background of the story—about Alex's jealousy of Laura, about her insecurities, about the crying. Joanna nodded along with the story, looking every part the concerned best friend. Until I got to the whole point of the story—"And then I told her that maybe Trent might like her, because of how he was looking at her during the party"—which was when Joanna's mood darkened significantly.

"You . . . you *what?*" she asked, her voice low and foreboding.

"Well, she was crying about how she was disgusting and unattractive because she thought I picked Laura to be straight for and not her, so I just—"

"*Ruined* my chances with him and *ruined* my *life*?!"

"Joanna," I pleaded, all of a sudden sorry she'd ever suggested our new no-secrets policy, "I didn't mean to—"

"Oh my *God*, Jonathan! You have got to be *kidding me!*"

Whoa! What the hell was going on here?!

"It's not like I made it up or anything! I *did* catch him looking at her like that, and I thought it'd make her feel better!"

"Why stop there? Why not just fucking *set them up?!*"

Joanna was really mad. Maybe it was the events of the past weeks or the fact that she was still in overdrive on her lust for Trenty-boy or something, but I'd never seen her so mad before. And it was pretty scary. I jumped up from the bed, afraid she might lash out and try to scratch my eyes out.

"How could you do that to me when you knew how I felt about Trent? When we'd just gone to the mall and everything was going so well! Couldn't you have just *not said anything*? *God* I feel so *stupid* now!"

"No no no noooo!" I cried frantically. "Like I said, I was lame, and it just slipped out! I just couldn't take the sight of her crying anymore and she was saying how she never got the guy and it reminded me of you and I just—"

"I don't wanna *fucking* hear it, Jonathan. The shit you started in this room has screwed up everything. I can't *believe* this."

Okay, Joanna was going nuts, and this was literally the *absolute last thing* I needed. I took a long, deep breath and tried to reason with her.

"Joanna, what happened to the no-secrets thing? I thought I was being a good friend by telling you—"

"*Fuck* the no-secrets policy, Jonathan! This is bigger than *anything* I could've imagined!"

"That's the stupidest thing I've ever heard. You're being way unreasonable."

"Unreasonable? *Unreasonable!* I'll show you unreasonable! Get out of here!"

"What?"

"Are you *deaf*? I said get *out* of my house! I don't want you here!"

"Joanna, you're clearly overreacting, why don't—?"

"*Overreacting?*" she yelled. "Leave! Out!" She got up from the bed and started pushing me out of the room and down the stairs.

"But I don't have my car!"

"And I don't have a boyfriend because of you! Just because *you* can't get the boyfriend of your dreams doesn't mean you should keep *me* from getting mine!" she screamed, muscling me through the kitchen toward the front door.

Now I was just as angry as she was. Irate. Fuming. Because she'd pulled out the big guns. She knew my weakness and was trying to exploit it.

"You're being such a fucking *bitch!*" I spat, gathering up my confidence. "Everything *always* has to be about you, doesn't it? I put up with your fucking crushes and pathetic boyfriends for *years*, and it's always me running at your beck and call to help execute these pathetic little plans you have for them! Outfits and makeup and *shopping excursions!* Well, I'm fucking *tired* of it, Joanna! I'm tired of dealing with your little neuroses and getting nothing in return. Why haven't *you* helped *me* get a boyfriend, huh? Because it's only about *you!* Why do you care so much about the Kylie thing? Because it's inconvenient for *you!* Joanna, Joanna, all about Joanna. And it always *has been!* And this whole thing is so *far* from my fault, it's not even funny! Because even if I hadn't blabbed to Alex about Trent looking at her, they'd *still have gotten together.* Why? Because he *liked her all along! And he DIDN'T like YOU!*"

With that, she reeled her right arm back and swung it forward, bitch-slapping me hard, right across the face. I couldn't believe it. I just looked at her icily, shaking my head from side to side. *I hope that was worth it,* I said to her in my head. *Because that's the last straw.*

"*GET OUT!*" she shrieked.

All I wanted to do was slap her back, push her, spit in her face. But I wouldn't sink to her level.

"I'm really glad we decided to be honest with each other," I told her.

And I walked out and closed the door.

"Hey, you've reached out and touched Carrie's cell phone. Now tell me why before I sic the cops on you. . . . How's that for clever?"

"Carrie, it's Jonathan. Joanna totally fucking flipped out on me and threw me out of her house because I let it slip about the Trent–Alex thing even though everything seemed fine-ish with her and me and Shauna and I'm a little . . . Look, just call me back. I need a ride out of BFE so I can get home. Hope you get this soon. Bye."

I pressed END on my phone and took a deep breath. I couldn't believe this shit. I could have killed Joanna for being so bitchy—not to mention over-the-top contradictory. Then again, I guess killing her would've been unreasonable, too. And illegal. And mean. Fuck! *I don't want us to have any secrets.* What was *that*?! Bullshit!

I wasn't about to try Laura's phone. I wasn't in the mood for a "See, I told you so" type of exchange.

And forget my parents. I was so *not* wanting to explain this to them.

I started scrolling down the numbers in my contacts list, trying to pick a random secondary friend who I felt like talking to. And I was finding no one.

Until I came upon R.A. MUTHAFUCKA!

Ryan Andopolis?

Why the hell not?

He thankfully picked up on the first ring.

"What's up, Parish?!" he said right off the bat.

"Hey, um . . . look, I'm stranded in front my friend Joanna's house," I said pathetically. "Do you think you could come pick me up?"

"Sure, man," he told me, not missing a beat. "What's goin' on?"

"Long story. Just let me give you directions."

. . .

I decided to tell Ryan—who was now sporting a couple days' worth of facial-hair growth—a much-abridged account of the twelve-car pileup that my life had become in the past few weeks. I left out Alex's and Trent's names, and didn't bother with telling him about the Shauna incident. And I definitely left out the Laura/Kylie details.

So basically he'd been told about my fight with Joanna, and what it'd been about. Whatever. That's all he really needed to know.

"That's crazy, bro," he told me after hearing the final details of the unexpected eruption of Mount Joannathan. "Sounds like a hell of a fight."

"Tell me about it," I said, dipping some fries in ranch dressing. We were at Denny's. He'd taken me there to soak up my sorrow with some grease before taking me home.

"Any reason you didn't call Laura?" he asked, then followed up quickly with, "Not that I mind, though . . . I mean, I'm always glad to help."

"Thanks," I said, surprised at his genuineness. He'd been a great listener the whole time, and he was really just what I needed.

"I mean, it's the least I can do—you were so cool last weekend. You know how many girls've felt up Clay in his textured shirts and gone 'Ooohh, what's thiiiis?'" He reached across the table and reenacted on my Target polo, mimicking the flirty teenage girl perfectly.

We both laughed.

"And soon enough, they'll start doin' that shit to me," he continued excitedly. "I should get some more clothes."

"Great," I said. "I'm glad I could help. Anyway, I just didn't wanna call Laura 'cause I'm not even sure if she *likes* Joanna that much . . . and I didn't want to get a lecture."

"Yeah, chicks can be like that. Lecturing, I mean. But Laura'd probably just do it to, like, protect you. I think she likes you a lot."

Eek. That was a little weird.

Then Ryan was quiet for a minute, and I could see him working out what he was going to say very carefully. "And hey, man, I'm not out to piss you off or anything, so don't flip out and puke all over me." We smiled at each other. "But from what it sounds like—like what you said to Joanna in your argument—she's got some kind of hold on you. And it sounds like you need some time to cool your jets."

"Cool my jets?" I mumbled playfully. "What the hell is that?"

"It's Andopolis Talk, man—get used to it!" he laughed, sticking a finger in my ranch dressing and licking it. "Anyway, I can understand where you're at right now. When I get sick of dealing with the football crowd and all that shit, I just gotta get out of there for a while, y'know? So, I call up old buddies from my last school, and we just kick it. It's totally chill, and I don't have to worry about stupid crap for a while, and it does me good."

I sighed, contemplating my situation. "Can I have one of your onion rings?"

"Be my guest."

I took an onion ring from his sampler and dunked it in my mayonnaise-ketchup concoction. It tasted awful. I put my cold water glass against my throbbing head for comfort. It felt nice.

"So, 'old buddies,'" I said. "What if I don't have any?" Because I didn't.

"I dunno, Parish. You don't have any friends at other schools?"

"Actually, I—"

Oh my God! Ryan Andopolis was a genius!

Carrie!

Dr. Phillips!

Gay friends!

Gaygaygaygaygaygaygay!

That was the answer!

"—I do, come to think of it," I finished. "I'll definitely have to think about that." I grabbed another of Ryan's onion rings, and it tasted so much better this time—hot and crunchy and comforting. Kind of like Ryan, I realized.

"Thanks, Ryan," I told him. "I feel way better now."

"No problem."

As I plunked down in bed, exhausted, my phone vibrated in my pocket.

CARRIE CELL CALLING.

"'Sup, bitch?"

"Jonny! I'm so sorry I wasn't around for your phone call! Are you still out there? What the hell happened?!"

"I'm home. Ryan picked me up," I said. "And I feel much better. I'll tell you everything in a minute. But you have to help me with something else first."

"Sure, sweetie, anything."

"I need you to call some of your old Dr. Phillips friends."

15. On a Night Like This

The Whore-sica turned on Turkey Lake Road and headed north toward Dr. Phillips and the party being hosted by Carrie's friend Eric. It was a really nice night—in the fifties, cool, crisp, and clear. Just the right temperature to break out the new long-sleeved pink-and-gray shirt I'd bought with the boys at Millenia the weekend before. I looked adorable. The outfit was perfect, the hair was perfect, and I'd gone to the Y after work so I felt all cute and pumped up.

But I was nervous as hell.

"Jonathan, stop *worrying* about it," Carrie said for about the fifty-eighth time. "You look great, I love you, and *they're* gonna love you. Just be yourself."

"My straight self or my gay self?" was my attempt at a lame-ass joke.

"Oh, shut up, you," she reprimanded me. "Tonight is all about the gay-gay-gay."

"Hence the music," I laughed as I turned up Pepper Mashay singing "I Got My Pride," a really fun thumpa-thumpa gay-club disco-anthem from a while back that Juan had given me on a mix.

"Exactly."

We danced around and belted out the lyrics as we came up to Dr. Phillips High on the left, and the roller coasters of Universal's Islands of Adventure on the right. I couldn't *imagine* having to go to school every day and have to hear the screams and sounds of fun just across the street. How shitty must it be to have to glance over and see a roller coaster fly by when you're on your way to chemistry or U.S. government? Probably very.

I actually sort of missed Islands of Adventure. Last year, Carrie, Joanna, Shauna, and I had annual passes, and any evening we were bored with nothing to do, we'd just hop in the car and head down I-4 to the park. It was great, because by five p.m., all the tourists who'd been at the park since the gates opened were dead tired. Eight hours of rides, lines, and heat generally did that. So, as the masses flooded out, we'd rush in, riding The Hulk or the Dueling Dragons one, two, eight times in a row. We'd usually wrap up the evening at T.G.I. Friday's on Kirkman and head to one of our houses for movies and a sleep-over. I missed that annual pass, but more than that, I missed having uncomplicated friendships.

But enough of that crap. I was on my way to meet some gay guys, and I was gonna have fun, dammit. I totally needed some gay friends, like Juan had said. Carrie turned on the interior light for a second and regarded a Post-it scrawled with illegible directions.

"You know, you really should take a penmanship class or something," I yelled to Carrie over the music. "If they offer that somewhere."

"They did, back in elementary school," she told me, turning

down Pepper a few notches. "Handwriting was the first class I ever got a C in."

"They should've held you back. I swear to God you should be a blonde. Give me those." I looked at the chicken scratch and had no idea what our next turn was.

"You can't read them, either?" she asked, and I shook my head no. "I'm gonna pull over." Carrie pulled the car over into the high school's parking lot. "Now, let's see, what does this say . . . Wordgrin . . . Voodvine . . . *Woodwine*? Is that a word?"

"It sounds like something from *Lord of the Rings* or something," I snapped impatiently. "Didn't you live here, like, a *year* ago?"

"You think I know where the hell I am . . . *ever*?" she said, laughing heartily. "Now shut up and help me!"

"Crap, Carrie," I whined. "This sucks. Unless we find Woodwine or Winifred or Voldemort Street, we're fucked."

Just then, I saw a lime-green VW Bug convertible drive by. Three sets of arms were stretched skyward, pulsing and shaking along to a Thunderpuss mix of Whitney Houston. I looked quickly at Carrie.

"Follow that Bug!" I cried, and the chase began.

Well, it wasn't much of a chase. The street was actually called "Woodgreen," and it was just a block or two away. There were a few cars between the VW Bug and Carrie's hot-pink Whore-sica, but we could still follow the sounds of Whitney's voice. After Woodgreen and another couple of turns, we were there.

"Don't worry," Carrie said for the fifty-ninth time. "Now, you carry in the beer. You'll look hot carrying in a twelve-pack."

"Okay," I said, breathing in deep and grabbing the case of Coronas. "Let's go."

We got out of the car and headed up to the front door. It was a cute house. Very simple, one-story, typical suburban house from the eighties or so. Not that kind of cookie-cutter, faceless suburban home, but still very typical in its intentions. Green front lawn, some nice flower beds, and a two-car garage. Carrie knocked, and seconds later a tall, cute blond guy answered the door, with—oh my God!—Dannii Minogue thumping out of the speakers in the background. Ahhh, I was home.

"Hi," Carrie said. "I'm Carrie and this is Jonathan. My friend Eric invited us."

"Ohmigod, of *course*, he told me all about you. I just started at Dr. Phillips last year, so I never got to meet you!" He was so sweet and sincere—and had the face of an Abercrombie model to boot. This evening was gonna work out just fine. "I'm Hunter," he said, extending his hand to shake ours. "Come in and get something to drink!"

"Thanks, Hunter," Carrie said, and we walked into the little entrance hallway.

Now it was my turn to take a stab at some conversation. "So where'd you move here from? If you just started at Dr. Phillips last year and all . . ."

"Oh, Jacksonville," he answered. "I went to D.A.—it's another performing arts high school."

"Oh, okay," I said, not sure what else to say.

"But then my mom got some big promotion and we had to move down here," he continued. "But I totally like it here. Way better than Jacksonville."

"Yeah, all I really know about Jacksonville is that the first time I went when I was little, it smelled really bad."

He laughed. "Ohmigod, *everyone* says that—that's so funny! Well, it's the paper mill—you get used to it, I guess. I never noticed."

"So no odd smells in Orlando to speak of?" Carrie asked him.

"Not really—just that bread smell on the way downtown, but that's kind of a nice smell," Hunter said.

"It's the Merita Bread Factory," I said. "We love driving by there."

"That's funny!" Hunter said, laughing. "So, if you guys are looking for Eric, I think he's in the kitchen. But go on into the party. There's dancing and music in the living room"—he pointed to the end of the hallway—"and there're drinks in the kitchen, and you can drop the beer in there, and on the other side of the kitchen we have DVDs going in the den. Make yourselves at home! I actually have to make a quick run for more ice."

"Okay, thanks," Carrie said. "See ya later." And Hunter ran down the hallway, grabbed a pair of keys off the hook, and went out the door. Carrie looked at me. "You excited, biotch?"

"Sure," I answered unsurely, but a little more confidently than I would have two minutes before. Hunter's radiant personality had put me more at ease.

We dropped off the Coronas in the fridge, grabbed drinks, and walked into the living room—and it was a *sight!* It looked like Hunter had bought about ten dozen packages of Christmas-tree silver foil—the kind that are bunched into a horizontal row and stapled together in a cardboard strip—and stuck them to his ceiling. All the lights were off except for some multicolored spinning lights on the tables and windowsills. A miniature disco ball hanging from the center of the ceiling caught the light from them and bounced and shot it back all over the room, creating a swirl of light and color. A dance-y Björk song thumped from the stereo, and there were about a dozen guys—ten of which were definitely gay—and eight or so girls gettin' down.

And you know the best part? They were all dancing like me! The swinging of the hips, the shaking of the shoulders, the occasional vogue-ing of the hands Madonna-style, the throwing up of hands and arms—it made me so excited. I didn't know *any* guys who danced as uninhibited and crazily as I did, much less to a Björk tune. Probably because I.

Knew.

No.

Gay.

Guys.

Until tonight.

We made our way through the crowd, Carrie hugging and screaming and introducing me to everyone. I couldn't keep the names straight at all, of course, but at least I was meeting people. We finally got to the kitchen, where she found her friend Eric—a kind of lanky, pale guy with a biggish semi-cute nose—and ran up to give him a huge kiss and slap on the ass just like the one she gave me the day we met (and many days since). The memory made me smile.

I grabbed myself a Heineken from the fridge and headed through the kitchen into the den to see what DVD was showing.

And that's when I just about died of excitement, because right there, on that big-screen TV in front of around eight guys, was Kylie Minogue, live from Manchester. One of my favorite concert DVDs of all time. It was at one of the last songs, "Better the Devil You Know." Three of the guys watching the TV were dancing around while sitting on the couch, and singing all the words. I took a sip of my beer and put it down on an end table and just drank in the whole scene. It's like I stumbled into an alternate universe where stuff I loved—Kylie Minogue, good pop music, and dancing crazily with and without alcohol as a catalyst— wasn't so unusual.

I reached back down and picked up my beer and was about to take a sip when I heard, "Hey, don't touch my Heinie." I turned around to face a very cute—make that *hot*—guy with buzzed blond hair. He wasn't too tall—about my height, actually—and had a similar not-too-built build and gorgeous dark eyes.

"Excuse me?" I said. "I'm confused."

He let out an easy laugh. "My Heinie," he said again. "I meant my *Heineken*—I know, *such* a lame joke, right? But you seriously *are* about to drink my beer, and I've never really gotten the chance to use such a geeky opening line in my life, so I figured why not? I'm Justin."

I couldn't believe he'd said all that in just about ten seconds. Well, I might be exaggerating a bit, but the boy could talk. *Shit*, he was cute. And sweet. And cute. Cute enough to think it twice. So what the hell was I doing just standing there? Remembering the fact that I was still alive and standing right in front of him, I introduced myself. "I'm Jonathan. And, uh . . . here's your Heinie back."

"Thanks, Jonathan, I don't know what I'd do without it." He did a little half-spin and checked out his own ass and let out a sweet little giggle. "So're you new to Dr. Phillips? I haven't seen you before."

"Oh, I go to Winter Park," I said. "I came here with Carrie Adams. . . . She used to go to Dr. Phillips."

"Holy shit, Carrie Adams is here?! I didn't even see her!"

"Well, we just got here, so . . ." I couldn't think of what else to say, so I just said, "Yeah."

"Are you a Kylie fan?" he asked, motioning toward the TV.

"You have no idea how big a fan," I said, almost choking on the irony.

"I know, I love her, too!" Justin said excitedly. "I just wish people in this country would just ditch the bullshit like Jessica Simpson and Mandy Moore and start liking *good* pop stars!"

"That's exactly what I think!" I said, getting a bit more comfortable. "That's so cool."

Kylie wrapped up her finale of "Can't Get You Out of My Head," and someone jumped up and changed the DVD. After a few seconds of waiting, FBI warnings, and such, up popped the menu for . . .

"Yay!" I started to exclaim quietly to Justin, not wanting to draw too much attention to myself, but I was interrupted by a collective scream of cheers and claps. Apparently, I wasn't the only one ridiculously excited about watching Christina Aguilera's *Stripped: Live in the U.K.* DVD.

The concert started out with the intro track to her *Stripped* album, with images on a big screen above the stage of X-Tina singing and writhing around, bound to a chair. It was such a cool intro. As Christina's vocals entered the music, I started to sing along in my head. Then I realized that the whole room and even part of the kitchen was, too, and I glanced back at Justin, who was looking at me and smiling and doing the same. I grinned from ear to ear and joined in.

At the end of the track, the curtain came down and the opening chords to "Dirrty" came in. I looked around the room. Some of the guys were up now, dancing around with one another, singing along like they were trying out for *American Idol.* I swear, it was like a *Rocky Horror Picture Show* viewing or something. Everyone was so into it!

"Speaking of pop stars who matter . . ." Justin said, nodding his head toward the TV.

"Seriously! I worship Christina. That voice . . . She just reminds me so much—"

"Of Whitney Houston!" Justin finished for me. "Is that what you were thinking?"

"Totally!" I said, a little surprised. "Hey, do you drive a VW Bug by any chance?" I asked.

"Yeah," he answered. "That's my baby—Christina, actually." He grinned. He had a gorgeous set of straight, white teeth. I *love* a set of good teeth.

"My car's name's Aretha."

"How classic. Wait . . . how'd you know my car, though?"

"'Cause when I heard 'It's Not Right But It's Okay' blasting from it, I knew it must've been coming to this party, so Carrie and I followed you here. We were kinda lost."

He laughed again. *God* what a sweet laugh. I felt like just grabbing him by the face and kissing him. "Well, I'm glad Whitney could guide your way. You wanna go get another beer with me?"

"As long as you keep your hands off my Heinie," I warned him.

"Hey, you can't steal my line!" He smiled and led me back to the kitchen as Christina tore it up on the TV. "And I can't promise you anything."

A couple hours later, Justin and I were still talking pretty much nonstop about . . . well, everything. There seemed to be this inexhaustible list of topics that interested the both of us, and there was hardly a second of silence. Carrie interrupted to say hi to Justin and to ask me quietly while Justin went to the bathroom how it was going and if I wanted her to keep me company, but I said no and told her to keep on mingling with all her old high-school buddies. I'd come get her if I needed her.

I found out so much about him. The conversation naturally progressed from pop music to other musical tastes, and I was glad to hear that his tastes were just about as wide and varied as mine. Of my bands/singers, he liked Garbage (not nearly as much as I did, of course), loved Placebo, and *adored* Tori Amos; he hadn't heard of Hooverphonic, Kosheen, or the Sneaker Pimps. *His* favorites were Coldplay (who I liked), Fiona Apple (who I loved), and Björk (who I *adored*). I hadn't heard of the Magnetic Fields, My Bloody Valentine, or Lamb. We promised to educate each other.

Then we moved on to other topics. Favorite movies. Family. Coming-out stories. Hometowns. Where we'd traveled. His top three movies were *Hedwig and the Angry Inch*, *Showgirls*, and *The Hours*; I lived for *The Birdcage*, *My Cousin Vinny*, and *Legally Blonde*. We both considered *Mean Girls* to be one of the most brilliant movies ever made. His parents were split up; he lived with his mom in Orlando, and his dad lived in Tampa, where he grew up. My parents were, of course, still together, and I'd grown up in Orlando and Winter Park. He'd been to some cool places—Paris, Barcelona, Puerto Rico. I'd been to Niagara Falls (like I said before, the Canadian side—wahoo!), New Orleans, and the Smoky Mountains.

By the time we got up to go dance, I felt like I'd known him for years. Well, weeks, at least.

"Wanna go cut a rug?" he asked me.

"Wow, I've never heard that one before," I replied. "I'll have to start saying that more."

"So is that a yes?"

"That's a *hell* yes. They're playing Christina, after all."

"Then let's go!" he yelled excitedly, startling me a bit, and practically leaped out of the chair and headed for the dancing room.

We smooshed our way into the crowd of people dancing, which by now had grown to a couple dozen. Just as we looked at each other, all of a sudden a little bit shy, Carrie ran up and interrupted.

"You ready, baby?" she asked, giving me a little pat on the ass.

"Already?" I whined. "I feel like we just got here."

"Remember how I told you I had to be home earlyish 'cause I'm going to my grandma's eightieth birthday party in West Palm tomorrow?"

"Oh, all right," I moaned, feigning exasperation. "I'm sorry, Justin. I gotta go."

"Do you want me to drive you home?" he asked. "I only had two beers and that was a few hours ago. I'll even walk the line." He started to walk heel-to-toe like a drunk-driving suspect would for a cop. "And I'll say my ABCs backwards. *Z, Y, X—*"

As he proceeded to count backwards through the alphabet, I was deliberating. I really, really wanted him to drive me home so we could talk even more, but I also didn't want to ditch Carrie, who'd been so good to me. So, as he got all the way to *P*, with Carrie laughing the whole time, I made my decision.

"That's really impressive, Justin, and I can tell you're not impaired in the least . . . but I think I'll have Carrie drive me back."

He made a sad face.

"But do you want my e-mail or something?" I asked quickly. "We should hang out sometime."

"Yeah!" he said enthusiastically.

"Great! I mean, sure, that'd be cool," I said, trying to sound a little less spastic. I went to the kitchen and found a pad of paper and wrote out my e-mail address and screen name for Justin. Then I ran back and handed it to him and said, "It was really fun. See ya later, hopefully."

"You, too," Justin said, and we hugged good-bye—a really nice, snug, I-really-mean-it kind of hug. Then he turned to Carrie and said, "It was *so* good to see you. Don't abandon us for so long again."

"I know, I know, I suck!" Carrie boomed drama-queen style. "It's definitely been too long—I'll keep in touch. Swear."

They hugged and kissed and then we were off. I totally didn't want to go.

"So . . . ?" Carrie cooed teasingly as we made our way to her car. "Have fun, stud?"

"I hate you," I said, totally deadpan.

"*What?*" Carrie yelled, seeming sad and deflated and angry and confused.

"I hate you for not bringing me around to these guys earlier. Justin is amazing!"

"Don't fuck with me like that again!" she said, punching me on the shoulder. "I thought you were really pissed at me! But, yeah—I can't believe it took me this long, either. I'm glad you had so much drama-free fun. Which is actually totally ironic since a lot of those guys in there are bigger drama queens than you can imagine."

"Yeah, but whatever—it was just so fun," I said happily as I opened the passenger-side door of the Whore-sica. "I hardly got to talk to anyone but Justin, but he was so . . . so . . . that's it. He was just *so!*"

"Okay, you make no sense," she told me as she plopped down into her seat. She reached over and put her hand over mine. "But I'm glad you had such a good time." And then she kissed me on the cheek and leaned back to her side of the car to start the ignition. "You were great. I told you you would be."

"Thanks."

"Oh, and hey—thank you."

"What for?" I asked.

"For riding home with me—you totally passed the test."

"Test?"

"Yeah! I was thinking you'd just plain-out ditch me when Justin offered you a ride, but I'm proud to see that you resisted. You're a good friend. Please don't ever ditch me for a guy."

"I swear, I won't."

She smiled big. "I'm totally kidding! Ditch me all you want! Get some *play*, for chrissakes! But just don't do it all the time—I like to feel loved every now and then."

"Okay! Okay! I get it!" I yelled, feeling my cheeks flush at the thought of making out with Justin. "And thanks, Carrie. For everything. Again. I love you."

"Back atcha, baby. Back atcha."

The next day, just as I was finishing off with my last customer and I saw my shift replacement coming over, Laura walked up and leaned over the customer-service desk.

"You blew me off yesterday, asshole," she said as I started to attempt a cheerful greeting.

Whoa! Bad Mood City!

"Yeah . . . sorry . . . about that," I managed to say, logging off my register and walking out into the store. She'd actually called me about twelve times, pretty much once on the hour from noon till midnight. (Weird, you think? Um . . . yeah!) I didn't know where exactly we stood on gay-boy interaction in Orlando on our arrangement, so I thought it best not to answer. "I could've sworn I'd told you about my . . . grandma's eightieth birthday down in West Palm Beach. . . ." I lied.

"No. You didn't."

"Yeah, I'm sorry, I thought I had. I was gone all day and, space cadet that I am, *totally* left my phone at home. So I didn't get any of your calls till we got home real late."

"Oh. Well . . . whatever." We started to walk toward the break room so I could clock out.

"Why do you sound so pissed?" I asked, a little put off by her attitude.

"Well, we'd been hanging out all week, so I just *assumed* we'd hang out on Saturday, so I made no plans," she said accusingly. "It was a waste of a day."

"I'm sorry," I tried in the sweetest, most sincere voice I could muster.

There was a long pause. Like she was appraising the validity of my excuse. Finally, she said, "It's all right. I'm actually sorry I psychoed out on you and called you, like, ten times. We just didn't get to have our weekly date 'cause you were hanging out with Joanna on Friday, so I figured it was gonna be yesterday."

Joanna. Crap. I hadn't told Laura about my psycho-rampage with Shauna at Halloween, and I definitely wasn't about to tell her about the Joanna disaster. At least not yet. It was all too fresh in my mind, and my face still stung where Joanna had slapped it. Figuratively.

"Yeah, that's true. Sorry we missed our date, then."

"Well, you could make it up to me. Wanna go for brunch at the Briar Patch?"

Um, not really, I wanted to say. *I was kind of hoping to skip out on another day with my fake girlfriend to bask in the post-meeting-Justin light of day.*

Just then I saw Mr. Ludlow coming toward us. Salvation!

"Good-bye, Jonathan," he said.

What?! No begging me to stay late? No hounding me to "help out"? I had to try—he was my only chance.

"Mr. Ludlow—are you sure you don't want me to stay later or anything?"

"Oh, no, no, you're always so busy on Sundays and I have a few other people who wanted to get some more hours," he told me. "So, go—enjoy the rest of your weekend." He glanced at Laura and smiled, seemingly impressed that I had such a gorgeous woman in my presence.

"Okay then!" I chirped, trying to sound happy.

"Well?" Laura said, tapping her foot. *"Brunch?"*

"Sure."

"Great!" a now-cheerful Laura exclaimed. "Hurry up and go clock out, silly!"

Jeez! Her moods could seriously turn on a dime. One second she's bitching me out and doling out the Kylieminders, and the next she's totally sweet and forgiving and understanding. (Well, gullible, actually, but what's the difference?) It was so weird. Maybe she liked spending time with me for more than just the deal. Maybe it was more than just for show for her. I mean, I enjoyed her company, too, don't get me wrong. But maybe she was liking it—or me?—just a little bit more . . . just like Ryan had said at Denny's. Maybe I *wasn't* just being paranoid about the kiss she smacked on me in the closet . . . or the incessant phone calls to check up on me . . . or the other random kisses in the near-empty hallways. . . .

Great. That was all I needed.

"So, I wanted to talk about Homecoming," Laura said, sipping her coffee. "I can't believe I've been so *completely* not on the ball with it, but we should talk about plans."

Homecoming. Actually, I'd been halfway dreading it and halfway wishing Laura would just let it slide by uneventfully. It was on Saturday, a little less than a week away. I mean, things had been stressful enough lately.

"Plans?" I said. My mind was too busy racing to form actual thoughts or sentences.

"Yeah, plans. I mean, it's your birthday this weekend, so do you have any restaurants you'd wanna go to before the dance?"

Now she was actually *including* me in the plan-making process? This was not Laura. Laura was usually businesslike, direct, and very take-charge when it came to making plans. I don't think I'd been consulted once about where to go on our dates. Except the one time I'd *insisted* on Amigo's. A boy needs his chips and salsa, after all.

"And who do you want to come with us?" she continued.

Another first. I could bring anyone I wanted? This was just getting weird.

"Jonathan?" she asked. "What's up with you? Did you have a bad day at work?"

"Huh? Oh . . . no."

"Then why are you so distant all of a sudden?"

Distant? Now she was definitely pulling real-girlfriend moves. Since when was my distance or lack of distance from her an issue?

"I'm not distant. I just . . . uh . . . It's not important to me where we go. And invite whoever you want."

"But who do *you* want to go?" she urged me. "It's your day."

I was hearing her at this point, but forming responses to her questions was beyond me for some reason.

"Look, let's change the subject. . . . There's something I've actually been meaning to talk to you about."

Potential Weirdness Alert. Potential Weirdness Alert.

"I was wondering," she said, lowering her voice, "how long you've known you were gay."

"Um." I swallowed. "I dunno. Probably since I saw the captain on *I Dream of Jeannie* on Nick at Nite—"

"So, what . . . you've known since you were, like, three or something? Really?"

"No. Well"—where was she *going* with this?—"I don't think I started to really *realize* it till high school. . . . Then it just took a while to admit it."

"But you've dated girls before, right?"

"Yeah, I mean . . . sorta . . ."

"Do you think it's possible that you could be wrong about being gay just as you were wrong about being straight?"

Now it'd gone too far. I was now officially worried that she liked me. Maybe she'd liked me all along. Maybe she was just making innocent conversation or something, but then again, wouldn't she *want* me to think that? I think that more than weird verb tenses in Spanish and T-tests in statistics, the most valuable thing I'd learned this semester was that Laura Schulberg was a beautiful, rich, powerful, and manipulative temptress. For shit's sake, one of her *screen names* was "Teen-Temptress69"! She knew exactly what she was doing at all times; everything she did was very calculated. Including the past few weeks.

It was actually all coming together for me now! Laura proposed this ridiculous relationship under the guise of a Kylie trip to London. This would snag me in. We would then date, making out from time to time (just to show off in front of people, "of course"), and see a lot of each other. Then, when the time was right, she would woo and coo me (Homecoming restaurant of my choice), be uncharacteristically and sickeningly sweet (let me invite whoever I wanted), take me out and get me drunk (the dance itself), then get me even drunker and make her move (Homecoming after-party). She probably figured that if it worked for Alex Becker, it would certainly work for the infamous Laura Schulberg.

A brilliant plan, really—and I was scared shitless.

After my long silence, Laura said, "Look, maybe we should just talk about Homecoming. I was thinking I'd get us a limo and champagne for on the way to the dance." *Ding ding ding ding diiiing.* "And I think there's gonna be some after-parties at the Portofino Bay Hotel." *Alert! Alert! Alert!*

It was time to get out of that restaurant.

"You know, I'm actually not really feeling well. It *was* a tough day at work." I rested my elbows on the table and dropped my head into my hands and started massaging my temples. "Maybe we could just get the check soon?"

"Well, sure, Jonathan," she said. "You wanna give me your hand and I'll press down on your pressure point—?"

"*No!* No, uh . . . no. Thank you," I sputtered out. She was *so* not touching me. "Just the check, I think."

I thought avoiding Laura at lunch during the week was going to prove difficult. But then I realized how well my fib about why I hadn't answered any of her calls on Saturday had worked, so I just concocted another. Since I couldn't use missing Joanna and Shauna as an excuse (I was still a little nervous about Shauna and so *not* talking to Joanna until she apologized to *me*), I just told her that I'd fallen behind in English class and that I had to read a bunch and work on a paper. So basically during lunch I was in the computer lab, screwing around, checking my e-mail, reading various bands' recent news stories, and generally wasting time.

So, how happy was I when on Tuesday, I saw an e-mail from Justin?! (Very, obviously.)

From: "Justin Kline" <JustinTime4aBadPun@yahoo.com>
To: "Jonathan Parish" <My_Disco_Needs_Me@yahoo.com>
Subject: To my music pimp

Hey, Jonathan! Just a quick e-mail to say hey before I go to school. I went online last night and listened to a few random Sneaker Pimps songs and totally fell in love. It's like, where have these people been my whole life!?!? Same for you, music

pimp: where have YOU been all my life?! Hahaha. ☺ You
should totally make me a best-of CD of them. I'm gonna
stop downloading their songs and leave it in your capable
hands.

Anyway, I had a way-whole-lotta fun at the party Saturday in
no small part thanks to you, so I hope you did, too. Hope all is
well in Winter Park Wildcat Country.

Later,
Justin

P.S. Pertinent info: 321-555-9823

Oh my God!!!! This was too exciting for words. I immediately
replied, hoping not to sound too dorky and eager, which was a
challenge, since this was my first gay-boy-to-gay-boy e-mail. Not to
mention that he'd given me his *phone number*! It was momentous,
really.

From: "Jonathan Parish" <My_Disco_Needs_Me@yahoo.com>
To: "Justin Kline" <JustinTime4aBadPun@yahoo.com>
Subject: You had me at "pimp"

Hi, Justin. Cute e-mail address, by the way. I wish I could come
up with a pun for MY name and then make fun of it. That's talent
right there. (This isn't bitchy sarcasm, for the record—it's fun
sarcasm.)

Anyway, I DID have tons of fun at the party, in no small part thanks to you. And no, I'm not copy-and-pasting from your e-mail. I just happen to feel the same way as you. ☺

As for Sneaker Pimps, I'm super-excited to make you a mix! Making mixes, especially best-of mixes, is one of my favorite things to do (other than sing and dance along to Christina and Garbage in my car). And if I'm making you a mix, you should make me a Lamb mix. I happened to get a couple of their songs yesterday, and I was really blown away! Especially with "Gorecki"—did they use part of that song in *Moulin Rouge*, by the way?!?

Anyway, at some point we maybe could get together to exchange said CDs. Lemme know.

See ya,
Jonathan

P.S. The digits (yup, I said it): 407.555.8383

There. I'd done it. I'd set up a possible date. Maybe it was bad luck to call it a date. Plus, I didn't know for sure if he liked me like that, or for that matter if I liked *him* like that. Then I'd call it a date-slash-meet-up-and-exchange-CDs thing. Anyway, no point in coming up with an official name for something that wasn't even happening yet. In fact, I spent the rest of my day not worrying about Laura, but wondering what I'd get in response to my e-mail.

By the time I'd gotten home from school, I had my answer:

From: "Justin Kline" <JustinTime4aBadPun@yahoo.com>
To: "Jonathan Parish" <My_Disco_Needs_Me@yahoo.com>
Subject: RE: You had me at "pimp"

Let's meet Saturday. Call me.

JK. (<— Not "just kidding"—my initials ☺)

> Hmmm.
> Saturday.
> Justin.
> Homecoming.
> This was a pickle.

"So, I'm thinking either Hue or Emeril's for dinner, but probably Hue because it's in Thornton Park so it's less touristy and there'll probably be tables for our party. Plus, Emeril's is at CityWalk, so *everyone* from school's gonna be eating there before the dance. And since it's already Thursday now . . . Wait, Jonathan? Are you there? I think your service is cutting out. . . ."

"Yeah, sure, Hue," I said to Laura, checking my reception. "I heard ya. Can you hear me okay?"

"Yeah, I can now. So, you're okay with Hue?"

"Mm-hmm," I mumbled. "Whatever." I looked over at Juan and gave him my please-shoot-me-now look as we walked into Chick-fil-A. We were taking our dinner break together from work.

"Okay, then, I'll talk to you later," she said. "Bye."

"Bye." I pressed END and sighed loudly. "Kill me!" I screamed to Juan. "I don't know what I'm gonna do!"

"You should just have Juan kill you so you'll shut the hell up already," Carrie said, standing up from a booth and coming to greet us at the door. "You must be Juan." She stuck her hand out to him. "I'm Carrie."

"Oh, please, honey," Juan said, pushing her hand away and leaning in to peck her on both cheeks. "This is how we greet from now on, okay?"

"I like this one," Carrie said, leaning over to me to kiss me hello. "Wanna eat?"

"Yeah, I'm *starving*," I said. "And we only have, like, twenty minutes. Thanks for meeting us—I've been meaning for you to meet Juan."

"No prob," she said. "I was next door at Barnes and Noble, anyway. Let's order."

We went to the counter and got our food. Then we picked out a booth with an oh-so-inspiring (hardly) view of the Barnes & Noble parking lot.

"So, Juan, what do you think of our little Jonathan's life lately?"

"Oh, *chica*, it's better than *Passions*." We all laughed at this. "But, I gotta tell you, I am *so* glad you got his ass out there to meet some *boys*! It was about damn time!"

"All right, all right," I grumbled, holding my hands up in surrender. "I know it was time—and yes, I'm sorry I didn't do it sooner."

"And me and my crew will have to take you out sometime now that you're almost eighteen," he said.

"Speaking of my birthday, what the fuck am I gonna do about Homecoming?"

"If you wanna go to Kylie, you better stick with it," Carrie said. "There are worse things than an all-expenses-paid night out with Laura Schulberg."

"Yeah," I said, "there are. A night out with Laura Schulberg when she's so obviously in love with me."

"Jonathan," Carrie said, "I don't really think she's in love with you."

"I dunno, girl," Juan said. "I was stocking CDs when I saw them talkin' in the store on Sunday, and I could maybe see it."

"My vote's still on no," Carrie said.

"Anyway, whatcha gonna do, girl?" Juan asked me.

"I really don't know. I'm wondering if all this is worth it. Maybe making new friends is more important than this ridiculous Kylie thing. . . ."

Code for: *Maybe getting to know Justin is more important than this ridiculous Kylie thing.*

"And by this spring, am I really gonna want to spend a week with Laura in London? I'll want to *kill* her by then!"

Code for: *Maybe Justin and I will be madly in love by then and won't be able to keep our hands off each other for a whole week.*

"I'm probably gonna just decide last-minute what I'm gonna do. I'm just sick of being in limbo about this whole thing. . . . I mean—" I let out a tiny gasp when I saw the restaurant doors open. "Holy shit, this town is *way* too small sometimes."

I gestured to the front door, and Carrie and Juan turned their heads to watch Joanna and Shauna come into the restaurant. Luckily, they hadn't seen us and went up to the counter to order.

"Fuck. *What* am I gonna do?"

"That's Joanna and Shauna," Carrie told Juan.

"Oooooh, shit, boy," Juan said. "You in trouble. . . . You could run."

"I'm not running! I have, like, six nuggets left!"

"This is so stupid," Carrie said. "I'm gonna go talk to Joanna."

Rather than argue with Carrie, I just let her go. I would totally lose the argument, anyway; it was no use in the first place. Carrie just always seemed to know what to do. I watched her go up to them, greet them kindly, and then start talking quietly to them. When I saw Joanna's head turn in my direction, I averted my eyes and continued talking with Juan.

"This is so goddamn ridiculous," I told him. "It just slipped—the whole thing was a mistake! Am I not allowed one of those every now and then?! I don't know why she's being such a bitch about it."

"I dunno, but that's probably not the only thing she's mad about."

"Well, still, it doesn't give her any right to slap me and then act like the whole thing was *my* fault. She's the one who got outta control. . . ."

"Hey," Carrie said, sliding back into the booth.

"Well?" I asked, noticing that Joanna and Shauna were going to the other end of the restaurant. "What'd she say?"

"Are you sure you wanna hear this?" she asked.

"No, but tell me, anyway."

"She said she's not talking to you until *you* apologize."

"*What?!*" I screamed loud enough for all of Chick-fil-A (and maybe some of the parking lot) to hear, on purpose. "I already *did*," I said, using my inside voice now. "And she should be committed if she thinks I have to do it again! Is she fucking insane?"

"No, Jonathan, she's just Joanna," Carrie sighed. "That's how she is. You know she's hardly ever the first to apologize—she's as stubborn as a fucking mule!"

"I know, but it still *pisses me off!* It doesn't give her an excuse—"

"I know it doesn't, honey. But it is what it is. . . ."

"'It is what it is'?" I cried. "How the fuck does *that* help me? Gimme your honey mustard sauce." I dipped a nugget in angrily and popped it in my mouth, then went for my coleslaw. "Did you happen to see what she ordered?" I asked.

"Yeah, a salad . . . What does that have to do with—?"

"See! She always gets the eight-piece meal so she can give me the slaw! She's even turning her back on me via *Chick-fil-A!* I'm gonna de-friend her on MySpace."

Carrie and Juan gasped.

"Don't do that!" Juan exclaimed.

"That's as bad as killing somebody," Carrie agreed.

"Well, maybe just off my Top Eight, then." I sighed.

What in the hell had happened to my life? In two short months, two of my three best friendships had been fucked over, I was in a ridiculous bribe-thing with a girl who I was fairly convinced was in love with me, and I was back in the closet! I longed for the simple days of repeated *Strangers with Candy* viewings and bad-horror-film marathons with my girlfriends, of attending parties where I didn't have to be flaunted around like a hot-straight-boyfriend piece of meat, of not having such a fucking dramatic time of it all. The one consistently bright spot in my life had been the football guys (Ryan most of all, after our talk at Denny's), Carrie . . . and now, Justin.

My phone vibrated in my pocket.

LAURA CELL CALLING.

Great.

"Hey, Laura."

"Hey, so I'm gonna probably book the hotel room for us for—"

"No," I said. "No hotel."

"What do you—?"

"No hotel. No dinner. No . . . I'm not going to the dance, Laura. I need a break from this."

"Wh—what? How the hell can you—?"

"Because it's *my* day, remember? My birthday. And since it's *my* day, I choose to spend it without you, without Tiffani and Tina and Chad, and without a thousand other jerks at Hard Rock Live." I looked up to see Carrie and Juan giving me wide-eyed stares, their jaws practically dropping into their dipping sauces.

"Well, what the *fuck* do you expect me to *do*?" Laura demanded. "You *know* I have to show up with you!"

"Like I said, I'm taking a break. So, I guess that means that *we're* on a break."

"You expect me to tell that to everyone . . . on *Homecoming night*?!" she screamed. "It's almost as bad as *prom*!"

"You know what? You should take someone else, or go solo, but I really don't care right now."

"You're *dreaming* if you think you can still get to Kylie, asshole," she said venomously.

"Bye, Laura." And I hung up.

I immediately searched through my numbers and found the one I was looking for: JUSTIN.

"Hello?" came Justin's voice after picking up on the third ring. "Jonathan?"

"Yeah, hey, Justin. How're you?"

"Good. What's up?"

"Wanna get together with some of my friends for my birthday on Saturday night?" I asked point-blank.

"Uh . . . sure, why not?" he said, definitely surprised by my lack of small talk. "Are you all right? You sound kind of . . . mad?"

"Don't worry—I'm not mad at you. But you're free Saturday night?"

"Absolutely."

"Cool. I'll call you with details later. But I'm on break from work, so I have to go."

"No problem," Justin chirped. "Thanks for calling!"

"Yup," I said. "Talk to you later. Bye."

"Bye."

I pushed END and looked up at Carrie and Juan, who were staring at me with a mix of puzzlement, astonishment, and pride.

"Juan?" I said.

"Uh . . . yeah?" He looked wary. "You're not gonna punch me or somethin', are you? 'Cause you actin' *loca*!"

"No. Wanna call up some of your pals and take me out on Saturday night?"

"Sure!" he said excitedly.

"And you're going, too, Carrie."

"Yes, sir!" And she gave me a little salute.

Feeling invigorated, I grabbed my Diet Coke and stormed right over to Joanna and Shauna's booth at the other end of the restaurant. I felt like my eyes were blazing.

Joanna looked up from her *salad* and snottily asked, "Come to apologize?"

"Yeah," I said, calmly opening up my cup and dumping the contents onto her healthy, anti-Jonathan meal. "Sorry."

18. Your Disco Needs You

That Saturday night was my birthday. After an amazing dinner with my parents and brother, I was putting the finishing touches on my hair when I got a call from Carrie's cell phone.

"Happy birthday, fucker!" Carrie sang. "You better stop screwing with your hair and be ready to run out the door!"

"How did you—?"

"I *know* you, baby! Now finish up your hair and come out to the street. We'll be there in, like, three minutes."

"Okay, okay!" I said, getting all giddy and excited. "What's with the 'we'? Who all's with you?"

"*Everyone!*"

"Everyone? What does that mean? How many—?"

"Just finish that fucking faux-hawk of yours and get your cute tush out the door." And she hung up.

I hung up my phone and put it in my left pocket. Then I opened my wallet and took out my debit card, cash, and ID, and put them in my right pocket. No need for a big, bulky wallet bulging out from my ass. One last look in the mirror. Cute skintight pink-and-black shirt: check. Diesel jeans that hugged my ass and hips in all the right places: check. Bright, rainbow-colored sparkly belt: *Kidding!* I mean, are you *serious*?!

I ran out my room and into the living room, where my parents were in their typical positions: my dad watching a movie, my mom with her book.

"Thanks for letting me stay out late tonight," I said.

"How late did we agree to?" my dad asked my mom.

"Well, no later than four," I answered for her. "The club closes at three."

"All right," Dad sighed. "We'll set the alarm for four, and if you're not here, we'll call you. Your phone's charged up?"

"Yeah."

"Well, have fun and *be careful*," my mom said.

"Thanks!" I leaned down to give them each a hug and a kiss, and I was off. "Love you guys!" I yelled as I closed the front door and walked onto our front porch.

That was when I saw it: the crazy big Astro van. The kind that seated, like, twelve and shuttled people to airports. It was kind of out of place on my street—it was old and gray and looked like it belonged on a construction site or something. I was pretty sure it was Carrie and Juan and his gang, but it looked kind of . . . I don't know . . . big and suspicious.

Then Carrie rolled down the front passenger-side window and said, "Well, get your hot ass over here," so I ran down my front walkway, and then the side door slid open and I was faced with Carrie, Juan, Justin (yay!), and a bunch of guys and a couple girls I'd never met before holding up a tray of cupcakes with candles on them spelling out the word "GAY."

"Happy Gay Day!" they all screamed and cheered. I started laughing my ass off and caught Justin's eye. He gave me a little wink. *Jonathan melts. . . .*

I blew out the candles and said, looking into the crowd of happy faces, "Thanks . . . everyone!" Then I jumped in the van and the door slid behind me.

"Well, start passin' those cupcakes around!" Juan called, now back in the driver's seat and starting up the engine. "Get this party *started!*"

The vanful of people laughed and began passing cupcakes among themselves. Everyone started introducing themselves to me. There was really no point. I'd try, but I probably wouldn't remember one goddamn name. But they were all so excited for me. Guys, girls, straights, lesbians, chubby, skinny, built, short, tall—it seemed that everyone was great and unique in his or her own way.

"So, you excited about finally being an *adult?*" "I love your shirt—where'd you get it?" "You ready to get *crazy?*" "So you've never been to a club before?" "You go to Winter Park? *I* was a Wildcat way back when."

It was overwhelming. Overwhelming but wonderful. Juan had an awesome group of friends. This was gonna be a great night.

"Hey," someone said to me as I fumbled with my seat belt.

"Hi," I said, and looked up. Justin had shimmied his way into the seat next to me. He looked hot. Not club-slutty or anything like that at all. Lime-green long-sleeved stretch dress shirt with the sleeves rolled up to his elbows (guess he had a thing for lime-green), supertight dark blue jeans. His buzzed blond hair was so sexy, masculine, rub-able. He smiled at me.

"So, you excited?" he asked. "I am. I still haven't been to Firestone and I've been eighteen for a month."

"Yeah, I'm totally excited. Thanks for coming. Now we can finally finish up that dance." Okay, totally cheesy, I know, but I couldn't think of what else to say. Luckily, for my sake, Justin didn't seem to mind the cheese.

"I know," he said. "I feel totally cheated. I hold Carrie's grandma in West Palm personally responsible."

And he listens! And remembers details!

"Yeah?!" Carrie yelled back from the front seat. "Well, my grandma said for you to *personally* fuck off!" And she laughed hysterically. She was in one of her crazy, infectious, going-out-to-party moods. I loved those Carrie moods. And that's when I unexpectedly thought, *I love my life*. I was eighteen, dammit, and I was ready to party!

The Club at Firestone is an Orlando landmark. Back in the fifties, when it was a real-life Firestone Tire garage, my grandfather actually *bought* his gas there . . . on *credit* . . . before credit *cards* were even around. And somewhere in between the fifties and the nineties, it was gutted and turned into Orlando's largest dance club. Before the rave laws changed, there was a weekly Saturday-night party that was called Sunday School because it actually let out on Sunday morning at around nine a.m. I remember, back when I was a little kid, driving by Firestone on Sunday mornings on the way to church (when we went to church) to see dozens and dozens of strung-out club kids spilling shakily and bleary-eyed onto Orange Avenue and thinking, *I want to go there someday.*

"So this isn't just, like, your I'm-going-out-for-the-first-time club experience," Justin said to me after I told him this story, "this is sort of the fulfillment of a childhood dream." We were walking up Orange Avenue past the courthouse. The Bank of America Building stood behind us. "It just sucks so much that this is one of the last gay Saturdays."

"Yeah, I read that online. But you're right about that childhood-dream stuff—I'm just glad we get to go tonight. I poked Carrie. "Didn't you ever drive by Firestone on Sunday mornings?"

"Uh, no . . . not really," she said. "My family didn't go to church—explains so much, right?" She laughed and twisted my left nipple. "Holy crap . . . look at that line."

Look at that line? More like, *Look at the men in that line!* I'd never seen so many gays at once. This was like that Dr. Phillips party times a hundred! Granted, a great majority didn't interest me in the least, but I did see at least a dozen hotties after scanning the crowd. The line of men—and a few women—snaked around the block. I couldn't believe that it was nearly midnight and there were still this many people waiting to get *in* the place!

The one-way traffic on Orange Avenue got a red light, and all of a sudden our little entourage bolted across to the Firestone side of the street. A couple of Juan's friends jogged ahead of us and ran up to the guy at the door. I couldn't tell exactly what was going on, but after some quick conversation, a hug, and a hand-shake, our group was motioned in ahead of the line!

We rounded the corner at the entrance and there it was.

Firestone. It was immense. Well, not like I had a ton of other clubs to compare it to, but it was pretty damn big. Immediately to the right was a long oval-shaped island bar with four bartenders inside and about thirty thirsty clubgoers on the outside. The area around the bar was filled with people either lounging on couches, scream-chitchatting over the throbbing bass, or dancing. Farther to the right was another room with what looked like a separate dance floor. Straight ahead and up a few steps was the main dance floor, which from where I stood looked like it held at least a few hundred people. And beyond the main dance floor, who the hell knew?!

The music was booming in my ear; I could feel the bass vibrating in my chest. It wasn't a song I recognized, but I liked it. Crazy techno-bass line, rapidly sputtering electronic beats, and a guttural, powerful black woman singer. All the ingredients for a Jonathan Parish–approved club song. I couldn't wait to get to the dance floor.

I looked over at Justin, who seemed to be thinking the exact same thing. A broad smile spread across his adorable face.

And then Carrie leaped between us and grabbed our wrists. "C'mon, boys!" she screamed into our ears. I swear, she must have been yelling at the top of her lungs, but I could still only barely make out what she was saying. "I wanna make a toast!"

And without waiting for a response, she clasped on to our wrists again and pulled us to the bar. She motioned at our group and a few of them ran over to join us. Five minutes of polite shoving later, we'd made it to the bar. Most of Juan's group had shots, and us underage kids had little cups of soda.

"Wait!" Carrie yelled at me. "You need something special!"

She leaped up and leaned across the bar and said to the Adonis-like shirtless bartender, "It's his birthday and he's only eighteen, but can you make him a special little shot, anyway? Like, with grenadine or something?"

"For you, doll, anything," he told her.

She leaned back and looked at me with lust in her eyes. "I like this place," she said. After getting my special shot, which seemed to have, like, ten nonalcoholic mixers thrown into it, Carrie yelled to everyone: "A toast!" The group leaned their heads in closer to hear.

"To my best friend, Jonathan Parish, on his eighteenth birthday. I loved him from the start, I love him now, and I'll love him even *more* now that he can finally get some *bootay! Ow!*" Everyone laughed and cheered.

Justin gave me a bashful smile and raised his cup. "To Jonathan!" he said. "Happy birthday!" And everyone toasted me and threw back their shots.

And then we headed to the dance floor. It was so crowded going up the short flight of stairs that we had to squeeze into a single-file line, Carrie and her hair in the lead, Justin right behind her, and then me and the rest of the group. As a sudden surge of smiley middle-aged men with bodies that put mine to shame ran down the stairs toward us, Justin quickly reached back to me and grabbed my hand.

"We don't wanna get separated," he yelled back to me, then smiled.

"Okay!" I yelled back, trying not to let my schoolgirl-esque giddiness show too much.

He pulled me up the stairs against the strong current of sweaty bodies, and all of a sudden I was on the dance floor. I stopped for a moment to gaze at it all: the giant disco ball, the hundreds of pulsating beams of bright light, the go-go-boy-topped black blocks, a fire-juggling performer onstage, and a sea of bodies dancing uninhibitedly to the music. If I hadn't seen the bartender make my birthday shot myself, I would've thought someone had drugged me. The whole thing was incredibly surreal. . . .

Then Justin tugged on my arm. He tilted his head toward Carrie, who motioned with her arms that we were heading deeper into the crowd. I looked at Justin, who shrugged and smiled at me, then continued to pull me along.

Have I *mentioned* how cute he looked?

We squeezed right into the center of the dance floor, directly under the disco ball. As if on cue, an ironically fast remix of Kylie's "Slow" blasted in, and I flipped out. I threw my arms up in the air and started shaking my hips—my whole body, actually—excitedly.

"You know who this is, right?" I said into Justin's ear.

"Of course I do!" he answered. "This remix is awesome! I wish I had it!"

"I'll burn it for you," I told him.

We were dancing, but not together. This wasn't like grinding on a bunch of girls at one of my parties; this was a *guy*. A guy I totally liked. And I was all of a sudden getting a little shy.

"Can I have this dance, ladies?" Carrie said as she sandwiched herself between our shaking-but-not-quite-touching bodies, her butt to Justin and her front to me.

"Why even ask?" Justin laughed.

"Shut up and *gimme* some of that!" she said, reaching backwards behind him and grabbing his ass. "C'mon, this isn't seventh grade—grind it, baby!" she yelled, pulling him closer.

"You kids're nasty!" Juan teased as he found a free spot on the dance floor next to us with some of his friends. "Mm-mm, no . . . make that nas*tay*!"

"You're next, *papi*!" Carrie said playfully. "I'll have to give these boys their privacy at some point."

Justin and I rolled our eyes at each other coyly and kept dancing. Carrie kept grinding on us, reaching in front of and behind herself, grabbing our arms and pulling them to encircle her. Eventually, our hands and arms were touching, and it was as if Carrie wasn't even there as she puppeted our dancing along.

As the song came to an end, blending seamlessly into the next, Carrie detached herself from our grinding pelvises and made her way over to Juan and his friends, leaving Justin and me to dance by ourselves. She turned around and winked when she caught my eye.

We were dancing, still about a foot apart, when Justin said, "Carrie's right—this isn't middle school anymore."

I glanced over at Carrie stuffing a dollar bill into a go-go boy's thong. "She's definitely got a point!" I said.

"So, shall we dance like the adults that we are?" And without waiting for an answer, he put his hands on my hips and pulled me closer. And all of a sudden we were dancing together. *Together* together.

Justin was amazing. This sounds cocky, but it was kind of like dancing with myself, which would mean he's pretty damn good! He was every bit as crazy, expressive, flexible, and flamboyant as I was as he gyrated, stretched, thrusted, danced, and lip-synched along to the song. I laughed as he grabbed me by my waist and pulled me close—crazy close—and proceeded to grind ghetto-style with me. I mean, I was no stranger to this kind of dancing, but I'd only done it with girls. This was fucking wonderful!

"You're a great dancer!" he yelled into my ear over the fierce beat and booming vocals.

"Thanks!" I shouted back. "I was just gonna say that to you!"

It was so surreal, dancing there in a sea of shaking bodies, surrounded by hundreds of other gay men, who maybe at some point in their life felt just like I did. Who maybe had an easier time of it, who were able to get out there and meet people immediately after coming out. Or who maybe had a worse experience than I did, got kicked out of their homes, or beat up, or spat upon for being "different." But all these problems, everything, seemed not to matter here, where everyone was so into the music, so happy to be out and dancing, so ecstatic to be among friends.

I realized at this point that I had been looking everywhere around me but straight ahead, into Justin's face. He looked like he might have been feeling the same emotions I was, dreamily gazing at his surroundings. Blue strobe lights flickered and sputtered across his face, making his movements reminiscent of some old silent film—but a modern version of one in rich, vibrant Technicolor. I smiled at the thought, and he turned his attention back to me and gave a perfect, shining smile.

We moved in closer, our faces millimeters from touching. The song that was playing told us to put our hands up—"Put your hands up! Put your hands up!"—over and over as a wailing siren built up and set our bodies to shaking so much I thought I would have a heart attack. A new lyric emerged through the din of the disco, telling us to put on our cha-cha heels, and I looked around me to see hundreds of arms straight up in the air and people smiling and singing and laughing along with the song. It was ridiculous (cha-cha heels?), but it seemed the entire club was really eating it up.

The next thing I knew, the song finally exploded after the last cha-cha-heels order, and it seemed that fireworks had gone off inside the club. I looked at Justin just in time (no jokes, please) to see him put his hands on my cheeks and pull me in for a deep, incredible kiss. The kind of kiss that sets off real fireworks. The kind of kiss that makes you feel alive. The kind of kiss that I really needed right then and there. From him.

"Uh . . . happy birthday," Justin yelled shyly into my ear when our lips separated. How he could yell shyly was a mystery to me, but that didn't make it any less cute.

Happy birthday to me, indeed.

Just then Carrie ran up to me and started patting me frantically on my arm. "Jonathan! I need you to—oh, shit!" She looked embarrassed. "Looks like I interrupted."

"It's okay," I said. "What do you need?"

"To pee."

"Aren't you sort of a big girl for that?" Justin asked.

"No, no, I was just in the girls' bathroom and it's full of guys 'cause the guys' room is all full. I just don't want someone to bust in on me while I'm popping a squat!"

"Okay, okay, I'll come and spot you. Are you gonna be all right by yourself?" I asked Justin.

"Sure, I'll just grab a few people and go to the hip-hop room over there," he said, his cute little body still dancing and bopping around. "Come find me in there."

"Okay," I said, and as Carrie pulled me toward the bathrooms, Justin jerked me back and gave me a peck on the cheek. "Thanks," was all I could manage, and I went back to follow Carrie.

The ladies' room had one lady, eight guys, and a drag queen in it. We got in line for a stall, and Carrie immediately laid into me.

"So, should I get you guys a stall to have sex in or something? 'Cause that's what it was starting to look like out there." She laughed one of her huge, actress-y laughs.

"Shut up!" I yelled, a bit embarrassed. "It's not like that. . . . I really like him. And I think he likes me."

"Jesus, it sounds like puppy love," she teased. "And I *love* it! Aren't you glad you know me?!"

"Yup, yup. You get me guys, and I give you bathroom security. It's a match made in heaven."

"You gonn' go in that stall, hon, 'cause ahm aboutta piss through mah duct tape," the six-foot-tall (six-six with heels) imposing black drag queen asked us. (S)he looked fabulous to me in that crazy green leopard-print dress and some major shimmering silver heels. All I could think was, *I love being gay and I love being eighteen!*

"Go ahead," Carrie said, who for the first time ever looked a little uncomfortable (how cute). "I can hold it."

"Not without buyin' me dinnah, you can't!" And with that (s)he cackled and ran in the stall.

After Carrie (and LaFawnda) relieved themselves, we left the bathroom and headed past the bar into the hip-hop den, which was basically a much smaller room with darker lighting. I was happy to hear Missy Elliott's classic "Work It" thumping as we walked in and found our little group. We all mashed in together and started dancing with one another, no one anyone's official partner. One second I was grinding on Carrie, the next I was having a Puerto Rican–style booty-shaking contest with Juan, and the next I was with Justin. Kind of like a dirty-dancing version of square dancing. So fun.

And all of a sudden, it unfortunately reminded me of one of my and Joanna's parties. In fact, that did sort of seem to be the only thing missing. I mean, yeah, the whole experience was awesome—what with going to my first gay club, dancing to great music with a dance floor full of like-minded guys, and getting an earth-shattering surprise kiss from Justin—but I really missed Joanna and Shauna. Without them to share the experience with, it wasn't quite the same. (Except of course the kiss with Justin; I didn't need to share that with them.)

Justin seemed to notice my shifting mood and asked if I was okay.

"Me? Oh, sure," I said. "Perfect."

"That bad, huh?" he asked. "Do you wanna talk about it?"

How sweet. And perceptive. And I felt like I could trust him, so I said yes.

We walked out the doors of the hip-hop room into the fenced-in outdoor patio, where a bunch of clubgoers were hanging out, and there was even a hot-dog stand! So over hot dogs and sodas, I went ahead and told Justin about everything that'd been going on since the beginning of October.

"Which brings us to me at the present moment," I said. "Feeling shitty about missing my girlfriends and how royally I've screwed things up."

"Sounds like you've had quite a month," he said. I'm glad he wasn't acting all weirded out by my unique situation. Then again, I kinda knew he wouldn't be—he was just that great. "And it sounds like you and your friends have a lot of fun together."

"Oh my God, yeah," I said, thinking back to the cutthroat board-game evenings, nights at Islands of Adventure, throwing wild parties, and watching *Golden Girls* reruns on Lifetime while making disgustingly fatty cookies and cheese dips. "They're actually the best. And they've always been there for me, before my gayness and even more so after. Things have just gotten really messed up lately."

"Yeah, but it's not all your fault, you know," he assured me.

"I know," I agreed. "I mean, Shauna made the pretty crazy mistake of wanting me to devirginize her. But then again, I was just as nuts to have sex with Alex in the first place, which was sort of the catalyst for all this insanity."

"Don't beat yourself up over it," Justin said sweetly. "No one's perfect."

"It's just that I'd put out the possibility, and Shauna misread it all and stepped just slightly over the line of our friendship. It was no reason to scream at her like I did. I can't believe I've let things sit like this for so long." I paused and thought about it some more. "And since I was usually the one to bring out Shauna's wild side, she probably just figured I could be the one to bring out her sexual side."

"Good point."

"I'm totally brilliant!"

We both laughed a little. This was nice—getting everything off my chest with someone who previously knew nothing about it. It totally helped. I stole a glance at his beautiful red neon–tinted profile as he looked off at Orange Avenue. The cool November breeze was ruffling his short, buzzed hair just the slightest bit.

He turned around quickly and caught me staring at him. I shifted my eyes to my Diet Pepsi can.

"Well, what about your other friend?" he asked. "The one who slapped you?"

"Joanna. Okay, hold on a minute, I was just on a roll," I said. "Well, she *did* bitch-slap me, but she was obviously just acting in the heat of the moment. And I was about one second away from pulling that same soap-opera move on her, anyway. And I'm sure that if I just sat her down and explained everything and apologized for what I did, she'd realize how rashly she reacted."

"Totally," he agreed. "I mean, it's worth another shot, right?"

"Yeah. Then again, she really pissed me off—I don't wanna be the only one to apologize. I've kind of realized how judgmental she can be; she can be almost hurtfully opinionated. I just don't wanna get shit on anymore, y'know?" I paused for a second and looked at the ground. "Then again, I could apologize for pouring a soda in her salad."

Justin let out an adorable giggle. "You poured a *soda* in her salad? Hardcore!"

"That's me, I guess."

"How long've you two been friends?"

"Three years." I chewed up the last bit of my hot dog. "And I guess I *have* sort of undermined our friendship, since my life for the past few weeks has basically said, *Yeah, I know you were the first person I came out to, and yeah, you've mostly been an amazing friend ever since then, and yeah, you love me like family . . . but I'm gonna go back to pretending I'm straight so I can go see a concert in London. Have a problem with it? Too bad.*"

"Wow."

"Yeah . . . I miss them."

"Sounds like it. But I don't think you have anything to worry about," he said, grinning, "since you're amazing, and I'm sure they're missing you, too."

"Yeah? Amazing, huh?"

"Absolutely."

This time, *I* kissed *him*. It was sort of like the move I'd pulled on Dade the bartender, but this time it wasn't just for the sake of kissing a cute guy. This time, it meant more. And it felt way better.

"Whoa," Justin said in a low, dead-sexy voice. "That was *great.*"

I gave a little self-conscious half smile. "I feel a lot better now—thanks."

"Anytime. You feel like dancing?"

"Yeah, let's do it."

And he took my hand in his and led me back into the club.

I felt a weight lifted off my shoulders already. Of course, my friendships with Joanna and Shauna hadn't quite been mended yet, but now that I'd effectively ended the Kylie arrangement, I was really seeing how important they were to me. The past few weeks *had* been pretty interesting, though, despite the ups and downs. I'd kissed my first bartender (oh, and yeah—my first guy, too!), had some pretty fucking fantastic meals, and had made a new friend in Laura. . . . Well, at least I *thought* I had. Until I realized that she'd just been after me the entire time in her patented manipulative and conniving way.

Laura Schulberg, that fabulous goddess who was making out with the spiky-haired blonde lesbian in the corner.

WHAT?!

Holy mother-loving crap!

There was Laura.

On a couch across the room.

Making out hardcore with some *girl?!*

And this wasn't some experimental, shy, pecking-on-the-cheek business—I'm talking hot and heavy, limbs so entwined with one another that I couldn't distinguish which belonged to whom!

Suddenly, my conspiracy theory fell to pieces as I realized what I should have deduced from the lack of tangible boyfriends, enthusiasm for making out with Carrie, and interest in my homosexual experience—Laura Schulberg was a *lesbian!*

A very rich lesbian.

Who was *going* to get me to London to see Kylie Minogue.

"Carrie, give me your camera phone."

"What?!" she yelled over Beyoncé. "I can't hear you!"

"Set your camera phone to flash and give it to me! And *hurry!*"

"Okay, baby, okay." She pulled her phone out of her pocket and fumbled with a few keys. "Why?"

I pointed to the wriggling mass of Laura's girl-on-girl make-out session and Carrie gasped.

"What're you gonna do?" she asked me.

"I don't know—but I definitely need evidence of this."

"What's going on?" Justin asked.

"That's Laura over there," I said.

"The one making out with that girl?"

"Uh-huh," I said, making sure the camera phone was working.

"Wow. She's hot."

"That's *all* you can say?!"

"I thought you said she liked you?"

"Well," I said, "I guess I'm not as brilliant as I thought."

I walked up as close to Laura and her friend (?) as I could without being noticed, held the phone up discreetly, and clicked the picture.

She didn't even look up.

After snapping the photos of Laura, I decided it was best that Carrie and I leave before we were noticed and my cover was blown. I asked Juan if it was okay if he drove us home early, and he said it was no problem, that he'd just come back to Firestone after dropping us off.

Justin tagged along, saying he'd had a really long day and was actually kind of tired, but Carrie gave me a knowing glance when he told us this. When Juan turned to leave and Justin went to follow him, Carrie grabbed me by the arm and said in my ear, "He's *totally* obsessed with you."

"Shut up," I told her.

"Ah, you love it!"

The ride home was pretty funny, what with me jumping up and down and going on and on about my good fortune—who would've thought I'd catch Laura making out with a *girl*?! This had to be good for me. I didn't quite know how, but I'd figure it out.

When I got dropped off at home at around two, Justin said to call him about hanging out the next weekend and gave me a quick little peck on the cheek good-bye.

"And *you* call *me* about those child-support payments," Carrie said, pecking me on the cheek like Justin just had. "You can't hide from your baby mama forever!"

I laughed and said bye and thanks to her, Juan, and Justin and made my way up to my front door, feeling wonderful. I unlocked the door and tiptoed to my parents' room. My dad jolted awake when I came in and, rubbing his eyes, said, "Hey, birthday boy . . . what time is it?"

"Two."

"What, you didn't close the place down?"

"Nah . . . I'll save that for next time. I'm home, so turn off your alarm."

"All righty. G'night."

I closed their door and headed for my room. After kissing Kylie hello, I went straight to my computer. After my speedy exit from Firestone, I'd e-mailed the picture of Laura and her make-out buddy to myself from Carrie's phone. So, as soon as I logged into my e-mail account, I downloaded it to my hard drive. Then I composed Laura a little message.

From: "Jonathan Parish" <My_Disco_Needs_Me@yahoo.com>
To: "Laura Schulberg" <VersacesMuse666@aol.com>
Subject: We need to talk.
Attachments: lauralesbo.jpg

Care to have dinner Thursday night? We need to discuss some stuff. I think the attachment says it all.

Hugs and kisses (hot, lesbian kisses),

Jonathan

I would have said to meet on Sunday, but I had some major damage-control plans already. I had to get back on good terms with Shauna and Joanna, and it was going to take a little effort.

19. Still Standing

Work at eight the next morning was surprisingly wonderful. It was a gorgeous Florida fall day, the birds were singing, and the customers were wonderful. Of course, some of this may have been due to the fact that I'd had that perfect birthday kiss from Justin just seven hours before, and that we'd agreed to get together the next weekend. And oh, it might also have been that I'd found Laura out—and I do mean *out*—and that my Kylie troubles might be over. It sounded a bit assy, but at least I finally had the upper hand. The only thing that was really troubling me was the Shauna/Joanna stuff, which I was confident would clear up after I did a bit of groveling.

"*Buenos días*, Juan," I chirped. "Beautiful day, huh?"

"*Ay dios mio*, honey, you are so awake! You didn't take a pill or somethin' from some stranger last night, did you?" he asked, all concerned. "I tried to keep an eye on you—you should *never* leave your drink unattended—"

"No, no, it's nothing like that," I interrupted him. "I'm just in a great mood! I had so much fun last night."

"Oh, good." He sighed with relief. "I'm glad we finally got your ass *out*!"

"Yeah, and your friends are great. Tell them thanks for every-thing."

"Sure, honey. They loved you. You know, you and your little boyfriend can come out with us again *anytime*—"

"Whoa, whoa, whoooa!" I said, holding up my hands. "I saw how you slipped *that* in there. . . . 'Boyfriend?' Don't jinx it, Juan."

"I don't think I'm gonna be jinxing *nothin'*, baby. That boy's crazy about you."

"Well, whatever—still, no jinxing. I'm paranoid."

"Got it. . . . Any returns for me?"

"Just this Gwen Stefani CD," I said. "The customer told me it skipped, but I think she just didn't like it. And since the album's mostly crap, I took it back and gave her store credit."

"I'll pretend I didn't hear that," he whispered, looking over his shoulder as the store manager came up.

"Jonathan . . ." the manager began. "I was hoping that you'd, uh . . . help us out with, uh . . . This kid got sick in front of the bathrooms, and I was hoping you'd—"

"Mop up his puke?" I asked. "No way."

"Uh . . . sorry?"

"I said no. That's the cart attendant's job. And besides that, it's actually noon, so I should be clocking out."

"Not staying late for us?"

"Nope . . . I have plans."

After clocking out, I took off my red Target shirt to reveal my Garbage concert T-shirt I'd been wearing underneath, stored my work shirt in a locker in the break room, and headed out into the store. I had some shopping to do.

• • •

By the end of the day, I'd been all over town, and had pretty much assembled what I thought to be the ultimate gift baskets to woo back my friends. Sounds lame, but a lot of thought went into each of them. And on each gift, I wrote a quick note on a pink Post-it.

For Shauna:

- A *Rocky Horror Picture Show* DVD, a memento of the first "friendship date" we went on, when Joanna was out of town. *Post-it: So we can do the Time Warp again . . . and again and again and again.*
- Ten Taco Bell Bucks, to spend at the Taco Bell we visited after the movie. *Post-it: Yo quiero Taco Bell! This was when I realized I could definitely love you—when I dared you to ask for seven sides of nacho cheese for no conceivable reason . . . and you asked for eight!*
- A bootleged Garbage concert CD from the same tour we'd seen together in Myrtle Beach. *Post-it: A little reminder of my most fun weekend with you . . . possibly the most fun weekend of my life!*

For Joanna:

- A pink three-ring binder, in commemoration of the time we first met. *Post-it: Remember having the same pink binders on the first day of geography? How did I (we) not know I was gay yet! (Side note: This was NOT easy to find!)*
- *The Birdcage* and *Dirty Dancing* on DVD. *Post-it: So you can reminisce about the first night we hung out and educated each other on our*

favorite movies. ☺ *Just add chips and Velveeta queso and it'll be*
practically the same!

- Chips, salsa, and Velveeta cheese. *Post-it: Speaking of Velveeta*
  queso . . .
- A pair of silk Victoria's Secret panties. *Post-it: To make up for*
  that little mini Christmas party you, me, Shauna, and Carrie had
  when I poured vodka over your panties and threw them in the
  fireplace . . . just to see what'd happen. . . .

For both:

- *The Golden Girls,* Season 1 DVD set. *Post-it: For us to hopefully share if*
  you can forgive me. Shauna, Joanna, be my Rose and Sofia for life. . . . ☺
  Carrie (Blanche) is down. If you like, we can discuss it over cheesecake.

I arranged the gifts into three Christmas baskets—one each
for Shauna and Joanna and one for *The Golden Girls*—as nicely as I
could. (Aren't gay guys supposed to have a natural knack for
stuff like flower arrangement and gift-wrapping? It's a fucking
myth!)

I crossed my fingers and hoped it would all work out.

The next morning in first-period statistics, I was met with the
same icy greeting (or lack of greeting, actually) from Laura that I'd
gotten last Friday, after our "breakup." She'd actually told everyone that she decided to end it because I was still acting "a little too
gay" and that she didn't think that my being "straight" was gonna
take. So, allegedly, I had rejected heterosexuality much like the

body sometimes rejects an odd piercing. Which was all fine by me, because I got to be gay again.

And she'd gotten out of Homecoming by saying she was going clubbing with the UCF student she'd been cheating on me with. Which technically I guess wasn't much of a lie.

I was actually sort of grateful for the way she told people she'd ended it. I mean, it's not like it made her look bad. After all, she *had* had me straight for a few weeks, as was evident in our numerous hot-and-heavy public make-out fests, but she could have said any number of things to make herself look even better. I could've been a jackass-y cheater. She could've found someone hotter than me. I could've gotten too clingy. But for some reason, she'd let me off sort of easy.

After yet another riveting statistics lecture, we were all filing out into the hallway when Laura grabbed my arm and pulled me into a corner. She started talking to me quietly as the last of the students made their way out, looking over in our direction.

Drama.

No matter what, she loved it.

"So I got your little e-mail," she said matter-of-factly. "So what? You've found me out."

I was temporarily shocked. I mean, I'd figured she was gay (or at least bi!), but I wasn't expecting a full-on confession/outing at eight thirty in the morning! And truthfully, I was a little hurt that she hadn't been honest with me from the get-go. Hurt, with a side of pissed.

"Uh . . . yeah, guess I did." Even when I had the upper hand, she could still find a way to be intimidating. But it was still early for me. My own claws hadn't come out yet.

"So we *should* talk about it, like you said. Can't you meet anytime before Thursday night?" She sounded irritated, angry.

"Not really," I said, now feeling my bitch-claws coming out. "Target obligations."

"Fine. Well. I guess you'll just have to keep me in suspense, huh?"

"Guess so."

"So. We're still broken up for this week. You're too faggy, I'm too straight. Stick to it."

"Why should I?"

"It's the least you can do."

"Fine. I got nothin' to lose."

At lunch, I went to my locker to retrieve the three gift baskets and said a little prayer to the friendship gods that they would do the trick. I mean, it would work on me, so why shouldn't it work on them, too, right? Hopefully I wasn't just a shallow jackass. So I made my way outside and went to our (well, Joanna and Shauna's, at this point) special lunch spot outside.

And there they were. Sitting Indian-style, facing each other, talking and giggling and sharing a jumbo-sized bag of Skittles. I wondered what they were giggling about—probably me, and about how funny it was that they both hated me so much. About how *hilarious* it was when I threw that hissy-fit with Shauna. And when Joanna slapped me across the face . . . *priceless.* Now I realize that this was just a smidge paranoid, but that's how I was feeling. I was actually really damn nervous. If I had been a cartoon, my knees would've been knocking together and I would be sweaty as a glass of iced tea on a balmy summer day. (Wow, that was *so* Blanche Deveraux of me. I think I'm ready for my debutante ball now.)

So I was pretty surprised when Joanna actually *spoke* to me as I headed toward them, teetering from side to side with the elaborately stuffed baskets.

"You look like Santa's gay underage lover," she said with no inflection of sarcasm or malice.

I didn't know how to respond, so I just said in the same unreadable voice, "Not underage anymore—my birthday was this weekend."

There was a ten-second period of excruciatingly uncomfortable silence before Shauna burst out, "*I can't do this, Joanna! JONATHAN!* We're so sorry. Happy birthday! We were gonna try to act mad at you to be funny but I just *couldn't!*"

Joanna rolled her eyes and, to my surprise, smiled, and reached behind her to pick up this huge Tupperware container of . . .

"*Dark chocolate macadamia nut surprise cookies!*" I screamed. Our special cookies! I was so happy. "When did—?"

"Yesterday," Shauna answered for me. "We just felt so bad— we've been awful about everything. And so we decided to try to make it up to you. Especially since it was your birthday and all. . . ."

"Oh!" I cried. "Speaking of feeling bad . . ." I put their baskets down in front of them. "I spent all day yesterday concocting the perfect gift baskets for each of you. 'Cause I felt so bad about stuff."

"I mean, it's our fault," Joanna said. "*We're* the ones who flipped out and got all awkward—"

"Yeah, it was all us," Shauna cut in. "I mean, I got all drunk and confused and . . . and Joanna just got mad and wasn't thinking, and—"

"And I know it wasn't your fault that Trent and Alex got together, because if Trent liked her, it probably would've happened eventually and—"

"Ladies, ladies . . ." I interrupted. "As much as I like to play the whole I-was-right-you-were-wrong game, I kind of fucked up, too. I mean . . . Okay, is it just me or is this *way* too happy-teen-movie-ending for you?" They both laughed and told me to stop stalling and go on. "Okay, so yeah . . . I got way too caught up in this whole Kylie thing, and in the past couple of weeks I've realized how stupid it was for me to go back into the closet and act all straight just so I could see a concert. I mean, to make *you two*—and Carrie—do it as well as me . . . that just wasn't fair. So, actually, I sort of blew up at Laura and essentially broke off our little arrangement."

"What?!" they both cried. "You didn't have to do that!"

"Don't say that," I said flatly. "You're entitled to have your opinion."

Joanna and Shauna looked at each other knowingly, and after a second's pause:

"Fine," Joanna said. "Good riddance."

"Thank goodness," said Shauna.

"Anyway, it was just a spur-of-the-moment thing. And it might not matter now anymore. But anyway, I'd just sort of decided that getting to know Justin was a better thing to do for myself than being closeted for the sake of a concert, so—"

"Who's Justin?" they asked in unison.

"Ooohhhh . . ." I said conspiratorially. "I have a lot to catch you two up on. But before I do that, I need to get some stuff straight."

"Please don't say yourself," Joanna joked.

"No," I said, chuckling a little. "I just need to be sure we're completely cool. And that the no-secrets thing is reinstated, and that we all *mean it* this time."

"Totally," Joanna said. "I'm sorry I was such a lunatic the last time we had this little talk."

"Yeah, but I'm dead serious," I continued. "I want us to be honest, and I need you to be a little more conscious of what you're saying—because you can be a little . . . mean . . . sometimes. Deal?"

"Deal," Joanna said.

"Yes," Shauna said. "No secrets. Honesty. Deal." She smiled. "Honestly."

"Good. 'Cause I love you guys way too much for this kind of crap to happen again. So . . . are we okay?"

"Well . . ." Joanna said, looking at the gift baskets. "That all depends on what you bought us."

And then she chuckled, and I knew stuff was gonna be just fine.

Carrie nabbed me on my way to Aretha at the end of the day.

"I skipped sixth period to work on a paper, so I haven't seen Joanna all day," she said breathlessly. "And I've been on the edge of my seat ever since. How'd it go?!"

I pulled the Tupperware full of cookies out of my bag and

said, "Well, I'll just let my birthday present from them speak for itself."

Carrie gasped. "Are those—?"

"You bet they are!" I exclaimed giddily. "All is forgiven. It was, like, *perfect!* We all sort of apologized at the same time. It couldn't have worked out better. Except now they're kinda sad."

"What about?"

"Well, about the fact that they missed out on my big gay debut in Orlando. I mean, they missed the party, they weren't there at Firestone, they haven't met Justin—"

"So what? Have them meet Justin."

"Well, we're going out this weekend. . . ."

"So take him out for a friend test-drive," Carrie suggested. "Take him to hang out with us and see how it goes. I think that can be a pretty big indicator of how much he likes you—how hard he tries for your friends."

"But he did so well at Firestone. . . ."

Carrie gave me a knowing look. She always had that look. "Yeah, but he was with me, who he already knew, and with a bunch of strangers who weren't your, you know, *real* friends. There wasn't any pressure. We were just all out at a club where people could barely hear each other."

"That's true, I guess." I thought for a minute. "Well, maybe we can all get together Sunday or something."

"What about Saturday?"

"That's a no-go—I'm hanging out with my parents Saturday. They were bummed they only got a birthday dinner out of me. But don't worry—I'll figure it all out."

"Rock on!" Carrie yelled. Then she did a crazy little dance. "*Damn*, Jonathan, you are such a fucking *stud* now!"

"Thanks," I said. "And thanks again for . . . you know . . . sticking by me the whole time. You've been awesome."

"I *am* awesome, Jonathan Parish. And don't let your gay little ass forget it."

"What is it about you? How're you so great? And how do you *know* everything all the time?" I paused. "Did you know about Laura's dykery?"

"I had a hunch," she said all-knowingly. "Especially at Halloween. I was picking up on some *major* lesbo vibes. How do you think I lured her away from her friends so easily to go smoke pot in that closet?"

"*God* I hate you!" I exclaimed.

"Well, don't feel bad, baby. I mean, I *am* bisexual—my gaydar for girls is much more advanced than yours. . . ."

"Then why didn't you *say* anything!?"

"Oh, I would have eventually. But first off, it wasn't really my place to out her to you, and I just wanted to see if you could figure it out yourself—it was kinda fun. And remember: I didn't know for *sure* or anything. And I would have probably said something really soon, but then there was that little incident at Firestone and I didn't have to." She smiled mischievously.

I sighed. "I guess so. Bitch."

"Hey!" Carrie smacked my ass, feigning anger. "And don't make me do that again, mister. 'Cause the next one's gonna *sting*! So when're you meeting with Laura?"

"Thursday."

"*Thursday?!*" she cried. "I can't wait that long! Your soap opera of a life is the only thing that keeps me *going*, Jonathan! Please don't make me wait that long or I might just *die!*"

"Are you kidding me?"

"*Nooooo!*" she bellowed. Then, back in totally normal Carrie voice, "I mean, why? Why do you have to wait so long?"

"Target."

"So switch shifts with someone. Don't *you* wanna meet with her?"

"Yeah, I guess I do. . . . Fine. I'll see what I can do."

"Yaaaay! Call me when it's done."

"*Christ*, Carrie! Introduce Justin to Joanna and Shauna. See Laura tonight. Call me when it's done. When do the orders *end?!*"

"When I stop being right all the time," she declared triumphantly. "Now get outta here. You've got some calls to make. Go, go. Shoo, shoo."

20. Confide in Me

"Hey," Laura said quietly as I slid into the booth at Denny's. "Thanks for meeting me here—and for not making this wait till Thursday."

"Yeah, well, Carrie said she couldn't wait to hear the results, so . . . I had to bump it up a couple days."

"Ohhhh, Carrie . . ." Laura sighed. "I'd be offended . . . if she wasn't so damn hot."

"That even gets her outta trouble with *me* sometimes, so I know what you mean."

Just as an awkward silence began, a waitress thankfully came over and took our orders. Unfortunately, when she walked away, I still didn't know how to fill the silence. I looked down at my hands. They were fidgety. I was already tearing up my napkin into little pieces. I had the upper hand in this situation, but I was still uneasy. I didn't know how to start. . . .

"So, it seems you caught me making out with my girlfriend."

Whoa. I guess she was gonna start things off. I think I said something along the lines of "Huh-whah-uh-well . . ."

But Laura seemed less than fazed with my very fazed response. She seemed more contemplative on what she'd just said.

"Wow . . . *girlfriend*," she mused. "I guess I've never called her that out loud before. . . ."

"So, that girl was your *girlfriend*?" I asked.

"Aren't you fucking *listening*, idiot?" she snapped, good ol' mood-swingy Laura back in full effect. "And her name's Julie, as an f-y-i."

"Julie . . . nice," I said. "I'm sorry; I'm just sort of shocked."

"Well if I had *you* fooled, then I guess I'm pretty safe as far as everyone else is concerned."

"And you had *Paul* fooled, too, obviously," I said. "Or were you his beard, too? Is Paul a big queer quarterback?!"

"Oh, no . . . Paul's about as far from gay as you are from straight." She paused and looked down to her hands, which were now folded up on the table. "In fact, the reason I asked you to be my boyfriend was because he was really starting to pressure me about . . . sex stuff."

"So Paul wants some action, so you come running to a gay guy," I said, smiling.

"Pretty much. It was getting a little tired going from *straight* boyfriend to *straight* boyfriend. So, I had Paul fooled, and I had you fooled."

I laughed a little. "You had me fooled so much that I actually thought that you liked *me* toward the end there."

Now it was Laura's turn to laugh. Cackle, really. She was cackling so hard I thought she might choke on the ice she had been chewing. "You're kidding!" she cried when she'd caught her breath. Suddenly, the laughter ended. She stopped cold. "Wait. Is *that* why you turned into such a fucking *prick* all of a sudden? I could've killed you! I still *could* kill you, you little bitch!"

"I'm sorry, I'm sorry!" I yelled, trying to stop her before her head exploded. "I was just confused, is all. You kissed me randomly at your party when no one was around except Carrie, and then in the hallways—"

"So what, Jonathan? Don't you kiss your other girlfriends hello and good-bye?"

"Well . . . yeah, I guess. But then you got all weird about Homecoming and then started talking to me about if maybe I wasn't gay or whatever, so I just thought that—"

"Thought *what* exactly, Jonathan?" she snapped. "That just because I was trying to get to know you a little better it meant I wanted to get into your tight little Diesel jeans? Well, let me tell you two things, buddy. One: Your pants are way too tight for me to even *consider* getting into. And two: I *do* like you. As a friend."

"You do?" I asked. "Well, I guess at this point I should ask if you *still* do."

"I dunno, Jonathan. You really pissed me off with the whole Homecoming thing. And I was sort of working up to coming out to you officially at the Briar Patch when you flipped out and asked for the check."

"Shit. I'm sorry about that. I was just über-paranoid. And sorry about the dance."

"Yeah, I was actually sort of looking forward to going with you. I mean, I feel like besides Julie, you're one of my closest friends."

"You do?"

"Well, yeah. I mean . . . you're, like, my *one* gay friend, and with my being closeted and all, you're kind of an inspiration to me."

"I'm an inspiration to *you*?" I asked. "You're the one with the girlfriend!"

"Yeah, well, who were *you* with at Firestone on your birthday, anyway?" Laura asked slyly. "I'm sensing a little giddiness on that side of the table. . . ."

I let out a nervous chuckle. "Oh! Ha-ha . . . well, I guess I've been cheating on you, too, for the past week."

"You two-timing son of a bitch!" she said, loosening up and kidding around with me a bit. "Tell me all about it—"

"Wait, wait, wait," I interrupted. "Could we please just rewind to the whole Laura-is-a-lesbian thing!? Does anyone know?"

"Just you," she answered. "And Julie, too, naturally."

"I'd hope so. Oh, and Carrie knows, too—she was at the club. But why are you closeted? I mean, it hasn't been that bad for me. Acting straight when I was with you was *way* more trouble."

"Look, not everyone can be like you," Laura said a little angrily. "We're not all blessed with your parents and with your confidence and—"

"Whoa! You're saying you're not blessed with confidence? That's a load of crap, Laura."

Laura sat still for a minute, looking like she was trying to say something and trying not to say something at the same time. "Fine. Then parents. I don't have your *parents*, Jonathan."

"Well, tell me then."

Laura sighed. A heavy, weight-of-the-world-on-her-shoulders kind of sigh. She looked down at the table, then took a deep breath and began. "My parents are hardcore Conservatives—"

"*Ewww!*" I shrieked. The surrounding three tables went silent for a second and looked over to us. "Sorry," I muttered to Laura. "It's kind of a knee-jerk reaction. Go on."

"Well, basically my parents are really conservative and think that homosexuality is going to ruin the nation, and if I came out to them, I think I'd get thrown out. And I'm *really* not exaggerating."

"You're kidding me."

"No, I'm not. I wish I was, but I'm not. They talk about the 'homosexual agenda' and shit like that. It's really sad."

"Yeah," I said, rolling my eyes, "like getting basic civil rights is some sort of evil plan of ours or something. If *Britney Spears* can get married for fifty-odd hours, *everyone* should be able to marry. And how can your dad talk about the homosexual agenda and ignore the fact that, like, half of who's buying up those fancy downtown condos of his are gay couples?"

"I guess everyone's money is green to him."

"Holy shit, Laura! Condos! You're getting one of your own when you graduate!"

"Yeah, as of now," she said. "But that's 'cause I'm still straight in their eyes. I'm bringing home guys, not dykes."

"Ugh, Laura, I'm so sorry," I told her. "I'm assuming you're not telling them?"

"Not till I get that condo. But even then I might not, because they might take it away from me. But at least if I'm closeted and away from home, I'll have a place for me and Julie to . . . ya know." She winked.

"Spare me the juicy details, Laura," I said. "I have enough images running through my head after watching you trying to suck out each other's tonsils at Firestone."

"Oh, yeah . . ." Laura said. "Firestone."

"Riiiight," I said, drawing it out for dramatic emphasis. "What're we gonna do about that?"

"You're not gonna fucking bribe me, are you?" she asked me. Come to think of it, it sounded more like a statement than a question.

"I just don't know. . . ."

"Well, I don't think you have it in ya."

Our food arrived, and we stared each other down as her Caesar salad and my sampler were placed in front of us. I actually didn't want to bribe her. After our little talk, I realized that Laura and I had more in common than we did before. I mean, our situations were totally polar opposites, but I could remember what it was like to be in the closet. To feel like if you told people, your whole world would come crashing down. Of course with me, I knew my parents and friends would be okay with it. But with Laura, I got the feeling she wasn't blowing things out of proportion. But we were both gay; we had that bond. Which I was learning could be very powerful indeed. I guess Juan had been right. I needed gay friends.

So I guess I didn't wanna have to bribe her after all. Since I was on this road to recovery as an actual human being, why mess it all up?

Then again, Kylie was showing no signs of coming to the United States anytime soon. . . .

But no. I had my integrity.

"Look, Jonathan," Laura said, breaking the silence. "I've been thinking. . . . I've learned a lot from dating you."

"Like . . . ?"

"Like it doesn't matter what people think of you. You should be who you are and not apologize for it. I was feeling worse and worse as our little tryst went on about making you change how you were . . . but come to think of it, you never *really* changed who you were. You just *said* you were something different, but you acted the same."

"I did?"

"Sure. Did you not notice the total makeover you did on a certain three football players? And why do you think I used the 'too gay' excuse to explain our breakup?"

"Thanks, Laura, that's"—I twirled a greasy onion ring around my finger, searching for the right word—"touching. And by the way, I think I'm gonna come back out of the closet, if that's okay."

"That's fine—but for now, can we just . . . leave it up to people's imaginations about what we did in the boudoir?"

"Sure."

Laura sighed contentedly. "And so I've decided that at UCF, I'm gonna go all out. And when I say 'out,' I mean it."

"What about your friends?" I asked. "They hardly seem like the most gay-friendly crowd. . . ." I thought about it a second. "But I could be wrong, 'cause Ryan, George, and Clay—they may be on their way. They're actually really nice guys."

"Well, they're probably going up to Tallahassee for school,

so I don't plan on seeing them much anymore. I want to start with a clean slate. And if they find out and can't deal, then fuck them."

"And if your parents find out . . . ?"

"Then we'll just have to see."

We both leaned back and let out our breath and smiled at each other.

"I'm actually pretty proud of you, you big softie," I told her. "Have you learned anything else?"

Her face broke into a huge grin. "Well, in all my research, I've *definitely* learned that Kylie Minogue's pop music is far superior to most everything we're exposed to Stateside. . . . *And* she's got a killer arse."

"I'm even prouder of you than I was thirty seconds ago," I beamed.

"And I think we should still go to London."

"*WHAT?!*" I screeched. More than a few tables turned around to look this time. "Are you kidding me? Don't play with my emotions. After this semester, I don't think I can handle it. I'll kill you if—"

"No, I'm serious," she assured me. "Happy birthday. And let's not get kicked out of here before I can eat this *fabulously* prepared salad. *God*, I can't believe we met here."

"Shut up, I *like* Denny's food. Stuck-up lesbo."

"Tasteless fairy."

We both laughed hysterically.

This was the fucking *best* thing that could've happened. I was beyond excited.

"So, yeah," she said. "I'm totally serious about this. We could go for a week or so, and there'll be some concerts right after graduation. And I'll see what I can do about meeting her and her tour manager. . . . I think it could be really fun."

"Are you *shitting* me?! *It'll be a TON of fun! I'M GONNA SEE KYLIE MINOGUE!*" Now the entire restaurant was staring at me. "Oh, get over it!" I yelled. "It's fucking *Denny's!*"

Singing and dancing along to my *Light Years* album, I was a million happy clichés on my drive home from Denny's. On cloud nine. On top of the world. Just to name a couple.

I was just pulling off Colonial Drive when I felt a familiar vibrating in my pants pocket. I took out my cell phone, saw R.A. MUTHAFUCKA! CALLING, and answered it.

"Ryan! What's up?"

"Hey, dude, how're you holdin' up?"

"Eh, y'know—I'm doing okay," I told him. "Kinda weird, though."

"Whaddya mean?"

"Well, I'm assuming Laura told you all why she dumped me."

"Yeah, man, I heard—'too gay'? That shit is gay—er, I mean . . . retarded."

"Good job, much less offensive," I joked. "But . . . y'know, she kind of hit the nail on the head there. . . . What I'm saying is, I'm pretty sure I *am* gay."

"Aw, dude, we all fuckin' knew it."

"Really?"

"Course, Parish. Well, I think it was official when you tried to convince us to get . . . what was it? Mani-pedis? You don't think we're *stupid* or somethin', do you?"

"No! Never." There was a quick silence. I wasn't sure quite how to continue, so I just went with my gut: "I guess this means that you're not gonna want to do any more shopping anytime soon . . . ?"

"Fuck you, man!" he yelled. "What kind of people do you think we are? We're still totally hanging out! You, me, George, Clay, Laura . . . whoever. You're a cool guy, Parish—just glad you finally decided which team to play for."

"Yeah—me, too," I said. "Even though dating Laura was pretty interesting."

"Shit yeah, J! She's *smokin'*!"

"Lucky little bastard!" Justin screamed from the backseat. "*I* wanna go!"

"Seriously, Jonathan, how lucky can you get?" Carrie whined. "Everything working out in the end? What kind of TV show *is* this?"

"*My life is not some goddamn show, Carrie!*" I yelled at her, laughing. "You need a new hobby."

"Maybe what I *need* are more interesting friends. . . ."

"I dunno," Justin said. "Come-ons from your straight girlfriends, dating-for-concert schemes, bitch-slappings . . . sounds pretty interesting to me."

"I'm over it," Carrie declared. She skipped the track in Aretha's stereo to "Koocachoo," our mutual favorite Kylie track. I'd introduced it to her on a mini road trip to Miami the summer before, and she'd been hooked ever since. We did a cheesy little jig to the James Bond–like intro and busted out into crazy tribal-dance convulsions when the drums kicked in.

"Is this rehearsed?" Justin asked, laughing.

"No . . ." I answered. "More like . . . memorized from extreme repetition."

"Huh," Justin said, and I could tell he was smiling without even looking in the rearview mirror. Apparently, I'd found a guy who could appreciate my little weirdnesses and dorkisms, which was refreshing. I knew we definitely had potential.

"So, Jonathan," Justin continued, "you think everything's gonna be cool with you and your girlfriends?"

Kylie sang something about the lights on Broadway as we sped past the downtown lights on Orange Ave.

"Well, yeah . . . I guess so . . ." I told him. "I mean, I don't know if things will ever be a hundred percent *completely* the way they were, but it'll be close. And after all the shit that happened, we'll definitely be more honest. . . . We promised that *for real* this time."

"Yeah, I mean, it's not like *poof* all of a sudden Shauna didn't come on to you, but it'll be cool soon," Carrie said. "And at least there's no bad blood about it. . . . And there *shouldn't* be—'cause you're just so damn irresistible!"

"Oh, shut up. . . . No, go on," I said. "No, shut up."

"*God*, you're a cocky little bitch, aren't you?" Carrie said lovingly.

"Thanks to you," I said even more lovingly.

"You should be," Justin said. "You *are* irresistible."

I blushed instantly, and was at a loss for words for about a split second before Carrie twisted around to yell sarcastically at Justin, "Oh, enough *flattery*, you already snagged him! Cut the shit, will ya?" And then one of those patented Carrie laughs that could raise the dead. "You just better hope his ex-*girlfriend* doesn't come crawling back."

"I doubt that," I told Carrie, rolling my eyes. "I'll just have to keep *your* greedy little paws off her."

"You act like I have one thing on my mind, Jonathan Parish, and may I inform you that—"

"She has a girlfriend, remember?" I cut her off. "They met online and are, like, in love. . . ."

"Oh. Right."

"So let's keep the sexual tension at a bare minimum with this one, sweetie," I suggested. "I'd like to keep her as a friend."

"I do, too, doll—I was just kidding," Carrie assured me. "And I can control my urges, you know. You don't see me straddling your cute little body right here on the East-West, do you?"

"Please, let's not start," I pleaded.

"You guys are too much," Justin was laughing.

"Oh, just you wait . . ." Carrie said.

Justin was a big hit with Shauna and Joanna. They took turns rubbing his fuzzy, shaved head as Carrie cued up the DVD player to watch *Pumpkinhead*, the oh-so-bad horror film we'd selected to watch in honor of the Thanksgiving season. And along with Justin's debut, I'd invited Laura to come over with Julie and make her big I'm-an-out-lesbian (to us only, for now) debut.

Laura brought caviar and a veggie tray.

I showed Laura and Justin how I make my famous chili-'n'-cheese dip.

Julie "brought" some kick-ass champagne, but I could tell that was from Laura, too.

I stored away our soda for a bit while Laura made a toast.

"To the most interesting semester at Winter Park I've ever had. I'm sorry about what my little scheme might have done to this group, but ultimately I'm glad it all happened. 'Cause you all seem like great people, and I feel very welcome. Thanks for giving me another chance, despite us all getting off on the wrong foot—to say the least. So, to bullshit antics, to Jonathan's belated birthday party, and to Kylie!"

We whooped and cheered and clinked glasses and sipped back Laura's very choice bubbly.

Things had come so far in the past few weeks. And I had a feeling they'd only get better.

For starters, I was already coming back out of the closet, first stop Ryan Andopolis of all people. (I know! Who'd've thunk it!) So apparently, I now had not only gay friends, but straight male friends too. And if things seemed to fit right, I was totally gonna set Ryan up with Joanna—she's really into Mediterranean guys.

As I sipped more of my champagne, I drank in the scene around me. Justin and Shauna were over in the living room, laughing and getting to know each other. Joanna was taking some spinach dip out of the oven, shaking her booty to the Christina Aguilera playing from the stereo. Carrie, of course, was grinding on me from behind to the beat and reaching her arms around my waist to grab a carrot from the veggie tray. Laura was doling out the caviar as Julie refilled her glass and pecked her on the cheek.

It all kinda reminded me of Juan's vanful of friends that I liked so much. Like the crazy mishmash of food assembled before us, so were we. All sort of mismatched in a way, but fitting together nicely. And this time, I truly appreciated it. I vowed to myself to never do anything else so crazy that would jeopardize or undermine these friendships I had. Because it was all too precious to lose. With these people, I felt like I had a second family, and it was so nice.

Eventually, we all settled down in the living room with our fine champagne or fabulous soda and our plates loaded down with egg rolls, caviar, raw vegetables, and who knows what else, and prepared ourselves for the cinematic masterpiece that was *Pumpkinhead*.

Life was good again.

Oh, and did I mention . . . *I GET TO SEE KYLIE MINOGUE!!!!!!!*

Acknowledgments

There are so many people I want to thank for making this book happen, from beginning to end, and luckily this isn't the Oscars—so no music is going to come on and scare me off. . . .

First of all, I want to thank my untitled novel-writing group—Nick Eliopulos, Billy Merrell, and Dan Poblocki—for letting me join on their second meeting, for their giddy enthusiasm over *Kylie*'s first pages, and for all the help and advice along the way. I think Dan thinks we're called "The Bitches," so . . . thanks, Bitches.

I also want to thank everyone who read the *Kylie* manuscript when it was ready for the world, especially the first official non-Bitches reader and star kid sister Katherine Medina. Much appreciation to Rachel Cohn, Janet Pascal, Kendra Levin, Joy Peskin, Regina Hayes, and Jim Hoover for their excitement and advice, and to David Levithan for—among many other things—hooking *Kylie* up with her ultimate home.

Thanks also to Katie Cicatelli for her unwavering support and enthusiasm over countless semi-fulfilling Jazzy's lunches, to Jack Lienke for the happy happy-hour sessions at Therapy, and to Susan Jeffers Casel and Greg Emetaz for helping me celebrate my book-deal news in style! Thanks also, Susan, for the stellar copyediting!

Thanks goes out to Aaron Riggins, too, for not only being an amazing friend, but for showing me an unforgettable (though we may forget some parts!) time in London when the two of us threw caution and good financial judgment to the wind and flew across the Atlantic to see Ms. Minogue in concert. Eighty-dollar bottles of champagne really *do* taste that much better when you're drinking them in the presence of your favorite Aussie pop star!

Hugs and kisses go out to the people who made my own high-school days and beach-house parties in Florida so memorable, including but not limited to Tanya Casey, Mariah Clarke, Ambry DeLater, Annie Gennaro, John House, Veronica McDougald, Susan Minard, Jennifer Neal, Rachel Raidiger, Erin Tanner, and Anneke Victorica. Thanks for your friendship and for the good times I'll never forget.

And to my parents, Carlos and April Medina, who supported my writing from a very early age, and my sisters, Katherine and Jessica—thank you for everything! For the love, the support, the trips, and the fun. I couldn't ask for a better family, really, and I love you all.

I owe Billy Merrell so much love and so many foot massages for not only being the best boyfriend anyone could ask for, but for his invaluable help brainstorming and revising the book in its early stages. Without him, this would have been a very different (and probably very unpublished) book. (And thanks also for your patience and for putting up with my screaming stubbornness. I love.)

To the wonderful folks at Simon Pulse, many heartfelt thanks. To Bethany Buck, for believing in this book from the get-go and for starting her own "Kylie Door" at the Pulse offices. To my editor, Jennifer Klonsky, for her excellent feedback and tireless grace in dealing with my many e-mails and concerns, and for being generally awesome in every way. And to Greg Stadnyk for my *amazing* cover, to Steve Kennedy for the striking interior layout, and to Katherine Devendorf, Carey O'Brien, Michael del Rosario, and I'm sure many others for bringing it all together.

And last but certainly not least, a thank-you to Ms. Kylie Minogue, whose music has always made me so happy. Thanks for giving so much of yourself to your adoring fans, and for showing such inspirational bravery in the face of adversity. Much love and respect! It was a pleasure seeing you in London, and writing about you in New York.

About the Author

© Billy Merrell

NICO MEDINA (www.nicomedina.com) was born in 1982 in Orlando, Florida, where he attended the nonfictitious Winter Park High School, which was fictitiously named *Playboy*'s top party high school in 2006 by *Orlando Weekly*. He then went on to receive a BA in sociology from the University of Florida before moving to Manhattan, where he has set up house with his boyfriend, Billy, their pug-daughter Paisley, and a mango sorbet–hoarding roommate named Nick. He began writing *The Straight Road to Kylie* (his first book) in 2005, partly to pay back the minor credit-card debt he accumulated after flying to London for floor seats to Kylie's Showgirl Tour, which he says was worth every penny.

As many as 1 in 3 Americans
who have HIV... don't know it.

TAKE CONTROL.
KNOW YOUR STATUS.
GET TESTED.

To learn more about HIV testing,
or get a free guide to HIV and
other sexually transmitted diseases:

www.knowhivaids.org
1-866-344-KNOW

What's life without a little . . .

DRAMA!

★ A new series by Paul Ruditis ★

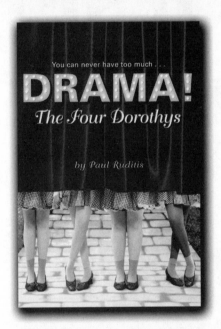

At Bryan Stark's posh private high school in Malibu, the teens are entitled, the boys are cute, and the school musicals are *extremely* elaborate. Bryan watches—and comments—as the action and intrigue unfold around him. Thrilling mysteries, comic relief, and epic sagas of friendship and love . . . It's all here. And it's showtime.

From Simon Pulse • Published by Simon & Schuster